THE HAND OF ADONAI:
THE BOOK OF THINGS TO COME

by
AARON D. GANSKY

Brimstone
Fiction

THE HAND OF ADONAI: THE BOOK OF THINGS TO COME BY AARON D. GANSKY
Published by Brimstone Fiction
1440 W. Taylor Street, Suite 449
Chicago, IL 60607

ISBN: 978-1-946758-00-2
Copyright © 2017 by Aaron D. Gansky
Cover design by Goran Tomic
Interior design by Karthick Srinivasan

Available in print from your local bookstore, online, or from the publisher at:
www.brimstonefiction.com

For more information on this book and the author visit: www.aarongansky.com

This is a work of fiction. Names, characters, and incidents are all products of the author's imagination or are used for fictional purposes. Any mentioned brand names, places, and trademarks remain the property of their respective owners, bear no association with the author or the publisher, and are used for fictional purposes only. Brimstone Fiction may include ghosts, werewolves, witches, the undead, soothsayers, mythological creatures, theoretical science, fictional technology, and material which, though mentioned in Scripture, may be of a controversial nature within some religious circles.

Brought to you by the creative teams at Lighthouse Publishing of the Carolinas and Brimstone Fiction: Bethany R. Kaczmarek, Rowena Kuo, Meaghan Burnett, Eddie Jones, and Brian Cross

Library of Congress Cataloging-in-Publication Data
Gansky, Aaron D.
The Hand of Adonai: The Book of Things to Come / Aaron D. Gansky 1st ed.

Printed in the United States of America

Praise for *The Hand of Adonai: The Book of Things to Come*

Aaron D. Gansky's Hand of Adonai Series is an escape into the eternal reality of things that are, that were, and that are to come. His storytelling mesmerizes. His characters engage so that the reader finds new friends to love and new villains to revile. I wish his series had been around for my children growing up but, no matter, for they awaken the child in me now, so I'll be giving Gansky's stories as gifts to everyone I know who loves an epic, eternal story of both great excitement and lasting worth.

~**Lori Stanley Roeleveld**
Author of *Running from a Crazy Man*

No matter what I might say in praise of this book, it wouldn't be enough. Wow, Aaron D. Gansky, what an imaginative and thought-provoking read! I have only one question for you: When will the next one be ready?

~**Ann Tatlock**
Author of Christy Award-winner, *Once Beyond a Time*

An underdog character fantasizes about leaving this world to magically transport into the Medieval-like digital game world she and her friend created? What's not to love? And it just keeps getting more exciting and twisty-turny from there. *Hand of Adonai: The Book of Things to Come* has everything I look for in good fiction: characters with a compelling growth arc, strong writing, a gripping story, intriguing turns of events. I particularly liked the characters Oliver and Lauren and found myself rooting for them. I'd recommend this book (and this author!) for all ages, not just the YA market. It's Christian fantasy at its best.

~**DL Koontz**
Award-winning author of *Crossing into the Mystic*
and *Edging through the Darkness*

The Lord of the Rings and *Tron* collide in this equally epic journey. The Hand of Adonai tests the limits of your imagination as two worlds collide in a most unusual way, pulling four teens from one life and thrusting them into another. Using their unique gifts and talents they must overcome obstacles, complete their quest, and defeat the evil that rules the land.

~**Caleb Lang**
Firefighter, Aspiring Author,
Avid Reader, and Huge Fan

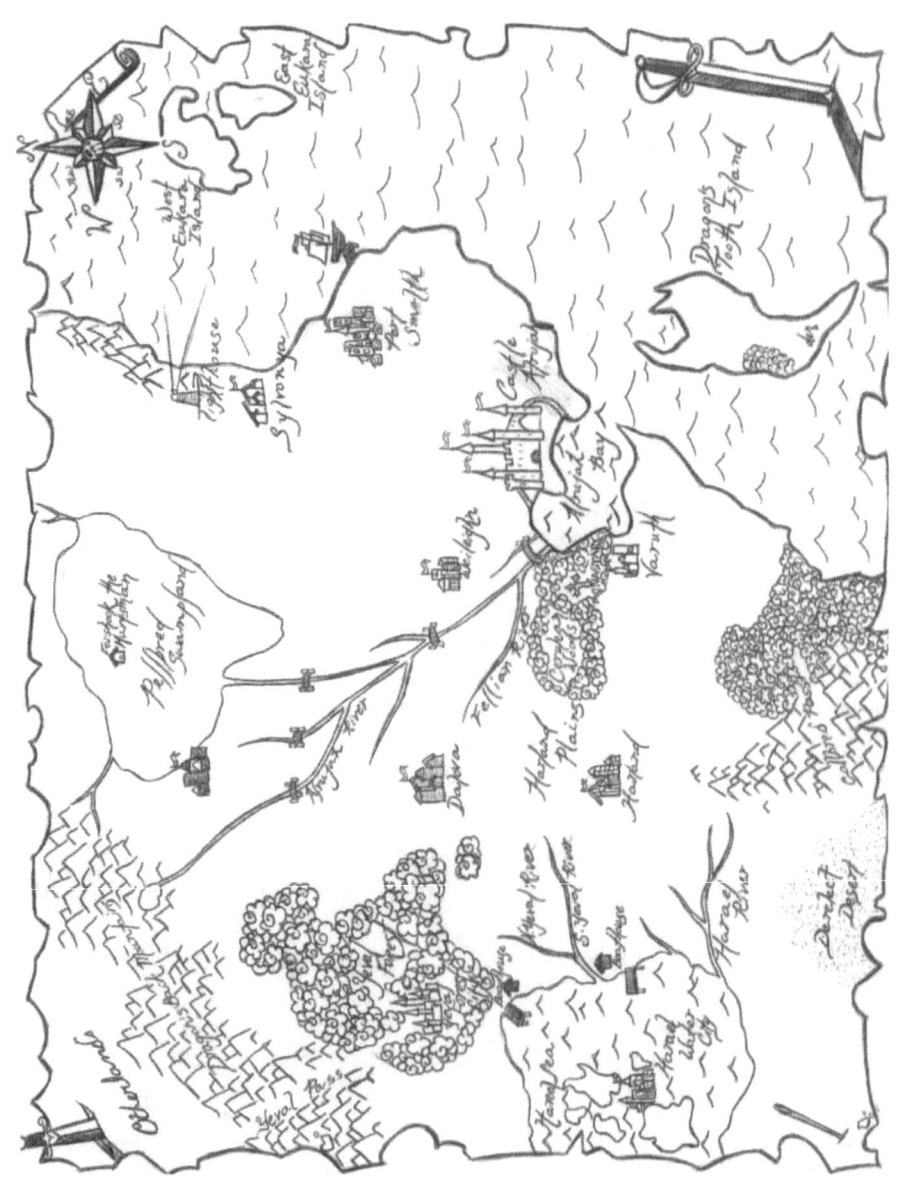

ACKNOWLEDGEMENTS

The Hand of Adonai series has been on my heart for a number of years. Seeing it come to fruition is a dream come true. But, as is the case with every book, this novel was not a solitary effort. It has undergone countless revisions, each better than the last. These revisions were made possible, thanks in large part, to two people: Steve McLain and Dennis Fulgoni.

Steve McLain's fingerprints are all over this manuscript. He helped me form ideas, wrangle unruly plot points, capture character voices, and solidify the end-game of the series. I cannot thank him enough.

Dennis Fulgoni and I got our Masters degrees together at Antioch University of Los Angeles in 2009. Since then, we've religiously traded work for reading. He keeps my prose clean and honest and never lets me rest with lazy language or tired clichés. He challenges me every step of the way, and my work is better for it.

I also had the incredible honor of working with Bethany Kaczmarek for the first (but hopefully not last) time on this book. Her editing skills are superb. I looked forward to each e-mail from her with comments on the manuscript. The process was not only enjoyable, but fruitful. Her keen eye and probing questions held my feet to the fire and forced me to make tough choices for which the book is better. I'm indebted to her and hope to work with her through the remainder of the series.

I'd also like to acknowledge Lighthouse Publishing of the Carolinas. I've had the privilege to know Eddie Jones for years, and I strongly believe in his vision. I'm humbled he's asked me to be a part of it as an author. And to Rowena Kuo, who runs Brimstone Fiction. Her management of the imprint is excellent, and she's always a pleasure to work with.

Lastly, I'd like to recognize the role my family has played in the publication of this novel. My father, even from my childhood, has encouraged me to write. He also suggested, one fine day, that I try my hand at YA fiction. Of course, I scoffed. But the idea stayed in my mind for some time, and this is the culmination of that suggestion. Thanks, Pops.

And to my wife and children who have tirelessly supported me and encouraged me, thank you.

Blessings of Adonai,

Aaron D. Gansky

Dedication

To Bailey Renee Gray
August 19, 2010

Save us a seat
At the feet of Jesus.

Prologue

Because of their wickedness, Adonai deposed the elves from the throne of Alrujah and again established humans as rulers of the land. He appointed King Solous to bear the weight of the crown. Through his bloodline shall Alrujah find salvation.

—The Book of the Ancients

King Solous set every pair of free hands in Alrujah scrubbing the blood from the streets. His general, Galdarin Korodeth, already had his troops remove the bodies of the men and the elves. Entire families, moving in from outlying areas, spent hours on hands and knees with buckets of soapy water and stiff-bristled cleaning brushes. The cobblestone streets would be stained red for years to come.

King Solous walked among the people, touching shoulders, whispering words of encouragement and thanks. Often, he'd find masses of children huddled together as they scrubbed, their parents looking on from down the way.

His heart broke. The children should be playing, should not have to see such grotesquerie. He knelt beside a group of young ones, took a brush from their bucket, and scrubbed the streets alongside them. Their conversation lulled, so he told jokes to lighten the mood. Uneasy laughter was better than no laughter at all. They'd lost enough of their childhood to the War of the Suns. Now, in victory, was the time to be jovial and lighthearted. This is why they'd fought in the first place—for freedom from the oppressive hands of the elves, for the right to rule themselves, for the right to enjoy life.

He'd earned the respect of the people in battle; now he sought to earn their respect in peace.

Behind him, the clang of armor brought Solous to his feet fast. But the soldiers had not engaged an enemy. Instead, they'd snapped to attention at the approach of General Korodeth.

Solous smiled. "Old friend. Have you come to help clean?"

"I wish I might, but matters of state demand our attention. The angels have again assembled in the throne room."

Solous touched the shoulders of the children nearest him. "Your work will be rewarded in the prosperity of Alrujah." As they walked toward the castle, Solous put his arm around Korodeth. "Did you ever imagine we'd be here? We used to dream of great battles, of commanding armies, but those were the dreams of oppressed children, born into the hand of slavery."

"We were fishermen," Korodeth said with a grim smile. "I'd hoped only to captain a boat."

"How old were we then?"

"Fourteen," Korodeth said.

"And now, the entire kingdom looks to us. Angels heed our call and follow our commands."

"Adonai has called us, old friend," Korodeth said. "He promised us the keys to the kingdom."

"I know, but I didn't anticipate this. Children scrubbing blood from the streets?"

"Not all streets are so stained. There are places where blood does not run," Korodeth said. He nodded toward the gates of the castle gardens. The silver-clad guards posted there snapped to attention, straightened their backs and pressed fists to hearts.

Within the castle garden, no blood stained the leaves of the trees, the grassy knolls, the crocuses and callas, or the violets and vincasor. Solous had taken great care to ensure no blood be shed within the castle walls. He could do little about the elven soldiers outside the walls, but Pacha el Nai, angel of Adonai, had personally walked Solous to the throne of Alrujah and negotiated the transfer of the throne from elves to men. That done, the men turned their attention to rebuilding.

"You've posted sentries?" Solous asked.

"At each entrance, both secret and public. Our most trusted soldiers guard your quarters and the throne room."

"Your talents stretch far beyond the battlefield, Galdarin."

"Thank you, my lord."

Solous stopped him just shy of the throne room doors. He lowered his voice to keep it from echoing down the stone halls. "Without you, we could not have won, even with the seven angels."

"Thank you, Solous. But Adonai's calling rests on your shoulders. Even without me, He would have enabled your victory."

Solous clasped the man's shoulder. "He sent you to me. Even before we were soldiers, even before we commanded armies. We fished beside each other. The miracle He's worked in my life is only matched by those He's worked in yours."

Korodeth smiled. "Come now. You must take the throne and act the king."

Solous nodded, then opened the doors to the white marble throne room. He passed the massive columns supporting the roof to the front where seven massive beings stood before him. He and Korodeth fell to their knees, pressed their foreheads to the marble floor. "You honor us with your presence, servants of Adonai."

Pacha el Nai, a massive angel three and a half spans tall with white wings stretching near to fifteen spans, led six other angels, all equally colossal. Still wearing his burnished steel armor from the final battle the day before, he slipped his helmet off and tucked it under his arm. A sword hung at each hip, one beside each leg. Even sheathed, they hummed with power. "Rise," Pacha el Nai said in the voice of two men. "Adonai alone is worthy of your honor."

Solous and Korodeth stood, ascended the dais to the golden, purple-upholstered throne. Solous sat, but Korodeth stood beside him. "You honor me by heeding my petition for an audience," Solous said.

Behind Pacha el Nai, Belphegor stepped forward. His head sprouted two horns a hand's length each. Armored in silver and gold, his legs bent at awkward angles. Unlike Pacha's white wings, his sprouted tawny feathers tipped with gold. While Pacha looked human, Belphegor had a faunish look. "Adonai wishes us to speak with you. But first, speak what you will. Why did you summon us?"

Solous gestured toward his old friend standing beside him. "Before your assembly, I wish to honor Galdarin Korodeth. Under the watchful eye of Adonai's servants, and with his blessing, I bestow upon him the title of Archduke of Alrujah. His honor exceeds that of all other men. Indeed, if I did not wear the crown, he would. Let it be known among those esteemed angels assembled today, and in the presence of almighty Adonai, that if ever my bloodline were severed, Korodeth, being chosen among men by Adonai as being noble and true, shall ascend the throne."

Korodeth immediately knelt, a paragon of humility and honor. He spoke with a reverence and formality worthy of a loyal subject. "May it never be, my king. Adonai preserve you and your line. May the calling of the line of Korodeth be to stand beside that of Solous from now until eternity."

Pacha el Nai said, "Adonai has heard your decision and honors your wish. May it be as you say."

Korodeth stood, his head still inclined to Solous. "I am unworthy of this honor, my lord."

"If you are unworthy, Korodeth, none in Alrujah will ever be esteemed worthy." Solous turned to the angels, put a fist over his heart. "Esteemed servants of Adonai. Give us his words."

Pacha el Nai spoke again. "Adonai blesses you, Solous, King of Men, and you as well, honored Archduke Korodeth, who leads both men and angels into battle."

"Adonai has been faithful," Tiamat said. "He has returned the throne of Alrujah to men. Rule under his name. Establish a kingdom marked by peace and prosperity." While not as tall as the other angels, he had the largest wingspan by far. His blue and gold feathered wings glimmered as if scaled. He wore no armor on his chest or back, but both arms were sleeved in a scaled blue metal embedded with rubies. His eyes burned cobalt, and lightning danced from feather to feather. He commanded weather, used strong spells to counter those used by the elves. Seldom did a blade come close enough to strike him.

Abaddon stepped forward. "Good king, Adonai has entrusted our service to your wisdom." He spoke with a buzz and a rattle. His obsidian armor matched his black wings. Broad in shoulder and chest, Abaddon wielded a two-handed sword with awesome ferocity and cowed the armies of the elves.

King Solous motioned to the guards posted near the entrance. "Bring stools for our guests to sit. This may take some time."

The guards vanished through the spotless white marble doors. Solous appreciated his decision to keep bloodshed from within the castle walls. His was a heart committed to peace, though the same could not be said for all the angels assembled before him.

Legion wore full plate armor fashioned entirely from bronze. His white wings reflected its light and glowed gold. In one hand, he wielded an enormous spiked mace. It'd take five men to heft its weight. In the war, what magic the elves used against him dissipated across his shield and armor. Few could stand before his might, and the angel reveled in his strength, relished his charge to overthrow the armies of the elves. He was a being created for battle and war.

Solous cleared his throat. "Your services?"

"The corruption of the elves began with Shedoah's hand. Adonai has thrown him beneath the deep of the Alrujahn Sea," Moloch said. He also had black wings. His cloak shimmered like onyx but flowed like fabric stitched with lightning. Thin in body and limb, he wielded the very power of life. To him alone, Adonai had entrusted this awesome authority. Solous's troops had taken to calling him the Angel of Death, a term which instilled fear on both sides of the war. He spoke little, but his mere presence unnerved monarchs and warriors alike.

Maewen, the only woman of the group, let her long golden hair spill over a circlet of bismuth. On her chest, she wore golden mail, and her legs were sheathed in scales of jasper. Emerald tipped both ends of her barbed spear. While smaller than the other angels, her battle prowess made her one of the most feared of the seven. "Seven seals bar his return." She spoke with the voice of a crackling fire, and her lips shone red.

The guards returned with the stools. Tiamat furled his wings and sat on the ornate red-upholstered stool. Back straight, his voice carried the weight and force of a tornado. "We have recorded our power in a book of magic."

Galdarin Korodeth said, "This book is already penned?"

"Aye," Maewen said, her voice an angry furnace. "Indeed, the very ink is imbued with our powers."

Archduke Korodeth folded his arms. "The book must be sealed, lest man or elf or dwarf find it and usurp it. Power like that could rend the world."

Of course. The wisdom of Korodeth became plain again. Mankind could not be trusted with such a force. Short of Adonai, only Solous had the ability to seal the book and the magic contained within it. He stood, moved to the glass case on which the tome was displayed. He whispered a few words over it, and the glass vanished. He took the book, felt the power surging through him. For a minute, he considered holding it, keeping it for himself. A book like this would virtually ensure immortality. Imagine what he could achieve if he reigned for centuries. What good might he accomplish?

But if he ever lost it? Man was not meant to live for hundreds of years. *Forgive my selfishness, my lust for power, Adonai*, he thought. He pressed his hand to the leather cover, tapped into the power entrusted to him by almighty Adonai, and bound the magic in enchantments stronger than Alrujah had ever seen. "There is no power within Alrujah that may shatter these bonds."

Moloch spoke, his voice a dusty buzz. "The elves practice strange magic, as do humans and dwarves. Today, there may be no power to break your bonds, but the power of the people grows. The book will not be safe here."

"It must be hidden," Abaddon said.

"Indeed," Solous said. Turning to Korodeth, he said, "You must hide the book. Tell no one of its location, even me. The secret must die with you."

Korodeth whispered in deference. "Your Graciousness, a matter so important cannot be trusted to hands other than your own. I urge you, good king, hide the book yourself. Indeed, is anyone else in the kingdom worthy of such a responsibility?"

"Such a task requires time. I have a kingdom to rebuild, trust between races to establish, and skirmishes to settle. Within the kingdom, there are no hands I trust more than yours, no mind so noble and able, no heart more humble, no wisdom more discerning. You alone are worthy to undertake such a task."

"If there were another, Your Graciousness. Perhaps one of the assembled angels?"

"This is a matter of men," Pacha el Nai said. "Adonai has entrusted the book to Solous. It is his to entrust to you."

Korodeth stood, put fist to heart, and said, "Very well. It will be as you say. With your leave, I will prepare myself for the journey ahead."

Solous nodded, and Korodeth made his way out the back of the throne room. King Solous turned to the assembled angels, still seated patiently. "Adonai wishes me to use your talents in the establishment of my kingdom?"

"He trusts your will. We are at your disposal," Maewen said.

Solous pressed his folded hands to his chin. He'd not considered how to use the angels after the war had been won. He'd assumed they'd return to the heavens and not return again until needed. How then, to use battle-scarred angels? How might they help reestablish the kingdom?

They must bring the people to trust in Adonai. A kingdom unified in faith would not fall. Korodeth would say the same thing. "Far be it from me to disagree with Adonai, though I am humbled by such an honor. His Hand has established my kingdom and will hold it fast in his grip. Be His fingers, then, and establish His church among my people. Watch over them. Defend them from the corruptive power of Shedoah."

"So be it," Tiamat thundered. "Where shall the churches be established?"

Solous sat, contemplated the map of Alrujah. Much of it would need redrawing, but the land itself, the cities, remained. What was destroyed would be rebuilt. He had only to discern which people would best respond to each angel.

Rising again, his finger on a map, he said, "Maewen. I've moved the elves to the island city of Harael. They are devastated from the war, and many still resist the rule of Adonai. They are a stubborn people, but your beauty and graciousness give you the best opportunity to gain their respect. Yesterday, they were our enemies. Today, they are our people; they are Alrujahns. You've shown your love for the people, and I pray you do so again.

"Moloch, you have gained the trust of the peoples of the Callbred mountains and forests. Their towns and villages have been ravaged by war. Use your powers to bring them life again.

"Abaddon, your battle prowess has impressed the swamp dwellers of Pellbred. They are a stiff-necked people, but loyal. Guide them in the practice of the worship of Adonai, and the swamp will again flourish.

"Tiamat, the coast of Alrujah will be safe under your watchful eyes. Your powers will protect our sailors and ensure the prosperity of our kingdom. The people of Sylvonya are thirsty for direction. Your strong hand will provide for their needs.

"Belphegor, you led the dwarves, who took up arms with humans to march against the elves. Your leadership helped us secure Dalova. I charge you now, protect the people whose hearts you've won, within the bellies of the mountains and hills, to establish the church of Adonai and lead them in the ways of our God.

"Legion, your troops overcame the elven stronghold in Yeval Forest. The people have come to call it the Bleeding Grounds, and they live in fear. Establish a strong presence as we rebuild what the elves accomplished. In Orensdale, you will build the church of Adonai and lead the people in peace as you led them in war.

"And finally, Pacha el Nai. To you, I entrust the very heart of Alrujah. By your hand, you overcame the fist of the elves in Alrujah. With your strength, you oversaw the transfer of the throne. Among all the angels, you shed the least blood but won the most victories. Your wisdom and love of peace must establish the church of Adonai here in Alrujah and Varuth, in Harland and Weileighn. The four cities compose the heart of Alrujah, our very economic and military strength. Keep us from corruption and greed."

The angels nodded in agreement and vanished with a flourish and shimmer. Solous dismissed his guards and again sat the throne of Alrujah, again felt the weight of the crown. He thought of the children and women and men scrubbing the cobblestone streets of Alrujah.

Adonai, he prayed, *accomplish Your will. Protect the book, that Alrujah may never again know war as it has known these long years.*

* * *

In the centuries after King Solous's reign, Alrujah's fortunes waned. The kingdom had fallen far from the prosperity and peace the fabled king worked so hard to achieve. The problems facing the kingdom weighted Archduke Pentavus Korodeth's heart.

He knelt on the white marble floor of the throne room of Alrujah. As Captain of the King's Watch, he was expected to give his report to his king and friend.

Ribillius was the twelfth king in the line of Solous. Korodeth wished the monarch had enough sense to realize what a gratuitous expense it was to sit on a throne fashioned entirely from gold. Ribillius hadn't fashioned the throne, but he refused to sell it, though the money would feed thousands. Far be it from Korodeth to mention this to his king. Ribillius would rebuff his suggestion as an offense to Adonai. The throne, the monarch was fond of saying, had been established by Adonai himself.

Ribillius stood and waved his guards away. The marble doors closed after them, and the king sat on the steps of the dais. He motioned for Korodeth to sit beside him. "You don't bring good news anymore," he said.

"There is little good to report," Korodeth said carefully.

"I find it hard to believe that in a kingdom the size of Alrujah, your spies can't find anything positive."

"Forgive me, my lord. I have entrusted my soldiers with finding potential threats to the well-being of your throne."

"There are always threats to my throne," he said.

"Never as many as now, my lord."

Ribillius crossed his arms over his heavy belly and sighed. "What news, then, Captain?"

"Orensdale has given itself to the worship of Legion. Sylvonya proclaims itself for Tiamat. Both cities have ceased trade with Alrujah, Varuth, Harland, Weileighn, and Dalova."

"And our people starve," Ribillius said, the heavy gold crown slipping down his forehead.

"Droughtworm has made its way within our walls as well, my lord. Each morning, my soldiers drag the dead to the sea. There are more each sunrise."

Ribillius stood, paced the throne room, ran his hands over the smooth marble columns. "Do you remember when we were children, Pentavus? The most we worried about was whether or not we'd be caught stealing pies from the kitchen. Now, there aren't enough pies to feed our people."

Korodeth stood, clasped his hands behind his back. "There is a way to heal the land," he said tentatively.

Ribillius shook his head. "Do not dishonor this throne room with your talk of Shedoah again. He is the reason we're in this mess. It is his touch that poisons the land, that breeds distrust among our people, that fuels the diseases that cripple our cities."

"You misunderstand, my lord. It is his hand that can heal us. I understand your devotion to Adonai, but your faith is misplaced. The prophecies say—"

Ribillius spun. "Prophecies? You mean lies. Shedoah is the deceiver of old. You've read *The Book of the Ancients*. You've read *The Book of Things to Come*. You understand what true prophecy is, and yet you cling to half-truths and lies? What of our fathers and their fathers? As long as men have sat the throne of Alrujah, we have dedicated our kingdom to Adonai. His power established our throne, and the suffering we face will not cause us to turn our backs on Him now."

"Our fathers were deceived. Their faith was strong, but misplaced. As is yours, my lord."

Ribillius's face flushed red. "If you were any other man, I would kill you where you stand. We've been friends since birth, but that alone will not stay my hand if you blaspheme again. Adonai's name will not be defamed."

"Then send me away, my lord. I will not turn from my faith, and you will not turn from yours."

"King Solous established your line to the throne. I cannot send you away. Even if I could, I would not. You are as close as a brother to me,

Pentavus. You are a loyal and trusted friend, misguided as you are."

Korodeth's heart fisted. What could he say to convince his friend of the truth of Shedoah? He'd tried countless times, and each time, was dismissed. "How do you explain the suffering? If Shedoah is chained in the deeps, if his power is sealed with seven seals, as you say, how may he touch the land? How may his influence or corruption conjure droughtworm, cause cities to renounce Adonai?"

Ribillius righted the crown on his head. "The seals must be weakening. *The Book of Sealed Magic* must have been found. Rumors of the Mage Lord must be true."

"They are rumors only, my lord. I've seen no evidence of a Mage Lord at work."

"You've told me the signs with your mouth. The droughtworm, the poverty, the distrust, the fall of faith. What more evidence do you need? We must find him, must restore the seals. Have your soldiers keep a close eye on Orensdale and Sylvonya. No—their faith has already fallen. He'll turn to cities closer to Alrujah, try to garner strength closer to the seat of our faith. Watch Dalova. Viceroy Gerald is a good man. We cannot afford to be without him."

"My lord," Korodeth said. He used a practiced deference and kept accusation far from his voice. "These commands have the feel of desperation, not of logic."

"How would you proceed were you in my place, Pentavus? Continue to let our people fall to starvation and plague? Wait until your precious Shedoah breaks his seals and turns us all to slaves, turns us all to corpses?"

"No, my lord. As always, you speak with wisdom." Korodeth put a fist over his heart and inclined his head.

Ribillius nodded. "I'm sorry, my friend. I didn't mean to snap."

"No apologies necessary, my lord."

The king returned to the dais steps and sat. "I have court in an hour. Leave me, my friend. Bring me news as it comes. And please, try to find something positive to report."

"As you will, so it shall be done." Korodeth exited through the back door, navigating his way through the dank stone hallways to his office overlooking the city square. The smell of death soured the scent of lilacs and lavender. He sat at his desk and pulled an ancient scrap of parchment from within. As he whispered over it, the paper shriveled with age.

Though his door never opened, Korodeth detected a presence

within his office. A moment of concentration identified the man as Argus Berand, brother of the traitor Trieli. As far as his Chameleon Soldiers went, Argus was one of the best. He'd proven his dedication and loyalty, not only to Alrujah, but to Shedoah himself. "You have news from Yeval Forest?"

The man removed his hood, exposing his face. The rest of him was armored in enchanted mirror-mail, making him invisible to the eyes, but not to Korodeth's keen perception. "We made it as far as Orensdale."

Korodeth did not turn his attention from the well of ink, over which he cast a simple enchantment. "What news?"

"They've burned the Yeval monastery and erected a church of Legion."

"Good," Korodeth said. The Shedoahn Prophecies continued to be filled. Before long, Shedoah would discontinue his willful submission to the false deity Adonai. He would rise and crush Adonai and again restore order and peace and prosperity to Alrujah.

But that could not be done as long as Ribillius sat the throne. "News of Varuth?"

"Firmly devoted to Alrujah and Adonai."

"And Dalova?"

"The same."

The time to act drew near. Korodeth scrawled on the parchment: "He who controls the daughter controls the king." He rolled the parchment, tied it carefully with black twine, and whispered a last enchantment over it. Only Ribillius would be able to read these words. A simple trick of twisting spells, but it would speak to his ability as a mage—something even Ribillius didn't know about. He handed the parchment to Argus. "Leave this where the king will find it. Do not be detected."

Argus replaced his hood. "As you will, so it shall be done."

Chapter One

And four shall rise. And they shall be in the world, but they will not be of the world. They will be in it, but will not belong to it. And one from Alrujah shall come alongside the four, and they shall act as one, and they shall free the land from oppression with a mighty triumph, and they will be called the Hand of Adonai.

—The Book of Things to Come

IN THE LATE AFTERNOON, Oliver found Lauren in her pajamas, ankle deep in the snow, a foot away from the edge of the steep cliff overlooking North Chester, Minnesota. The wind circled around her feet and pulled the bottoms of her pink pants near up to her knees. Ice crusted the tops of her slippers. She stared out over the valley. No footprints; she'd been there a while. The snow reddened her ankles, and he wondered why she hadn't worn socks.

He came up behind her quietly and slowly. "You okay?" he asked.

Lauren didn't move. "We're on the mountain."

"I know."

"Not this mountain. In Alrujah. Vesper's Mountain."

Oliver took a few more steps and stood next to her. Of course she'd be thinking about the video game they'd created together. She always was. Then again, he was, too. Still, her fascination with it, her fantasies about leaving earth and being magically transported into a digital world, concerned him. She was too eager to leave the real world, and that would only make it harder for her to live in it. "Are you sure you're okay? Your mom is worried."

The dampness of her cheeks had crystallized into ice diamonds. Had she been crying or just been cold? "I'm surprised she realized I was gone," she said.

He took his jacket off and put it around her shoulders. "I'm worried, too."

She turned back to the valley. Snow slipped from the slate sky. It covered the buildings below. The gray clouds obscured the sunlight, made it feel much later than four in the afternoon. Already, the shops and homes below had their lights on. All of North Chester did, for that matter.

Lauren standing this close to the cliff made Oliver nervous, made him wonder what exactly she had in mind. "Can we go inside?" He folded his arms over his chest and shivered.

Lauren put her head on his shoulder. He liked the gentle weight of it, how he had to bend a little to his right so she wouldn't have to stand on her tiptoes. "Don't you ever want to go? To get away from here?" Her voice wavered, either from sorrow or from her chattering teeth.

"Of course I do. Wouldn't spend all my free time running code if I didn't."

"I mean really go. No more school, no more bullies, no more embarrassment or harassment. In Alrujah, I'm a princess. Here, I'm a fat loser nobody."

"Come on," he said and shivered again. "It's not that bad."

She pulled her cell phone out of the pocket of her pink flannel pajama bottoms. She punched a few buttons and handed it to Oliver. Sarah the Skeleton, the "hot" girl from chemistry, had sent her a message. *If I wuz as fat as u Id kill myself.*

Oliver sighed and put his arm around her shoulder. "First of all, you're not fat. Second of all, she's retarded. You have to know that."

"She's not retarded," Lauren said. "And she's not the only one who thinks that. Maybe she's right."

Oliver thought of the cliff, how close she stood to it. "Let's go inside and talk, okay? Sarah's dumb. She thinks anyone over fifty pounds is fat. It's not your fault you're not a skeleton like her."

Lauren faced him. She held her arms out to her sides, palms facing him. "Look at me, Oliver. Tell me I'm not fat."

She sounded like a wife asking her husband, "Does this dress make my butt look big?" No answer would suffice. Still, he had to say something. He thought for a minute of how to say what he wanted to say but didn't act fast enough.

The red on Lauren's cheeks deepened, embarrassment adding to the crimson chill. "See, you can't say it."

He crossed his arms, tucked his hands into his armpits and shivered. "Other people may think you're fat. But I don't. Neither does your mom. It's not your fault. The doctor said once he finds the right medication, you'll start to slim down some."

Lauren wiped at the iced line of tears trailing down her cheeks. "Stupid thyroid," she mumbled. "Bailey Renee calls me fat, too."

"She's your little sister. She's supposed to call you fat." He gritted his teeth to keep them from chattering and pulled her head to his chest. Remarkably, the chill of her ears pushed through his sweater and shirt, froze his chest above his heart. She'd been out here far too long. Hypothermia long. He had to find a way to get her inside, but she'd have none of that talk until he'd soothed her self-loathing.

He put his arms around her and held her tight. He could warm her a bit while he tried to talk her away from the edge. She shivered. He said, "You may not have a magazine-type body right now, but you are beautiful. You have a face that inspires poetry."

She laughed. "Wow, what a line. You should save it for Erica."

Erica. He thought of her dark eyes and her black, black hair. "Somehow, I don't think Erica would appreciate it the way you do." Snow melted on his blue sweater. A minute later, the flakes froze to the cotton and made it stiff with an icy crust. Ice streaked her wavy blonde hair. "We're going to freeze out here. Let's go in."

"I'm tired of being a nobody."

Lauren wasn't a nobody. She was his best friend, and God loved her very deeply. Still, he'd told her all that before, and she shrugged it off. She didn't like hearing how valuable, how loved she was, how much God loved her, how she was a child of God. She wanted only what she couldn't have—the approval of shallow teenagers. Instead of basing her self-worth on what God thought of her, she depended on the opinions of too-skinny students. He wanted to tell her again, but it'd do no good. She'd only argue with him and refuse to go in until he'd agreed how worthless she was. So, instead of repeating the old debate, he simply held her tighter. "Let's talk inside. It's cold."

She laughed. "I can't feel my feet. I can't walk."

He took her laughter as a good sign, though he failed to see the humor of numb feet. Sighing, he turned around and knelt in the snow.

"What are you doing?"

"Piggyback ride. Come on."

She laughed again, a high staccato sound like the chirping of a bird. "I'll crush you, Oliver."

"No chance. I'm as strong as a bull."

"You're a toothpick is what you are. Put you and Sarah the Skeleton together and you might weigh a hundred pounds."

"I'm Vicmorn, the mystic monk, m'lady, and I'll carry you with the power of Adonai to your castle in Alrujah."

She put her hands on his shoulders, wrapped her legs around his sides. With her chin on his head, she mumbled, "Whatever, crazy monk. Now, giddyup, horsey."

Oliver complied. He stood up, careful not to lose his balance or grunt. She'd take either as a condemnation of her weight. Instead, on his back, she felt the way he saw her—a thin girl, a heavy heart. His legs, now numb with cold, pushed forward. Each step pressed his ankles further into the snow. He wouldn't wobble, wouldn't even breathe heavy. He wanted her to feel weightless. It would only be a matter of time before the doctors found a balance of medication that would slim her down to the weight she should be, her real weight. Maybe she'd be happy when she was thin again. Had her happiness simply gone into hibernation, or had it quietly died for good?

When they got to her porch, Oliver wiped his feet. He set her down, took her slippers off, now wet and hard with ice, and set them next to the door. She leaned her forehead on his shoulder and said, "I don't want to go back to school tomorrow."

"You and about ninety percent of the school population." He hugged her. Not a romantic hug—a comforting embrace, one that told her that—even though they loved other people, and even though those people didn't love them back—they at least had each other. "Including me."

* * *

As always, dinner started quietly. Oliver sat next to Lauren, which had become the norm over the last few weeks. Lauren was thankful he stuck around more. It made her family a little more tolerable.

Lauren hardly touched her chicken and stuffing. She stared more than ate, using her fork to pick the chicken apart. Good as it smelled, she wasn't hungry. Anything she put in her mouth would end up on her hips anyway. Safer not to eat.

"Excellent dinner, Ms. Knowles," Oliver said. He shoveled the last bit of stuffing into his gaping maw, wiped his mouth, and sat up straight. He folded his hands in his lap like some kind of reform school student. Sometimes, she really hated how perfectly polite he was, how kindly he treated her family. Maybe because they treated him so nicely in return. At times, she believed her mother would trade her for Oliver, no questions asked. What parent wouldn't want a thin, well-mannered, straight-A genius?

Her mom's bangs slipped from behind her ear and swished across her face. She readjusted them. Smiling, she said, "Thank you, Oliver." Then, without the smile, "Eat your food, Lauren."

"Not hungry."

Her mother, shoulders slumped and eyes heavy, sat at the head of the table, the place their father used to sit. Instead of the stiff-backed oak chairs everyone else sat in, she sat in a black leather computer chair. She'd hardly taken off her gray suit jacket before she served dinner from the crock pot. "Don't make me go through all this again, please, Lauren. Hungry or not, you have to eat."

Bailey Renee, in all her perfectly slim beauty, sat at the foot of the table, opposite their mother. Oliver talked a lot about God, but Lauren couldn't understand why God would make Bailey Renee so beautiful and Lauren so ugly. Talk about unfair. Bailey ate twice as much as Lauren and stayed twig thin. She played varsity basketball for North Chester High and maintained a 4.28 GPA. Academically, she could give Oliver a run for his money. She'd pulled her light brown hair into a ponytail. Wisps of bangs tugged themselves free and framed her face like a portrait. Nose deep in a calculus book, she went out of her way to ignore Lauren.

Beautiful, smart, athletic, loved. Perfect. The exact opposite of Lauren. It's like they didn't even share a gene pool. And it all came so easily to Bailey. She hardly had to work at any of it.

Freshmen weren't even allowed in calculus, but the counselors made an exception for Bailey Renee. Didn't everyone? Wasn't she the standout exception to humanity? Nothing could be more irritating than having a sister who excelled at absolutely everything.

The only thing Lauren could do that Bailey Renee couldn't was drive. And even when Lauren picked her up from practice after school, the other girls on the team looked at Lauren funny. They'd stare at Bailey Renee, then at Lauren, as if to say, "You're related to that?"

"How was your day, sweetie?" her mother asked Bailey Renee. Bailey was "sweetie." Lauren was "Lauren."

"Good," Bailey said.

Lauren pushed her stuffing around. Her fork scraped the ceramic plate.

Her mom sighed and dropped her fork. The steel rattled as it bounced off the table. "You know what? I give up. I don't even know what to do with you, Lauren."

Oliver fidgeted in his chair. The fingers of his folded hands tightened as he stared at his plate.

"What?" Lauren asked, as if she didn't know which lecture was coming next.

"Every day it's the same thing. I have to scream at you just to get you to eat. I have to threaten to take away your stupid video games to get you to do your homework. I have to put passwords on every computer in this house so you don't waste all your time on that dumb game. Your grades are slipping, and you don't even care."

"I have a 4.2, mom. My grades aren't slipping."

"You had a 4.4 last year."

"I can't believe you're even saying this right now."

Her mom pressed on. "And you don't eat, either, no matter how many times I tell you to. Honestly, do we need to put you in counseling? Seriously?"

Bailey Renee glanced up from her book. She grinned at Lauren.

Lauren dry swallowed. Her words came out as a whisper. "Are you saying I'm crazy?"

"That's not what I'm saying at all. I'm just worried, and I'm tired, and I can't do this anymore. I work hard to make sure I can put food on our plates, and you don't even touch it. Do you know how frustrating that is?"

"Maybe you should quit," Lauren muttered.

"Excuse me, young lady?"

Bailey Renee said, "Settle down, Lauren. You're such a drama queen."

Oliver could help. Why didn't he defend her? Instead, he stared at his hands in his lap, then pushed himself from the table. "I should go."

"No, you can totally stay," Bailey Renee said. She stared at him with a wide grin. "You can show me that scripting language and physics engine you designed."

"Sit down, Oliver," Lauren's mom said. She pushed her hair behind her ear and wiped her mouth with a paper napkin.

Embarrassment and outrage heated Lauren's throat, burned the back of her eyes. She wanted to throw the plate at her mother; she wanted to kick the chair. It was bad enough being the ugly duckling, and now her mom thought she was crazy? She took a deep breath, dug deep in the pit of her stomach, and found the worst thing she could say. She pointed a finger at her mother, poking the air in front of her. "No wonder Dad left you."

"Lauren," Oliver said quickly.

"Whoa," Bailey Renee whispered. "Harsh."

Too late. Her mother's face turned from irritation to absolute despair. She opened her mouth to say something, but didn't. Her jaw hung half-open like an unhinged door.

Lauren stood up fast, dropped her fork, and stormed out of the room.

* * *

The last time Oliver had knocked on Lauren's door, they were in third grade. At some point in their friendship, which stretched back to kindergarten, knocking had become superfluous. But he knocked now, a gentle knock, a modest supplication for permission, not just to enter, but to speak.

"Go away," she said.

"It's just me."

"I know."

He opened the door anyway. She sat on her bed, legs crossed, Xbox on. The shelves lining her walls—something her father had installed for her before he left the family ten years ago—had once been filled with stuffed animals. They'd long since been replaced by books. She may not get straight A's, but few people on the planet read more than her. And, impossibly, she'd somehow filled as many journals as books she'd read. Most had to do with Alrujah—the world that formed in her mind, that took its roots in her journals, in her sketchbooks. It'd taken Oliver the better part of a year to compile all her notes, all her sketches, into the master file for the game. But he hadn't minded. She'd conceptualized a real, breathing world.

The 32-inch LCD TV on her desk provided the only light in her room. He'd grown accustomed to her sulking in the dark. And, as always, she took her anger out on her Xbox. She played some button-mashing brawler, though she'd beaten it several times. She wasn't in the mood for a challenge now. She wanted to use the avatar she'd designed, some ridiculous female ninja, to slice through competitors with graceful ease. Right now, she wanted to see something bleed. "So how long am I grounded?"

"You're not," Oliver said. He sat on her chair and rolled back over the wood flooring so he could better see the television, then put his feet up on her bed.

"How long do I have before she wants me to move out? Do I get to pack my things first?"

Oliver tried to suppress his frustration with Lauren. She hadn't always played the victim like this. But in middle school, when other students started shedding baby fat, hers clung to her bones relentlessly. Sure, she'd lost friends over it, the plight of the unpopular, but he'd lost just as many, maybe more, just for sticking by her side. How often had she thanked him for that?

He understood how hard it was to be unpopular. Truth be told, he was every bit as physically unattractive as her. What with his loppy arms and too-thin waist, his patchy beard and uncontrollable hair. But he didn't care, didn't let others get him down.

Maybe, he thought, it stemmed from her father leaving. It must. Oliver, at least, had two parents at home who reminded him how much they loved him. They sacrificed for him, supported him. Poor Ms. Knowles just seemed too tired to be as supportive as she wanted to be.

But Lauren didn't have the patience to see that. She'd been hurt enough by words to know how to use them as a weapon. And so she erected her vocabulary as a defense strategy. She'd hurt those who hurt her. He sighed. "You made her cry. Did you know that? She left the room right after you, but I heard her crying through her door."

Lauren paused the game. She set the controller on her pillow and lay down. "She called me fat and crazy. What was I supposed to do? I'm tired of being fat and stupid and unlovable. For once, it would be nice for someone to look at me without cringing. You have no idea what it's like." Her voice got softer as she spoke.

But he did have an idea, a very good one, in fact. He'd tried to tell her that on several occasions, but she'd have none of it. No room for Oliver in Lauren's pity party. So he pushed on, determined to be the strong one, determined to be the encourager. Isn't that what God had called Christians to do? To love and encourage?

He stood up and stretched his legs, tired of the constant battle he fought to combat the damage done by insecure, selfish teenagers. He'd done what he could with Lauren. Tonight, whatever seeds of love and encouragement he tried to sow would end up in the gravel beside the road. Crows would snatch them up, eat them before they had a chance to put roots in Lauren's hard heart.

His phone beeped, and he checked it. *Coming home soon? It's a school night.* "Mom wants me home. But before I go, I want to say a couple things. I want you to listen, okay?" He spoke with the gentleness he'd learned from his father, spoke with patience and perseverance. "First of all, you're not fat. I'll say that every time you say you are. Secondly, you need to apologize to your mother. I don't think you understand how deeply you hurt her tonight."

"Serves her right," Lauren whispered.

"Please, Lauren. You really have to stop. I know your mom hurt you, but she at least meant well. What you said—" he paused. "It was mean and vengeful. That kind of attitude is only going to make you feel worse." He pulled his jacket on and fixed the sleeves of his sweater. "Good news, though. We're close to a Beta. I'll have one ready by the end of the week. Two days, if I can get some time to focus on it."

Lauren sat up. "Really?"

"Really."

"Playable? Really really?"

"Really really playable."

She grinned. "Well, go home and get to work." She pulled her journal from under her pillow. The worn leather torn near the front corners, the binding creased and worn. She tossed it to him. "I came up with more stuff if you can work it in."

He went to catch it but fumbled it instead. It collapsed to the floor and pages spilled out. Ah, awkward adolescence. He had no idea how athletes kept their feet straight. He could hammer out thousands of lines of code in a couple hours, so why should simple hand-eye coordination give him such grief? "I'll get right on it, Princess."

She laughed like the caw of birds. "Good. Now get going, you crazy monk."

* * *

When Oliver got home, he stayed in his car. He turned the engine off and pulled his phone from the center console. Snow collected on the edges of the windshield. He waited for a few minutes, letting the warmth from the heater dissipate until the air inside the car took on a chill. He composed a new text message to Erica, as he did nearly every night. This time, though, he decided to actually send it. *What r u doing Tues after school?*

The air cooled rapidly. His finger felt stiff, almost numb. He swallowed his unease like a pill. His breath came out in tendrils of mist. He put his jacket on. His phone beeped. *Who is this?*

He should have known better. He wasn't even supposed to have her number. A week ago, as he walked down the science hall of North Chester High School, he'd overheard her giving it to a friend, and he memorized it.

He should have introduced himself, maybe said something witty, something funny and memorable. But Oliver wasn't known for his wit.

He put the phone in his pocket, buried his hands in the folds of his jacket, and closed his eyes. He started the car and let the engine heat up again. His parents would hear him. His '82 Honda was neither a classic nor quiet. But he couldn't go inside until he'd said his piece. If he went inside, his parents would want to talk. They'd want the full run-down of his day, and he'd give it to them. Then, he'd lock himself in his room and get lost in the coding of Alrujah. He wouldn't text Erica until two AM, likely. Too many distractions within the walls of his house. His car was quiet, peaceful, cold. Here, he could concentrate on not making a fool of himself.

Of course, he hadn't done too good of a job so far. But he was tired of loving and never daring to say anything about it. If Lauren wasn't brave enough to talk to Aiden, the North Chester High School football all-star, then Oliver would be the brave one. He pulled the phone out again and texted, *Oliver from Bio.* He put his hands in front of the heater.

How did u get my ###?

He knew she would ask this eventually, and he'd devised an answer. *On Facebook.* He had, the day he heard Erica give her number to the friend. Wanted to double check to make sure it was legit. Plus, Facebook seemed much less stalkerish than the full truth.

A beep. *Whats up Tues?*

The snow melted away when it hit the pewter gray hood, still warm from the drive from Lauren's. *Want 2 show u something in the comp lab. A game I made.*

Talk 2 me 2moro

Oliver grinned and closed his phone.

Chapter Two

They will come like a thief in the night, the four fingers of Adonai, and then the thumb. They will hold strange mysteries, and cause Alrujah to stumble. They will be a burr in the boot of kingdoms and cities. Mighty will be their powers, and all Alrujah will tremble before them.

— The Book of Things to Come

L AUREN HATED THE CAFETERIA. She much preferred eating in the computer lab, something Mr. Benson let her and Oliver do, but no one else. Mr. Benson was out sick today, though, and the sub left for lunch. Besides, for whatever reason, Oliver insisted on sitting here today, which was weird, because he hated this place as much as she did.

They put their lunch trays on the table in the far back. Lauren faced the back wall so she wouldn't see all the popular, thin kids staring at her and giggling. No one else sat at the table, and likely, no one would. The one advantage of not being popular—for the most part people left you alone. Even her too cool younger sister.

She wondered what month they'd made the grilled cheese sandwich. It looked, amazingly enough, soggy and crunchy at the same time. And the cheese hardly melted. American cheese, to top it off, which struck Lauren as neither cheese nor American. It didn't look like cheese, smell like cheese, and sure didn't taste like cheese. She'd do better to not eat, which is exactly what she did.

Oliver, however, finished his sandwich in a few bites. He washed it down with skim milk and eyed Lauren's plate.

"Help yourself."

"You need to eat," he said.

"I'll eat when I get home. Trust me. That sandwich looks like a relic from the Civil War."

"You sure it's not because … you know."

She'd been eating less and less since her weight went up a couple years ago. The doctor told her to make sure she kept eating as normal— the weight gain had little to do with her caloric intake and more to do with her thyroid. But he'd also warned her not to overeat. Even if she didn't eat, her weight would likely stay the same, maybe even increase. She just needed to be patient while they tried different doses of different drugs to find the right medication. She looked again at the pills in her hand, which she'd gotten from the school nurse before the lunch period. It said right on the bottle, do not take on an empty stomach. She popped the pills anyway. She could handle being dizzy and moody, but not being 200 pounds. "Just eat it."

"If you insist. Thanks." He snatched up her meal and finished it as quickly as he had the first. His face split with a dopey grin.

"It couldn't have been that good."

"The sandwich? Terrible. But today's going to be a good day. I can feel it."

His giddiness meant something good must have happened. "Did you finish the code?"

"Worked most of the night on it. I'm running on about three hours of sleep, but I might finish it up after school if I can stay awake." He gulped the last of his milk. "And I texted Erica last night. She wants to talk to me today."

"No way." Her eyes widened. "Serious?"

"Totally." Oliver looked up behind her.

Erica walked toward them. She wore a black skirt, black and green striped stockings that went up over her knees, a black halter top, and black vest. Her hair was black, her makeup was black, her shoes were black. Lauren wondered if she were simply covering for being color blind.

Before Erica was close enough to hear, Lauren leaned forward and asked Oliver, "Are you going to ask what's up with the gloves?"

No matter the weather, Erica always wore a pair of thin black gloves with the fingers cut off. They looked like peasant's gloves, beggar gloves.

"It's fashion. Get with it."

"No one else wears them."

"Not yet. She'll set a trend. Watch." He stood up and waved.

Erica rolled her eyes. She set her tray next to his and sat down. She scowled at Lauren. "Who's this?"

"Lauren, my best friend."

"Pleasure to meet you," Lauren said. She put her hand out, but Erica stared at her.

"So what, you're like my stalker or something?" Erica asked Oliver.

"I'm not a stalker. I'm making a game. Well, we are. Me and Lauren. A role playing game. Thought you might be interested in it."

Erica's black lips pulled into a sneer. "A video game? What makes you think I'd be interested in that?"

Oliver's face fell. He shrugged his shoulders. "Thought you might think it was cool."

Lauren's stomach growled. She pushed the gnawing hunger out of mind. Oliver was embarrassed, humiliated. Without even trying, Erica managed to trivialize the one thing she and Oliver had worked so tirelessly on for the last few years. No one thought it was important but them, and Lauren was getting sick of it. She was getting sick of a lot of things. Her face heated. Irritation and anger welled up in her like they had last night. She leaned in real close to Erica. "We were thinking of putting you in the game."

Erica grinned with half her mouth, amused, but not willing to laugh. "Really."

Lauren said, "Of course. We need a wicked witch, and you fit the bill perfectly."

Erica worked her half-grin into a half-frown. "Sounds about right. Fat girl insecurity. I've seen it before."

Lauren wanted to cry, wanted to punch Erica. She didn't do either. Instead, Oliver spoke up, much to Lauren's surprise. His soft voice sounded confident, which confused Lauren completely—how could he keep his calm? "Hey, come on, Erica. Come on, Lauren. Let's not get so mean. Get to know each other."

Erica stood up, leaving her tray of food. Lauren couldn't blame her for that. "She's not worth it," Erica said.

Not worth it? The little witch. Lauren's insecurities snapped into irritation, into a vengeful thirst for malice. "So what's with the gloves? I mean, I get that it's cold, but your gloves don't even cover your fingers. It's not fashion—none of the other goth girls wear gloves. Especially not in the spring and summer. Not like you do. And, to be quite honest, they're kinda trashy. They look like something a homeless bum would wear."

Erica's hair bristled. She turned around, ruthless eyes masking a deeper sadness. For a minute, Lauren almost felt sorry for her. "What's with your fat face?" Erica said. She turned back and walked away.

Oliver threw his empty milk carton at Lauren. "Nice going."

"What?"

"She hates me now. She didn't know me before, but now she hates me."

Lauren shrugged. "No. She hates me. You, she likes."

"I doubt it."

"I seriously don't even know why you like her. She's a witch."

Oliver put his hands behind his head and stretched his elbows wide. "Ever think she's mean as a defense mechanism? That maybe something happened to her to make her sensitive and insecure and the only way to defend herself is through sarcasm and social isolation?"

Lauren's blood froze. "You're talking about me, aren't you?"

"We all have problems, Lauren. It doesn't mean we have to be so cruel to each other, to your mom or sister or even Erica."

"I can't even believe you're saying this right now. She called me fat and insecure."

"I'm not taking sides. I'm worried about you."

"You sure have a funny way of showing it."

Oliver looked up behind her again. It must be Erica, back for more. She didn't turn around.

"Hey," Oliver said.

"Everything cool here?" someone asked. The voice sounded familiar, a boy's voice, deep and dreamy.

Crap. Aiden. And here she was all fat and blotchy faced with embarrassment. She closed her eyes and prayed he'd go away.

"Yeah. Grab a seat."

Impossibly, he put his tray next to Lauren and sat down. "You're Lauren, right?"

Her mouth instantly went dry, and she became hyper aware of her hands. What should she do with them? They sat there looking stupid and ugly.

"Yeah," Oliver said.

"You okay? Looked like you and that other girl got into a bit of a fight."

She couldn't believe her ears. Did he really ask if she was okay?

"We're fine," Oliver offered after she sat there in silent awkwardness.

"Okay, cool. Hey, you're Bailey Renee's sister, right?"

Disappointment stabbed her, and Lauren closed her eyes. She'd wondered how long it would take him to figure out her relationship to Bailey. She expected him to make the connection when they'd been paired up in Algebra II. That was a good day. She'd gotten over her nerves quickly and had a good talk with him. Of course, they never talked again.

It only made sense he'd be into Bailey Renee. The hot new kid, all-star football receiver could never be interested in a loser fat girl. Not like her.

"Yes," Oliver said. "Why?"

Aiden pushed his curly sand-colored hair back. "This is kind of embarrassing. So Bailey Renee's dating a friend of mine, and she told me you were really good at English."

Lauren cleared her throat, surprised Bailey Renee said something nice about her. She dug deep and finally found her voice. "I guess so."

"She's rocking an A+ right now," Oliver said. "She's killing that class."

"Thank God, because I'm totally not, bro. Coach says I got to pull my grade up or I'm off the team. We've got finals coming up, and I can't mess this up. I'm supposed to rewrite an essay and retake a few tests next week. Can you help me out?"

Her stupid fat hands sat on the table like two seals sunning themselves on tide rocks. "Uhm, I think so. I mean, if I'm not grounded for forever." Hope, ridiculously light and cheery, settled on her heart and tickled her with feathery wings.

The final lunch bell rang. Aiden stood up and straightened his purple and white letterman jacket. "So can we talk after school? If you need a ride home or whatever, I can get you one. Franky is already planning on giving Bailey Renee a ride home, so he can take us too, if that's cool."

"What? No, yeah. I drove, but whatever. I'll call my mom and find out if I can stay late or something. Meet me at the computer lab?"

"For sure." He smiled.

Lauren dizzied.

* * *

Thanks to funding from a grant Mr. Benson earned, the computer lab of North Chester High boasted some of the best technology in the state of Minnesota. Located in the basement level and big as two classrooms, the lab had stations for up to fifty students laid out in two horseshoe shapes, each lining the outer walls.

When Lauren and Oliver arrived at the lab, Oliver's mom, Mrs. Shaw, opened the door for them. She wore jeans and an orange turtleneck. She had a walkie-talkie clipped to the waist of her jeans and a pair of sunglasses on top of her head to keep her black hair out of her face. Lauren actually liked her more than her own mother at times.

"Thanks for staying in here with us, Mom," Oliver said.

"No problem, baby. Anything for you and Lauren."

Oliver slung his backpack under a computer station and flipped the computer on. He spoke softly, but firmly. "Can you do me a favor and never call me 'baby' at school again, please?"

She laughed and pinched his cheek. "Awww … am I embarrassing you?"

Lauren's lips pulled into a sad smile. It'd be nice to have a mother embarrass her with love instead of insult.

"Seriously, Mom. I love you and all, but you don't have to broadcast it."

Mrs. Shaw gestured to the empty room with both arms stretched wide. "Broadcast it to whom, exactly? Are we on some reality show I wasn't told about?"

"You know what I mean," he said. He pushed a flash drive into the USB hub and began copying files. "We should only be here for an hour or so. I'm going to show someone Alrujah, and Lauren's going to help someone with his English."

Mrs. Shaw said, "Oh? Oliver's not using names. You two must like these other nameless students."

Oliver blushed. "Seriously, Mom. Please. Be cool this once, okay?"

Mrs. Shaw sat at the teacher workstation and logged into the computer. "Wow. They sure do grow up fast. How about I chat with you over the intranet? Or on Facebook. What do you think?"

He sighed. "Just don't pinch my cheek or call me baby."

"Got it," she said. "At least Lauren's here. I can still talk to her, can't I?"

"Of course you can, Mrs. Shaw," Lauren said. She opened a highly organized document detailing every facet of Alrujah. She leaned closer to Oliver and whispered, "At least she didn't suggest you go see a counselor."

"So how are you, sweetie?"

It was nice to be called "Sweetie" for once. Bailey Renee didn't understand how lucky she was to have the affection of their mother, to be called sweetie by someone who meant it. She said, "I'm okay. How are you?"

Mrs. Shaw's walkie-talkie squawked. She shot up fast and headed out of the room. "Hang on a second, guys. Actually, this may take a bit. I'll be back when I can. Be good." She disappeared from the lab, probably to help break up an after-school fight. As a part-time proctor for the school, her duties included being on call for emergencies on Mondays, Wednesdays, and Fridays.

Shortly after, Aiden came in. His iceberg blue eyes froze her, and she felt like a flower blooming in reverse. "There you are," he said. He sat at the computer next to her. He smiled. "I like your sweater. That's a cool shade of purple. Like the school spirit."

Oh. My. Gosh. "Thanks," she said. "I like your…" She paused. She wanted to say "everything," but didn't want to come on too strong. "I like your arms."

"My arms?" he asked, half laughing—a sound like a song. "Right. Thanks. Anyway, here's my essay." He handed her a black jump drive.

Lauren took it, making sure her finger lightly brushed his—a gentle gesture, easily explained away as an accident. But, when their skin touched—the tip of her forefinger and his thumb—she thought her skin might erupt in electricity.

"What's this here?" he asked, pointing to her file of information about Alrujah.

"Nothing," she said quickly.

"That's a whole lot of bullet points for nothing."

Oliver turned in his seat slightly. "Actually, it's information for a game we're creating and …"

"Oliver!" Lauren shouted.

"What?"

"You guys are making a game?"

The flame of her embarrassment ignited beneath her cheeks. "Oh gosh."

"A role-playing game, called Alrujah. She does all the writing for it, and I do the graphics and the development—physics engines and all that."

"Bro, that's intense."

"Can you please stop talking," she whispered to Oliver.

Erica walked in, her black hair pulled into a rat's nest on the back of her head. A silver stud rested like some steel orb on her left nostril. She'd gotten fancy with her eyeliner and made some elaborate pattern at the corner of each eyelid, an ornate, flowery design all in black, traced down to her high cheekbones. Black lipstick covered her lips like a bruise, and her purple eye-shadow made her eyes look swollen and puffy, like she'd gone ten rounds with an expert MMA fighter. Uncountable studs and rings ran up the outside of her ears. If Lauren didn't know better, she'd have guessed Erica took her fashion sense from texts on ancient Egypt.

"Hi, Erica," Oliver said. "Come sit down."

Erica stared at Lauren. "Honestly, I'd rather not. Not if she's going to be here."

"Something wrong?" Aiden asked.

"A whole lot of things," Erica said.

Lauren rolled her eyes. She didn't want Erica there, but Oliver liked her. Otherwise, he never would have asked Lauren to put her into the game. "I can leave," she said. She stood up and Aiden put his hand on her wrist.

"Hold on, you shouldn't have to leave. You have to help me with my essay. You guys can't even be in the same room?"

Erica sent the same knife-tipped stare toward him. "The jock needs help on an essay. There's a switch."

"The game won't take long. It's not even fully finished. Still have another night's worth of work to go, but it's really cool, I promise," Oliver said.

Erica folded her arms across her chest and dropped her bag in the chair next to Oliver. She stood over his shoulder. "Be fast. I have other things to waste my time on."

Oliver smiled. He opened a file browser and began to show her the artwork he'd digitized, even the demo he'd made a few months back.

Lauren couldn't figure out why Oliver smiled at her, why he gawked at her like she was a celebrity. Erica had been rude to him since he met her, but still he took every insult like a compliment. What would Lauren do if he and Erica ever started dating? Probably never see him again. No way Erica would let him hang out with her, and there's no way he'd ever pick her over Erica. *Settle down*, she thought. *I'm making up problems that don't even exist.*

She wondered again how someone like Aiden ended up sitting next to someone like her. But it happened. And he hadn't once said anything about her weight. For a short second, hope stretched its wings. What if Aiden wasn't the typical date-the-perfect-cheerleader jock? But danger always hovered over hope. The strange politics of popularity ruled high school with clear, undeniable, irrefutable laws: Popular jocks didn't date loser fat girls. She put it out of her mind and focused, instead, on his paper. "Okay. What you want to do is start off here with a stronger thesis statement."

"A thesis statement?"

"Yes. The sentence that says specifically what your paper will explore and what it will prove."

"Lauren, you're going to have to slow way down."

* * *

Oliver clicked at his computer long after the sun had set. He checked the clock on his screen—two in the morning. He had to get up in four hours to get to school, but he couldn't bring himself to stop working on the game. Too close to quit now. Another minute of debugging final code and he'd be ready to compile and compress the Beta, nearly a week earlier than he had expected.

He'd always been driven to finish, but the thought of impressing Erica pushed him that much harder. Erica didn't hate him, amazingly. She talked with him, sat with him, and met him in the computer lab where she actually seemed excited by what he'd put together, as excited as she could seem while still being tragically cool. "Pretty dope, I guess," she'd said. "Kinda chill you put it all together." It wasn't much, but it was enough.

He tapped furiously on the keyboard. The soft icy glow of the screen dimly illuminated his room. He scrolled through thousands of pages of code, making minute adjustments, checking and rechecking for consistency. He should remain humble, but pride swelled in his chest and filled his lungs. Most professional design teams took years to develop games half as complex and fluid. And he had written it all, every line of code. Every idea from Lauren's imagination found a home in what she lovingly called "Oliver's file of gibberish."

What Lauren saw as gibberish, he saw as *Deep Red*, a groundbreaking new scripting language that would revolutionize the gaming industry. When he ran the file, the world would understand.

His phone beeped, and he jumped. It took him a minute to find the black cell phone in the darkness of his room. He flipped it open. He recognized Erica's number. *U up?*

Smiling, he pumped his fist in the air. *Whats up?* He debugged the last few lines and began the process of compiling and compressing. After putting the first DVD in the disk drive, he pressed the execute button. The computer whirred and his screen dimmed a bit. Another beep, but not from his computer. *Game looks cool. Laurens a witch.*

He frowned. *Laurens nice. Get 2 know her. Game will be playable 2moro.*

He leaned back in his chair and rubbed his eyes. Exhausted, he refused to sleep until he'd finished the game. It would likely take three DVDs, nearly full, to fit everything he needed, an hour long process at least, even with the fastest DVD burner money could buy.

Beep. *Sounds chill.*

He grinned. *C U in Bio.* He sent his final message and closed his eyes. He didn't mean for it to happen, but the gentle hum of the disk drive lulled him to sleep.

Chapter Three

The suns shall stay in the sky, and the battle shall continue. The Great Evil, Shedoah, Deceiver of Old, will cast shadows on the land, and all Alrujah will tremble at his voice. The people will cry out for a savior, and their cries will be heard by Almighty Adonai.

—The Book of Things to Come

LAUREN HADN'T EVEN OPENED her eyes Tuesday morning when she realized something felt different. The blanket was too heavy, as if there were many smaller blankets instead of one big one. And her face was freezing. Had she left her window open?

She put her head under the blankets and tried to warm her cheeks, but the sheets weren't hers.

They were soft, made of the finest white linen. And, distinctly, she smelled irises and honeysuckle. Something was definitely wrong.

Slowly, she poked her head out. Instead of her room, cold, gray stone walls, jagged and uneven, surrounded her. A glassless window was cut out on the opposite end of the room. Instantly, she recognized where she was. She had drawn this place in her journal. It was her room, or, rather, the room of her alter-ego, Indigo.

"Oh. Em. Gee," she whispered.

Immediately, she leapt out of bed. Behind her, a full-length mirror hung on the wall. She closed her eyes, slowly turned around, and hoped to God she would see what she hoped she would.

She was thin.

She touched her face. Her dreadfully and uncorrectably curly hair had been transformed into wispy blonde locks, nearly white. She wore a thin, white nightgown. The chill in the air raked across her and left a trail of goose bumps on her pale, perfect skin. Mouth open, she ran a hand over her shoulders and down around her arms. She wrapped her fingers around her wrist, and they touched. She pressed both hands to her flat stomach—she couldn't remember when it had been so toned, so firm. For a minute, she wondered if she woke up in Bailey Renee's body.

"Best. Dream. Ever," she whispered.

Slowly, she reached for her ears. On the tip of each, she felt a nub, a hardness, a tiny point. Imperceptible to anyone else, but she knew what the tips meant: she was a half-elf.

God, please don't ever let me wake up, she thought.

The stone floor drained the heat from her body through her bare feet. She tucked her hands under her arms and tried to still her chattering teeth. Despite the biting cold whipping in through the window, she took a moment to inspect the rest of the dream world. The window overlooked the castle gardens, primarily dotted with irises and honeysuckle. Gray stone paths weaved through the immaculately manicured purple and white flowers. Yellow spider trees stretched out from the flowers with long, knobby branches. They looked, as she had hoped, like spider legs. In the spring, they would bloom with yellow four-petal flowers. Their leaves, like elephant ears, grew large, providing incredible shade from the heat of the dual suns during the unrelentingly hot summers.

In winter, farther from the orbit of the greater sun, Alrujah ran cold. A light dusting of snow floated in through the window. A bird landed on the window sill—the same bird she'd drawn in her journal. Like the yellow spider tree, it was uniquely Alrujahn. Larger than a sparrow, but smaller than a raven, the bird had purple feathers and eyes black as tar. Elongated wings protruded out from its body. It alighted on the sill and stared at her. Lauren looked away quickly. "This can't be real." But her heart told her it was. Hope, that feathered pest, perched in her heart again.

A resonant voice called from behind the splintery wooden door. "Indigo! Indigo, wake up!" The voice sounded raspy, exactly as she'd described it in her journal.

Her journal! She had to find it. She dropped to her knees, ignoring King Ribillius's call, and searched desperately under her bed for the leather journal. No luck.

"Indigo!" The door shook under the heavy blows of King Ribillius. It bowed like it might shatter at any moment.

Her stomach tightened like a fist, and she said, "I'm here, Papa."

* * *

When Oliver woke up, he couldn't hear the sound of the DVD

burner working. Panic seized him—had the file crashed while he slept? Would he have to start over from his last back up? It would take hours to rebuild, and Erica would be waiting to play it after school.

He snapped his eyes open and threw his covers back.

His computer was gone. Had he been robbed? No, his desk was gone, too. He blinked. Slowly, his brain woke up.

This wasn't his room. This bed, small and wooden, had only the thinnest of mattresses—little more than numerous blankets folded over and sewn together. "What in the world?"

The blankets he'd covered up with were not blankets at all. They were skins—bear skins, deer skins, and … what was that? A pelt covered in gray and black fur, with six brown stripes running diagonally down like flights of stairs. "A Sasquatch pelt?"

This had to be a joke. The only place he'd ever seen anything like this was when he digitized a picture Lauren sketched in her journal. No one else knew about it. No one else cared.

The bed, the stone walls, the glassless windows—must be the monastery. His heavy blue robe stretched to the floor. Snow whirled outside like television static. "A dream?" Purple and yellow flowers split through the thin layer of snow. Irises and honeysuckle perfumed the air. "It's a dream!" he shouted.

The door to his small room swung open. An older man with white hair and an identical robe stood in the threshold. Eljah Morrow, his digital father. He looked sternly at Oliver and shut the door behind himself. "So much for your vow of silence," the old man rumbled.

The line, one of the first he'd coded, sounded familiar.

The chill in the air, the goose bumps rising beneath his blue robe, the scent of wintry tree branches and frozen soil—unmistakable and far too vivid to be a dream. Which meant, by process of elimination, that he was truly in Alrujah. No dream had detail this immaculate, and Oliver seldom dreamed at all. A significant lack of detail and organization marked the few he'd had growing up. They were hodgepodge compilations of random events, fears, and hopes. Too much order—the monastery with its slick damp walls, Eljah Morrow standing every inch as tall as Oliver, the rough beard on his face—marked the scene real.

He pinched his hand. The sharp pain confirmed his conclusion. He folded his thickly muscled arms and wondered if he'd woken up in Aiden's body. He'd never had muscles like this before.

He hung his head and closed his eyes. He had to think. Everything in his body affirmed the situation's reality. Every shred of logic in his too-rational brain denied it.

"Don't worry, Vicmorn, my son. You'll not face discipline for your broken vow."

Should he play along? Should he follow the script? Could he do anything else? Did it even matter?

Eljah continued. "I've received a message from King Ribillius this sunsrise. His kingdom is in danger, and he has requested you make haste to Castle Alrujah. He seeks the blessings of Adonai."

Unable to think of anything else, Oliver played along with the script. "But why me, Father?"

The old man smiled, the corner of one side of his mouth stretching up toward his ear. He reached under the collar of his cloak and pulled a golden amulet from his neck. "Because, Son. Your time has come. You are the leader of our people's spirit. We knew this day would soon be upon us. King Ribillius asked for you by name, Vicmorn."

Years ago, he wrote this entire exchange. Lauren may have handled the overall story, but he handled the minutiae of his character: Vicmorn, the mystic monk, a man after Adonai's heart, whose prayers healed. *It's like I'm dreaming the code. Maybe I need to take a break from Alrujah.* But still, the idea of a dream just didn't seem right.

It couldn't be real, no matter how real it seemed—the cold of the room, the slight heat from the breath of the old man, the smell of potatoes and herbs on that breath, or the weight of the golden amulet hung around his neck and tucked under his blue robe. He would wake up any minute, in his real bed, or, rather, in his chair, with the hum of the DVD-ROM spinning madly.

"The letter was marked urgent. The messenger is waiting to take you to Castle Alrujah. Gather your things."

Oliver nodded and opened the trunk in the corner of the room. He wished he'd put more in it. Instead, he had to make do with an old harspus wood prayer staff, leather pants, and a brown burlap shirt. They wouldn't do much against the cold, but he'd not considered the warmth of the clothes when coding them.

He pulled the thin, rough shirt over his head, the cold pants over each leg, and he found himself longing for a pair of jeans fresh from the dryer. Tugging his heavy robe over his head, he hoped the thick fabric would guard against the frigid wind. He replaced the hood over his head and hugged the old man. It felt, he thought, a lot like hugging his real father. "I'll return quickly," he said, "if Adonai wills it." The scripted lines came naturally. The ease of the words impressed him. Playing along might be fun, as silly as it made him feel. He'd not meant these lines to be spoken out loud, and yet here he was, standing in front of a digital person, speaking to it as if it had any intelligence of its own.

He hurried out the door of the monastery, into the cold mountain air, and straddled the white horse the messenger held bridled. He'd never ridden a horse before, but he held the reins like an expert. Easy as riding a bike. "To Castle Alrujah," he said, eager to see what lay ahead in the strange workings of his subconscious. Lauren would get a kick out of it when he told her at school. This dream would stick marrow-deep in his bones.

The young messenger mounted his brown horse, struggling with the weight of his armor. He leaned too far back and fell over. Getting up, he set his jaw tight and tried again. Finally, positioning himself awkwardly but stably on the saddle, the boy grinned self-consciously at Oliver. "This armor is heavy," he said, an offer of explanation Oliver hadn't asked for.

Oliver hadn't remembered coding the messenger to be so young, or so clumsy. Come to think of it, he couldn't remember a messenger coming along at all. An addition of his subconscious to the dream? Or an indication that this wasn't a dream at all. The evidence seemed to support the latter, while logic suggested the former.

An overwhelming strangeness caught the chill air in his lungs in a half-gasp. It was like swimming or flying for the first time. Alrujah was just as he imagined it, exactly as he designed it, but jumping in with both feet, being completely immersed in the water of the pool or the air of the sky, left him weightless and breathless.

* * *

Panic and excitement warred within Lauren. Both suns rose over the horizon through her window. The light refracted off the snow as it fluttered from weighty gray clouds. She thought of the cliff outside her house, and how she and Oliver had stood at the precipice two days ago. Did her wish come true? Had she been transported by some work of magic, some miracle, into the world she'd created?

She ran her hands over her skinny, toned arms compulsively. She didn't believe it, but she wanted to. The door burst open, and she leapt back with surprising speed. She'd never been able to move so fast.

An aged man, heavy in the belly, crashed into the room. "Indigo," he said. "You must leave. Immediately."

She wanted to say, "I'm not Indigo," but she didn't. She couldn't. Her entire heart told her she was. She wanted this to be real. She would play along and see how far she could make it. "Father, be calm. What is it?"

"This note." He handed her a page rolled like a scroll. She couldn't read the writing, but she recognized some of the symbols. Why had she insisted on a different alphabet? Still, whether she could read it or not, she knew what it said. She had written it in her journal years ago. "He who controls the daughter controls the king."

"This means nothing," she said, following the script. She'd written it so long ago, the words felt fuzzy, thick on her tongue. Still, they rolled out with a natural ease, as if she'd said them before, as if she'd say them again.

The heavy man bellowed to the hall, "Guards!" Seconds later, two thickly armored men marched into her room brandishing broadswords and heavy, square shields. "I'll not have my daughter kidnapped and used as a pawn!"

Lauren stared at her hands, her pen-thin fingers. They'd been so fat and useless in North Chester. Here, they felt mobile and dexterous. "It doesn't have to be like this, Father."

"I won't have it." His stern face flushed with anger and fear. The skin of his cheeks erupted with redness, his eyes narrowed.

She recognized his heavy gold crown resting on his hoary hair. Diamonds and multi-colored gems surrounded a center jewel, a midnight sapphire, which shone indigo when it caught the light. The Crowned Sapphire of Alrujah had inspired her character's name. "What would you have me do, dear Father?"

"The tower is the only place you'll be safe." He spat his words out quickly, with finality.

"I'll freeze in the tower. Besides, they would look for me there. We can't risk an assault on the castle."

"Let him come," Ribillius seethed. "We're more than capable of defending our walls, our homes."

"Think of the casualties, Father. A battle like that would decimate our forces. And I'd be vulnerable to any aerial assault the Mage Lord may launch against me. I'd be nearly defenseless."

The king took her knobby elbows in his hands. "You are not queen yet, young lady. Let him sack the city, so long as your neck does not break. No price is too high to pay for you."

"You must think as a king and not as a father. Your people trust you with their lives. Don't throw them away needlessly. Send me away. It's the only way I'll be truly safe."

He laughed. "Send you where? Where may you hide? The swamps of Pellbred? The Dragon's Back Mountains? Perhaps the Ruins of Norgren? Evil is no stranger to Alrujah, my dear. Droughtworm infests most of our cities. I cannot keep money in the hands of my people. We have few friends within the walls of other cities, my love. They do not understand the peril we are in. The influences of the Mage Lord are evident, but the people do not believe he exists. They blame me, my love, and will do anything to get to me. No, you are only safe here where I may protect you."

Droughtworm? She'd not written that in the script. Nor had she mentioned poverty. In her journals, Alrujah was a place of influence and wealth, and Ribillius was well-loved and respected. "I know a place," she said, sticking to the script. She had no idea what else to say. She leaned toward him until her lips neared his ear. His salty stubble scratched her cheek. "Yeval Forest."

"The Bleeding Grounds? No," he said quickly. "It's far too dangerous. You would never make it."

"I'm perfectly capable of providing for myself."

"Leave us quickly," Ribillius snapped. The dutiful guards clinked out of the room and closed the door. "I've already lost your mother because of her involvement in the Council of the Order of the Protectorate. She vanished from me years ago, and the Council will not tell me what happened to her. I will not give you up to them yet. The time may come for you to rule the land as a member of the Council and as a queen, but that time is not now. The Shedoahn Order has its spies everywhere, and it is unwise and unsafe for you to even mention Yeval Forest."

Lauren sat on her bed and put both her hands over her heart. This was not in the script. Sure, she knew Yeval Forest, knew the Council of Yeval secretly ruled over the land of Alrujah with more power than Ribillius himself. But his paranoid speech about the Shedoahn Order rattled her. She'd never heard of it.

Her throat tightened, and her head dizzied. "The what?"

He knelt before her. With a gentle hand, he cupped her neck and ran a finger over her smooth cheek. "Indigo, if you must go, I understand.

But please tell me you won't seek out the Council."

His tears washed away whatever notion she had about this being a dream. Sadness lined his face and made his cheeks glisten with wetness. She missed her father then, her real father, and loved Ribillius even more for being everything her real dad should have been.

She backed herself into a corner, sat on the floor, and pulled her knees into her chest. She wrapped her arms around her legs and rested her head on her knees. *This can't be real.*

Ribillius asked, "Indigo? Are you well?"

"No, Papa. I'm not." Her spirit stretched, as if her chest were being pulled open and her heart put on the rack.

He knelt beside her and pulled her into his arms. "I will not let him find you. You have my word." He whispered to her, ran his fingers through her wispy hair. "I will send you away, but not to Yeval. And you will not go alone."

Lauren concentrated on slowing her breathing, on maintaining control over whatever slippery grip she had left on sanity.

Ribillius kissed her head, and she wished he'd never leave her, wished she could stay here with him, wished she could have a father again. But, in her infinite stupidity, she'd created a situation that forced her away from her father. Her presence at the castle endangered too many people. It endangered her father.

Chapter Four

In those days, the monks who honored Adonai were gifted with a portion of His power. With His power, they healed humanity, shielded them from the onslaught of the elves, summoned angels to aid in the battle for Alrujah. In all of this, they honored Adonai, and pleased Him.

—The Book of the Ancients

Y NOW, OLIVER SHOULD have been awake, so why wasn't he? The dream persisted unrelentingly, and, no matter how much he enjoyed riding a horse, the weightlessness and speed, the rhythmic stamping of hooves, the cold air pressing his cheeks, each passing moment made him a little more uneasy.

What if, despite all logic and reason, the whole scenario was real?

The cold of the leather saddle between his legs numbed his thighs. The chill of the pommel nearly froze his hand. Alrujah confirmed its reality through all five of his senses. His dreams were never this vivid, never this ordered or this real.

Beautiful Alrujah brimmed with danger. He had no doubts he could live here happily for some time, but only if he could avoid being ripped apart by ravenous monsters.

His mind broke in again, protested his assumption of reality. This simply couldn't be real. He wouldn't give in to childish fantasies of being swept into distant kingdoms to fight dragons, not like Lauren. Sure, he loved the game with his whole heart, but he understood what was real and what wasn't. At least, until now, he thought he had.

Oliver was a man of numbers and data. But being pulled into some strange fantasy land was exactly the kind of thing Vicmorn the monk would accept on faith. And with each steaming breath of the steed beneath him, Oliver felt more like Vicmorn, who would assume Adonai had supernaturally placed him in a position to be active in His will. If Adonai could do that, then couldn't God? Of course He could, but would He?

The black-barked harspus trees thinned and gave way to flat

grasslands on either side of the winding Fellian River. The messenger, who rode ahead of him, pulled back on his reins and his black horse halted past the tree line. He took his oversized helmet off and set it on his pommel. A tangle of brown hair hung over his ears. The horse neighed and shied back a step.

It was just Oliver's luck to finally get Erica's attention and wake up in some alternate reality. "Yeah, I know we were supposed to meet at the computer lab after school again, but I kind of fell into the game I created, and I was too busy running around pretending to be a martial-arts monk and trying to find a way to get back to reality to make it by three o'clock. Want to go to prom this spring?"

Under the dark clouds, the gray waters of the Fellian River rushed through the cavern it carved for itself like nar'esh poison through a vein. The two dominant towers of Castle Alrujah loomed through the fog hanging beyond the river. They stretched toward the soft glow of the suns. From this distance, they looked like two lower case i's. "Why are we stopping?" Until then, they had ridden the horses hard. When the king demanded an urgent reply, things happened quickly. He'd sent his two fastest horses and his fastest rider. Clumsy as he was, the boy could ride. Oliver hardly kept pace.

The messenger pointed downstream. He struggled to keep his arm up under the weight of the polished steel. "The river beast."

Downstream, a blue scaly head split the silvery water. Its jaw hung agape. Thousands of sharp, jagged teeth, stained red with blood, lined its maw. Oliver had nearly forgotten this part of the script. The serpentine neck stretched backward in the shape of an S.

The messenger spoke with the reedy voice of a child. "If we stay far enough back, it should leave us alone. But if we approach the river now, it may anger him."

"He won't come down this far."

"How can you be sure, Brother Vicmorn?"

Technically, the messenger should call Oliver "Father." It was his new rightful title. The passage of the amulet to him signified an elevation in rank among the Monks of the Cerulean Order. But this was not the time or place to correct the young man. "Trust me." He slipped a hand under the collar of his robe and ran a finger over the golden amulet his father had given him. The ancient prayer amulet had been handed down from Adonai himself, so the story went. It granted the wearer, according to the lines of code he'd compiled last night, special powers of prayers, prayers uttered in the midst of battle and at times of need, which pretty much covered the rest of the game.

The messenger licked his lips. "We should wait and make sure the beast turns back."

Oliver shook his head and pulled the hood of his robe over his head to keep his ears out of the wind. "Do you wish to tell the king why we're late?"

The messenger looked from the bluish beast to Oliver, as if weighing which option would be more terrifying—facing the wrath of the river beast or the anger of King Ribillius.

Oliver closed his eyes, hand on his amulet, and said a silent prayer in a language he hardly recognized. As foreign as the words sounded, Oliver strangely understood them.

The Ancient Language. He remembered meticulously coding the bizarre language Lauren created and copied down in her notebook. Why she'd insisted on an alternate language boggled his mind, but he'd went with her on it. He feared she might pull up stakes if he refused.

The beast craned its neck up, and finally, turned away from them and moved off.

Oliver positioned his horse next to the messenger's. "In time, you'll learn the courage of Jaurru."

"I doubt anyone is as courageous as him," the messenger said, though his face split with a hopeful grin.

The horses clopped across the rickety bridge spanning the rushing waters of the Fellian River. An angry chill tinged the air over the waters, bit at the skin on his face. They moved swiftly, but cautiously. The river beast buried its head beneath the waters. The shadow of the massive beast moved away from the bridge, exactly as Oliver had prayed it would.

At this point in the game, the point of view should have switched over to Jaurru, but it didn't. For a second, Oliver half expected to wake up in Jaurru's body and play that part. But he didn't. He rode his horse toward Alrujah and to the castle within its walls. Further evidence that this must be a dream.

Or, it might be a residual code. For Vicmorn to get from this location to the castle, he would have to travel. The computer must have filled in the gap in the coding. He'd designed it to do exactly that—to reason, to make ends meet. Not to put too fine a point on it, the game's artificial intelligence, which he'd designed, was the most complex reasoning computer script available. He'd designed the feature to allow for maximum individuality for the player. Here, though, his heart beat a little faster. No counting on the script to guide him. With AI governing the game, anything could happen.

* * *

Among the items in the chest in her room, Lauren found a white-hilted dagger in a white sheath and a hooded white fur-lined cape. She draped a white fur belt over one shoulder and under her arm so the hilt of the dagger rested on her left side above her hip. Theoretically, the cape should increase the strength of her spells by five percent. Strangely, once the cape draped over her shoulders, strength ran through her, as if she'd taken a deep breath of cold air—a crispness in her blood, an awareness of the environment around her. Or had she mistaken her relief as strength? Relief to have something over her thin dress, something over her beautifully round shoulders, to keep the chill off her slender neck?

She fastened the cape under her neck. It stretched down to her calves. She pulled it around herself, admired the gold trim along the edges and the midnight sapphire clasp.

The chill of the snow fluttering in through the window and the depth of the purple feathers of the bird staring at her suggested reality. Her initial surprise and shock thawed with the rising of the twin suns. The room, the suns, the bird, and snow were as normal as a hardboiled egg for breakfast.

Her father's raspy voice dripped with genuine love. She hadn't heard anything like it in a long time. More alarmingly, she loved him, too. She shouldn't. He wasn't real. Couldn't be. None of this was.

But it had to be. All of it.

Before she opened her door, she took a deep breath. She knew what would happen next. She would maneuver down the stairs of the castle, navigate the halls until she came to the throne room. By the time she arrived, Vicmorn would already be standing in front of her father. He'd be tall like Oliver, but stronger, and he'd be wearing the heavy blue robe of the Monks of the Cerulean Order. Within the hour, she'd leave the castle and travel to Varuth for the night.

This must be what it would be like to wake up from a coma. You open your eyes and everything is different. Everyone has changed and you don't remember anything. Everything is new and exciting, familiar and terrifying.

If she had to wander Alrujah with nothing but the cape on her back and the dagger on her side, it would be good to do it with a friend. Or, at least, someone that was supposed to be a friend. And, if things played out the way they should, Ribillius would send Jaurru, the King's Guard, and her father's most trusted man, with her. Lauren had designed Jaurru to resemble Aiden in nearly every way, from his curly sandy-blond hair to his slightly crooked teeth. He would come to love her, or to love Indigo. Either way would be fine with her.

The more she thought about it, the lighter she felt—too light. She looked down, bending her slender neck, to see her feet floating inches above the slick stone. "Well, that's just perfect," she said. She sighed, opened the door, and pulled herself along the wall. If she pointed her toes down, the tips of her white fur boots hovered only a half-inch above the ground. Unless someone looked closely, they might not notice.

She thought of weights, of barbells and medicine balls and boulders. She thought of herself in North Chester, of Sarah the Skeleton's text. *If I wuz as fat as u Id kill myself.*

Her toes touched the ground. The relief it brought didn't do much to ease the poisonous memory of Sarah and all her dreary soulless clones.

She moved down the stairs, insecurity heavy on her shoulders again.

Soldiers in polished steel packed the windowless, torch-lit room, all with swords drawn and held in the air toward the king. Each knelt with his head bowed. Lauren had drawn this scene in her journal years ago, but experiencing it made her breath catch in her throat. A man in a blue robe stood in front of the crowd. He alone refused to kneel, and her father looked furious.

"I bow for no one but Adonai," the man in blue said.

Vicmorn's line. Penned by Oliver. Lauren had thought this entire exchange was a stupid idea, but Oliver insisted, so it stayed in. Collaboration required give and take. Sometimes Oliver took more than he gave, at least in the context of Alrujah. And why shouldn't he? He did all the computer work. She only wrote the story and did the sketches.

Vicmorn's voice sounded like Oliver's. No surprise. He was tall and lanky like him, too.

"You will bow to me, Brother Vicmorn. Your father had no trouble acknowledging my reign. Why this sudden betrayal? Why this treason?

I send for you to petition Adonai on my behalf, and you come at me with insults?"

Showtime. She rushed to Vicmorn's side, bowed to Ribillius, and said, "Father, forgive him. His refusal to bow is not an act of treason, but one of dedication to Adonai. Who better to petition our God than one who is wholly committed to Him?"

When he looked at her, Ribillius's anger melted from his face, replaced instead by worry and concern. "Forgive me, my precious daughter. You are right. My concern is only for your safety."

"What is your prayer, my lord the king?" Vicmorn asked.

Ribillius stood from the throne and took Lauren by the hand. He turned her to face Vicmorn. "For my daughter's safety."

"And this," Vicmorn said with a nod toward Indigo, "is your daughter?"

"It is."

Vicmorn stared at her, angry or confused. "I sense you are in danger. I sense you wish to journey far away from Alrujah."

Her face fell. For the second time in less than an hour, two primary characters broke away from the script. Had Oliver changed these details without mentioning it to her? No, he wouldn't be that selfish. But no other option presented itself, unless …

He couldn't be. She mouthed the word, "Oliver?"

Vicmorn whispered, "Aye, Lady Lauren."

The heat drained from her face, and her fair skin ran white as paper. Were they both part of the same dream, or was this a simple twist in her dream, another wrinkle to further unsettle her?

Vicmorn knelt quickly, as the script called for, put a hand on the prayer amulet, and closed his eyes. He began speaking in a different language, one Lauren didn't understand. She wondered if Oliver had actually learned the language she'd made up, or if he mumbled for show.

When he finished mumbling incoherent nonsense, he stood again. "I've petitioned Adonai on your behalf. He warns of imminent danger. He promises safety for your daughter, but not here. His plans for her lie elsewhere."

The king bowed his head, crushed. "Where?"

"Where does not matter. Only when. She must leave immediately. I am to accompany her."

Ribillius asked, "You?"

"And with me, the favor of Adonai."

The king nodded. "So be it. In addition, Jaurru shall accompany you both." At these words, the soldiers, who had been kneeling, blades outstretched, all stood and replaced their swords in their sheaths. They moved as one, and the thunderous metallic clapping of their clanging armor shook the room.

"Jaurru," Ribillius shouted.

No answer.

Vicmorn looked at Lauren, who shrugged.

The king stood. "Jaurru!" he bellowed.

Still nothing.

If this weren't a dream, and if she and Oliver had been pulled into the game, could Aiden have been pulled in as well? If he had, he'd be more lost than her.

Chapter Five

In those days, men defended themselves with weapons forged of steel and iron. They cried out to Adonai, and Adonai heard them. He delivered them from the slavery of the Otherlanders and brought them back to Alrujah and raised up the Dragon's Back Mountains to defend the land from those who seek irresponsible power.

—The Book of the Ancients

BAILEY RENEE SLUNG HER backpack over her shoulder and made her way to Lauren's room. She'd better be up. If she overslept again, Bailey Renee would kill her. She hated always running late to school. The tip of the sun inched over the mountains. The yellow of it looked like a yolk, while the whites of the sunrise egg spread out over the jagged tips of the distant Sawtooth Mountains. She flipped on the hall light and knocked on Lauren's door. "You better be up," she said.

But Lauren didn't say anything. Normally, by now, she'd have heard her groaning and kicking her covers off, or else she'd chastise her for being rude and immature or whatever. But she always said something. Now, the only noise was the slight thrumming of the overhead ceiling fan as it woke up and ran a few slow laps around the central hall light.

"Are you still pouting?" She shifted her backpack from her right shoulder to her left. Her calculus and biology books felt like they'd been printed on stone or lead. She didn't particularly like her schedule—school in the morning, basketball in the afternoon, homework until bed—but it would all pay off senior year. She hadn't worked this hard to get lazy and throw away her dreams of being valedictorian and earning a full ride to Stanford.

Stanford sounded good right about now. Sunny California never dipped under seventy degrees. Did it even snow in California? It must, somewhere. But when she thought of the state, she imagined beaches, crazy college towns, friends laughing while hiking in the middle of winter through thickly wooded passes near the bay.

She checked her watch. If they were going to be on time, they'd need to be out the door in twenty minutes. "Get up, Lauren. If you're going to get ready, you have to do it now. Don't make me ride the bus again. You know how much I hate riding the bus."

She tested the knob. Locked.

Hadn't Mom said not to lock doors? Lauren would be in some seriously hot water when Mom heard about this. If she didn't fix her attitude, she'd find herself on some shrink's couch by the afternoon. "Lauren, come on! Stop being such a drama queen. Let's go."

The ceiling fan thrummed rhythmically. The motor whined.

She *really* hated the bus.

Bailey Renee pounded on the door. "Seriously! Get up!"

No wonder Lauren didn't have a boyfriend. No one liked unceasing pity-parties. Bailey Renee wished Lauren would, for once, get over herself and accept reality. Who cared how much she weighed? She'd have a lot more friends if she had more confidence.

Bailey sighed heavy enough for Lauren to hear through the door. "Fine. I get it. You don't want to take me to school. Whatever. I'll ride the bus. I'll give you your space. But don't forget to pick me up after practice, okay? Franky can't give me a ride today."

Nothing.

"I won't tell Mom you didn't give me a ride in, okay? I get that you're still mad. But if you don't pick me up, I'll have to call Mom to get me, and you know how mad she'll be. I'm serious."

Nothing.

Bailey Renee shook her head. In a high, mocking voice, she whispered, "Drama."

* * *

Oliver tucked the golden prayer amulet under his robe and slid one hand into the sleeve of the opposite arm. He gripped each of his elbows. His arms fit easily in the loose blue cotton sleeves.

Ribillius's crown slid forward on his head. He looked past Oliver toward the rear pillar and gestured with a quick wave of his hand. A lightly armored soldier stepped forward. Unlike the other steel-clad knights, he wore light chainmail, a shirt bearing the crest of Alrujah—a Razorbeak with its head tilted toward the western sun, purple wings pointing to both suns, which were little more than two white circles on either side of the crest—greaves, and no helmet. He kept his black hair shorn short, close to his scalp. Instead of a sword on his back, he wore several daggers on his belt, one for any occasion. Most of the blades were only a few inches. One looked closer to a foot. Any bigger and it'd be a short sword.

Oliver recognized him immediately. Captain Korodeth led the king's network of spies and recon soldiers. Essentially, he filled the role of medieval CIA director. Because of this, his men moved swiftly and stealthily. Heavy armor hindered more than it helped. He and his soldiers wielded speed as a weapon.

"Find Sir Jaurru and bring him here immediately," Ribillius said.

Oliver did not like the tone of the king's voice. If Aiden had been pulled in the way Oliver and Lauren had been, he would be confused, and being summoned to an angry king could change the course of the game exponentially. It could ruin their chance of getting home.

"Father," Lauren said. She sounded frightened but confident. "There must be good reason for Jaurru to be absent. Allow me to go with Captain Korodeth. My abilities may be needed."

The king considered this and nodded. "Very well."

"And Vicmorn should come as well. Perhaps he needs a monk's prayers."

Again, the king said, "Very well."

Instantly, the three weaved their way through the back of the castle toward Jaurru's personal quarters. Oliver used his prayer staff as a walking stick. With each step, the thick harspus rod tapped the cold stone floor. Relieved to be out of the throne room, he still battled his nerves. How would they explain this to Captain Korodeth? Would they be able to? Should they?

They walked quickly to the back of the castle, their footsteps echoing off stone walls. Oliver said a quick prayer, not to the god of the game, but to God, the real God. He could work here as easily as He could in their normal lives. In fact, He had probably brought them here. No other answer satisfied.

At the back of the castle, they jogged up seven flights of stairs. Ordinarily, the effort would have left him winded and weak-kneed, but it didn't. He was as strong at the top of the stairs as he was at the bottom. In a moment of lucidity, he understood—though Vicmorn may look vaguely like Oliver, especially in the face, his thickly muscled body made Oliver's look like limp spaghetti-noodles. He couldn't imagine how excited Lauren would have been to wake up inside Indigo's body.

"We check his room first," Korodeth whispered, every bit as paranoid as she'd designed him. The daggers on his belt swished as he moved down the corridor with surprising quickness and stealth.

Once they arrived, Korodeth knocked on the door. "Jaurru!" he called.

A lump swelled in Oliver's throat. Someone moved on the other side of the door, but he didn't hear the heavy clanging of armor. "How many times do I have to tell you? I'm not Jaurru." The voice sounded irritated. Oliver recognized it as Aiden's. Not good, at all.

Korodeth pounded again. "Jaurru, the king summons you! What mischief is this?"

Lauren said, "Perhaps his mind is under a spell. Perhaps his memory has come under attack."

Perfect, he thought. What an improvisation. He'd have to follow her lead, think on his feet, improvise lines that may help get them back on track, back on the script. "I've seen this before," he said. "At the monastery. Travelers come in, their memories cluttered and confused."

"Are you able to help him?" Korodeth asked. He worked to sound concerned, but distrust lined the edges of his voice.

"Aye. But I must do so alone."

Korodeth narrowed his eyes skeptically. "Young Vicmorn, you do not hold the same trust your father holds with us."

"You trust my father, and he trusts me. As does King Ribillius, who sent for me by name. I will prove my trustworthiness in this small matter so you may see that I am trustworthy in more important matters."

Korodeth eyed him, ever suspicious, but finally produced a black steel key from a ring on his belt. They'd hardly jangled as he'd moved down the hall, and Oliver had almost forgotten he wore them. Now, looking at the numerous keys to the castle on his belt, Oliver thought Korodeth looked like a medieval janitor. A particularly dangerous janitor at that.

Korodeth slipped the key in the lock and opened the door. Oliver slid in and the door closed behind him.

Jaurru's quarters looked more like an armory than a bedroom. In addition to a straw practice dummy in one corner, several racks of swords, shields, and axes lined the walls. They gleamed in the light of the lesser sun, which poured in through a window on the east side of the room. Several skins lay carelessly piled on the redwood bed.

Aiden, dressed in loose fitting cotton pants and a light white shirt laced in the front, looked at Oliver. His face moved from confusion to rage and back. "Oliver?" He stared out a window overlooking the sprawling city beneath. "Seriously, bro. This is the weirdest dream ever."

Oliver removed his hood slowly. "I don't think this is a dream." He set his staff on the bed.

"No way. This is a full-on dream. Or I took up drugs and don't remember it."

How could he explain this in a way Aiden could understand, especially since he couldn't understand it himself? "It doesn't feel real to you?"

"Of course it does. But it can't be real. You're a brain, aren't you? You should know this is a dream."

Oliver sighed, decided to take a different approach. "You ever take Theoretical Physics?"

Aiden turned away from the window. "They look like ants down there, bro. We're pretty high up, aren't we?"

"Seven stories, yes. But it doesn't matter right now."

"Nothing matters." He ran his hands along the gray stone walls and took a sword down from the rack nearest the window. "In a few hours I'll wake up and head to school. I'll find you at lunch and tell you all about this trippy dream." He twisted his wrist and the sword looped around to Aiden's left. He repeated the motion on his right side. The sword moved through the air with a subtle whoosh. It moved in forward circles, then in reverse circles. "You and Lauren are working on some fantasy game, aren't you? Wouldn't it be a trip if this were your game? Like, if I predicted what your game would be like. I could totally give you some ideas from this dream."

"We don't need ideas. And yes, this is our game." How strange to say it out loud, how clunky and awkward the words felt in his mouth. He cleared his throat. "You ever see a movie where people move through dimensions?"

"Sure. Love movies." He put the sword back on the redwood rack.

"Ever see Tron?"

"Sure. Dude gets sucked into a video game."

"I think that's what happened to us."

Aiden laughed loudly, as brash as Jaurru. "Sure, that makes much more sense than me having a dream. Why am I even talking to you? Maybe I'll jump out the window here and fly around this place. Get a bird's-eye view." He turned back to the window, and Oliver caught him by the elbow.

In less than a second, Aiden reversed Oliver's grip and threw him against the wall. Swords and axes clanged on the racks. Oliver impossibly caught himself against the wall with both hands and feet. In a split second of weightlessness, he leapt back at Aiden, his foot in front of him. It sliced through the air toward Aiden's chest.

Aiden jumped out of the way at the last moment. He yanked a sword from the rack and spun around to face Oliver, the tip leveled at his neck.

Oliver moved on instinct. As Aiden lunged at him, his full weight behind the attack, Oliver ducked to one side, grabbed Aiden's wrist, and pulled it under his other arm. He twisted the wrist until the blade broke free. In one fluid motion, he caught the hilt of the sword in his left hand and smacked Aiden in the ear with the flat of the blade.

Aiden stumbled back with a sneer and cupped his ear with his hand. He pulled it down to check for blood. "How in the world did you do that?"

"This isn't a dream."

Aiden grinned. "As long as you have my sword, I think I'll take your word for it."

Oliver let his breath out. He handed the sword back to Aiden and hoped to God Aiden wouldn't attack him again. "That's what I'm trying to tell you. As stupid as it sounds, I think we've slipped into some sort of alternate reality."

Aiden kept his eyes on Oliver as he took the sword. "How can you be sure?"

"Because we created this place. Every detail, from the castle to the Fellian River, to the Monastery of the Monks of the Cerulean Order. I've spent the last seven years of my life creating a computer code to bring this world to life. But I didn't anticipate it actually becoming real."

"So this *is* your game?"

"It's the only logical answer. I was running the Beta code last night, and then we three woke up here."

"Three?"

"Lauren and I. And now you." Oliver moved toward the door.

"Not cool, bro."

"Seriously not cool. You have to understand, we didn't mean for this to happen."

Aiden lunged at Oliver, sword outstretched. He twisted his body in midair and barrel-rolled. Oliver hardly had time to move, and the edge of the blade caught the fabric of his robe.

Aiden, still airborne as he flew past Oliver, flipped forward, somersaulted in front of the door, reversed his grip on the sword, and stabbed backward behind him.

Again, Oliver had only seconds to react. He fell backward, and the tip of the blade came within inches of his chest. Oliver threw his hands over his head. "Take it easy!"

From outside the door, Korodeth called, "Is all well?"

Aiden dropped the sword. The cold metal clanged on the stone flooring. He took two steps away from the weapon and put his hands on his head. "I'm not going to lie. I almost killed you right then."

Oliver whispered. "I know." He stood up slowly and rubbed the back of his head. Every muscle tensed, ready to leap out the window if Aiden grabbed the sword again.

Aiden started pacing, his hands behind his head, fingers interlocked, as if he were about to explode into a long set of sit-ups. "Okay. Alright. Alternate reality. Sure. So why me? How did I end up here? Is everyone from North Chester here?"

"I don't think so. I sure hope not." Oliver picked up his prayer staff and held it tightly. If Aiden lost his cool again, he could use this as a simple means of defense—if he anticipated another random attack in time to save himself. "We modeled Jaurru's character after you."

Aiden's eyebrows lifted. "Really? Why?"

Oliver had no interest in saying anything to anger him more, had no interest in staring down Jaurru's blade again. "It was Lauren's idea." Immediately, he regretted it. He'd sold Lauren out for his own well-being. "And mine, too. We thought you fit the part."

"Bro, you guys hardly know me. You don't know my life."

"You seem chivalrous. You seem honorable."

He shook his head. "Thanks, I guess. So, how do we get home? Can't you dial up a portal or something? Because I'd kind of like to get home. We got playoffs this week, and if I don't make practice, coach won't let me play."

Oliver tugged at the amulet under his cloak. His eyes wandered off to the ceiling. Playoffs were the least of his worries, but Oliver didn't want to tell him that. Instead, he said, "A portal's not a bad idea. I hadn't considered it before. If we can get *The Book of Sealed Magic*, maybe we can open a portal back to our world."

"What are you talking about?"

Why hadn't he thought of it earlier? It made sense—to beat the game, they had to conquer the Mage Lord and find the book. As speculative as it was, the portal idea had the most promise. And the idea gave them purpose, a definite goal to strive toward, and an excuse to follow the script. "I think I can get us home. You're going to have to trust me, though. Get your armor on and grab your sword. Hurry. Stick close to me and Lauren and follow our lead."

Aiden touched the suit of armor in the corner of the room opposite the bed. "You mean this isn't some sort of medieval decoration?"

"It's real enough. Real as everything else in this world."

"Totally don't even know how to put this thing on. Looks dangerous."

Oliver moved back toward the door. "I'm sure you'll figure it out. Unless you want me to stay and help."

"No chance." Looking at the suit again, he shook his head and said, "This is way messed up."

Chapter Six

Because of this, Adonai changed the name of His chosen general from Raasnus, which means strong one *in the old tongue, to Solous, which means* righteous avenger. *He would end the reign of the elves and punish their idolatry and wickedness. He would rule Adonai's kingdom with wisdom and justice.*

—The Book of the Ancients

WHEN AIDEN FINALLY CLANKED out of his room in his heavy armor, Lauren wanted to launch herself at him and throw her arms around him. The urge welled up equally from the Lauren part of her and from Indigo. But she restrained herself and kept her composure.

If she had thrown herself at him, it could have been a fatal mistake.

As the king's personal guard, Jaurru wore a heavier, more ornate armor than the simple steel-clad soldiers in the throne room. While his still gleamed as brightly as theirs, his helmet sported three bladed ridges sweeping from the front to the back, each terminating in a gruesome point. The polished steel was painted with Alrujah's purple in stripes along his arms and legs. The emblematic Razorbeak adorned his chest and kite-shaped shield. Bladed points extended from the joints of his elbows up the back of his arms, and similar tines pointed up from his knees. The shield itself had edges sharp as swords. The suit served as protection and as a weapon, an extension of the deadly skills of the soldier wearing it.

She couldn't help but stare, though she told herself not to. What would happen if they made eye contact? He must hate her. He'd blame this mess on her. She'd insisted Jaurru look like Aiden, act like him, too. She could handle being ignored by him, but not being rejected.

"Are you well, Sir Jaurru?" Korodeth asked.

Aiden didn't look as confused as she thought he might. "Sure, I guess," he said.

"He is well now, Captain," Oliver said.

"Good. The king summons you." He turned on his heels and headed back toward the throne room.

Aiden's eyes sauntered over her. "Lauren?"

She wanted to say yes but found her breath locked in her chest. Instead, she nodded.

"Wow," he said. "You're …"

Oliver said, "Let's worry about that later, big guy. Right now, we've got a king to see." He hurried after Korodeth toward the staircase.

Aiden clanked alongside Lauren, watching each of her movements. "I can't even believe … I mean … wow."

Not exactly the response she'd figured he'd have, but she'd take it, and not ask questions. Maybe Oliver hadn't told Aiden it was her fault Aiden had been pulled into the game, too. Maybe he had, and Aiden didn't care. Either way, she wouldn't let this opportunity pass. She'd enjoy his stupefied, dumb-struckness.

Oliver and Korodeth, a few steps ahead of them, disappeared down the spiral staircase when she realized she'd not said a thing to him since he came out of his quarters. She should say something to break the increasingly awkward silence. "Nice armor." The statement came out more as a question than anything.

"Yeah, it is. Pretty gruesome. Look, I don't mean to stare. I'm sorry. You're so different." Aiden, with his long stride, took the steps two at a time.

She took the steps quickly, holding her cape up so she wouldn't trip on it. "Believe me, I know."

"And your dress."

Instead of being flattered, irritation washed over her. For a minute, she almost wished she were fat again, so he'd learn to love her and not whatever digital body she'd given herself. So she shifted the conversation. She whispered, loud enough to be heard over the clanking of the armor, but quiet enough so Korodeth wouldn't overhear.

"Okay, crash course, hot stuff." Had she really said, "Hot Stuff"? She moved on quickly, hoping he wouldn't catch her faux pas. "In this world, I'm Indigo, daughter of King Ribillius."

"So you're a princess? You're wearing a very princess dress."

"Keep your voice down," she said, touching his arm. His armor was absolutely freezing. "Yes, I'm a princess. Anyway, the Mage Lord has …"

"The Maze Lord?"

"Mage, as in magic. Try to keep up. Anyway, he's threatened my life, so I'm leaving the castle to hide somewhere. My dad doesn't like the idea, but too bad for him."

"Wait, your dad or the king?"

"Same guy."

"Your real dad's here, too?"

Lauren swallowed. "No, just listen. We're almost there. We're going to go in. Follow our lead. You're Jaurru, the king's personal guard. He's going to send you with me to protect me, even though I don't really need it because I can use magic. Or at least, I'm supposed to be able to. Haven't quite got it figured out yet."

"Okay," he said. "Feels like you're teaching me how to write an essay again," he said and grinned.

"This is serious, Aiden." The stairs flattened out, and they proceeded down the stone hallway to the throne room, quickening their pace to catch up with Korodeth and Oliver. "Try not to say too much. And if you do have to talk, try to at least sound like a medieval knight."

"Got it," he said.

The hallway of the castle expanded, and they passed through wide doors into the throne room. Aiden mimicked Korodeth's bow. His eyes went wide, as if he were trying to do a dance he'd never seen before. Lauren bowed, but, true to his character, Oliver remained standing.

"Rise, loyal subjects. Jaurru, where were you?"

"He was, as I had feared, the victim of a spiritual attack," Oliver said. "His mind and memories were scrambled by the enemy, but I was able to overtake the enemies' stronghold. He's of sound mind once more, my lord. I've erected defenses to ensure it does not happen again."

"Is this true?" the king asked Aiden.

Aiden cleared his throat. "It is, my lord." Each word came out slowly, deeply.

In a few more minutes, the three would be on their way, alone at last, able to speak openly about the situation and find a way to get home. For now, Lauren's nerves racked her.

Ribillius stood, as she had written it so many years ago. He took a golden scepter in his hand. A giant spherical diamond adorned the top. "Knights of Alrujah. We face dark times. The enemy gathers strength and threatens our very lives. But now, they have named my daughter a target.

"For too long we have waited for the mysterious Mage Lord to show himself. But no more. His anonymity ends today. Today marks a shift in the coming war. It will be the day all Alrujah remembers as the day we reclaimed control. Today, we march, we infiltrate, and we root out the Mage Lord wherever he may be."

Ribillius's thunderous tone echoed through the throne room.

Anxiety froze Lauren's lungs like she'd inhaled helium. The threats of the Mage Lord were supposed to remain secret. Her father was supposed to rule as if the Mage Lord didn't exist. The war was supposed to come to Alrujah. If the game changed, if it didn't follow the script, how would they know what to do? The freeze of the helium worked through her chest and down to her stomach.

Ribillius no longer sounded like a loving father. He sounded like a king, a king hungry for expansion and for power. She knew his inner workings and his fear, his insecurities and his doubt. She knew him as a mother knows her child. She had seen him crush several elf rebellions and punish, harshly, traitors to the crown, but she had never seen this side of him, the side of him that demanded blood. His voice carried a very clear message, more so than the words his mouth formed. His voice announced blood would be shed, and *he* would shed it if no one followed. He spoke like an avenging king, an avenging father.

"Today, Alrujah declares war on the Mage Lord and his followers. Today, we issue our own threats, our own decree. Alrujah is free and will never again live under the tyranny of a maniacal king!"

The room shook with the cheers of soldiers stomping in unison, each lifting their swords toward the ceiling. The cry of the soldiers pierced Lauren's back. Her legs buckled. Aiden's hand grabbed her elbow in a strong, robotic grip.

Amidst the cheers, Ribillius leaned to Korodeth's ear.

Lauren had to stare intently at his lips to see what command he might issue.

Ribillius said, "I want to know who the Mage Lord is. I want him rooted out and brought before me. By any means necessary. Bring his corpse if you must. You are my eyes. You are my ears."

"As you wish," Korodeth said. He hurried from the room. As the doors swung open in front of him, three soldiers dressed in similar garb melted from the shadows and followed him out.

Lauren hadn't scripted any of this. These must be changes Oliver instituted without talking to her. She should be irritated. She should have some say over these things. But the thought of covert soldiers slinking in and out of shadows was too cool. He must have known she would have approved.

Based on Ribillius's actions and the little she knew of Korodeth, the game may have changed completely, and their hope to get home may have, like the mystery soldiers, slipped from the shadows and away from them forever.

King Ribillius raised his diamond-topped scepter—encrusted with jewels and inlaid with silver—in the air matching the soldiers' salute. "Knights of Alrujah—prepare for battle. Every man old enough to hold a fork must be fitted with a sword and shield. You will train, you will lead. Now, go."

The soldiers thundered out. Lauren feared the king would give them different orders. He'd not followed a word of the script since Aiden's arrival. She wondered if there might be a connection.

With the throne room clear of the knights, the king dropped to his knees and pulled Lauren into his arms. Ribillius's chest heaved with gentle sobs. "I can't lose you. Not like I lost your mother."

"You won't, Papa." She let herself melt into her pretend father's embrace. In the script, Indigo cried at this point. Lauren didn't have to force the tears. She didn't want to go. She was genuinely afraid. She wanted to stay with her father, no matter how pretend he may be. As long as she was in Alrujah, he was real.

Oliver put his hand on her shoulder. "I will go with you."

The king pulled back and said, "Jaurru. You will accompany them. Watch over them. Protect them. When we've found the Mage Lord, I'll send word."

"But how, Father?" Lauren asked.

"I will send a razorbeak to deliver messages."

"How will they find us?" She asked because they were finally back on script. She wanted to keep things moving and hoped they would progress the way she and Oliver had drawn them up.

"Lakia the Caller will accompany you."

Oliver looked up, his eyes bright.

Erica.

Chapter Seven

Adonai made them each, the elf and the dwarf, the nar'esh and the angel, but the first of His creation was the human. He breathed upon them, and His breath blessed them. They achieved their endeavors and sought peace among the races and the beasts.

—The Book of the Ancients

Lauren knocked on Lakia's heavy wooden door. Two black iron strips ran horizontally across it to hinges on the side opposite the handle. "Lakia," she called softly. The two of them—Lakia and Indigo—had grown up together in this castle, Indigo from the time of her birth, and Lakia from the age of six.

No answer, but someone stirred. It sounded like blankets and pelts moving over each other, sliding together like soft music. She tried another tactic. "Erica?"

After a moment's quiet, "Who's there?"

The cold of the stone floor seeped through her white boots. "It's Lauren."

No answer.

Oliver leaned in close, his forehead only inches from the door. "And Oliver. We can explain."

Still no answer.

"Want me to kick the door in?" Aiden asked. He grinned. Lauren thought he might be joking, but hope sparkled in his eyes. He sounded like Jaurru.

Lauren wasn't surprised. She felt more like Indigo with each passing minute, even the magic coursing through her, through her blood. It was like being very awake, very aware. All her senses worked seamlessly together with her environment, as if she could change it by the power of her will alone.

Even the cold, which never left her alone, was a part of her, an extension—almost as if the cold could talk to her, and she to it. "I have an idea." She grabbed the handle, squeezed it hard, and closed her eyes.

It was cold, but her hand radiated heat. The hotter her hand got, the colder the handle became, until it snapped off in her hand, dusted with ice crystals.

Oliver's eyes grew wide. Aiden stared, his smile replaced by an awe-struck gaze.

"What?" she asked.

"How …" Oliver stammered.

Lauren shrugged and pushed the door open. "You should go, Oliver. She probably still hates me. And you can blame it on me if you want."

"It's no one's fault," he said.

Aiden stared still, his face blank except for surprise.

Lauren smiled. "Impressed?" she said flirtatiously.

"Wow."

Oliver said, "Oh brother."

* * *

Lakia's room, though smaller than Jaurru's quarters, dwarfed Oliver's monastery room. The morning breeze whispered in through two bell-shaped windows cut into the wall opposite the door. Erica sat on the bed, her knees up, staring at the back of her hands. When he came in, she immediately shoved her hands under the thin pelts spread over her legs.

She wore a white and purple nightgown, something ridiculously thin. He wished he or Lauren had thought about the practicality of the costumes they designed. The skin on her arms bristled with goose bumps. Dagger, her oversized wolf, sat in the corner, staring at her.

Quietly, Oliver asked, "You okay?"

"I'm so not okay."

"I guess you're pretty confused." He walked closer. He wanted to put a hand on her shoulder or sit next to her, but within a girl's bedroom, the gestures would be far too forward for a monk.

"My hands," she whispered.

"What about them?"

Her eyes were sad. He almost didn't recognize her without her dark makeup and black clothes. She looked good this way, different, definitely, but good—softer, prettier.

"Where are my gloves?"

Oliver scratched at his chin. Already, stubble had formed on his pale skin. "Yeah. I didn't put those in the code."

She looked back to her hands under the pelts. "What are you talking about?"

He folded his hands and the sleeves of his robe fell over his wrists to his intertwined fingers. "We've been pulled into the game Lauren and I designed. And we didn't exactly put your gloves in the game."

"Are you insane? I mean, like truly crazy?"

"If I am, we're all facing the same problem. Aiden's here, too."

"Great. I'm stuck in some nerd world with a geek, a jock, and a spaz." She glared at him. "Listen, I need gloves."

At first, he wanted to ask if he was the geek or the spaz but decided it didn't matter either way. "You're willing to take my word for it? You don't think you're dreaming?"

The pelts moved in small lumps, like hamsters crawling over each other. She rubbed her hands together. "If it is a dream, it's not mine." She sounded frustrated, irritated even.

If she wanted gloves, he would get her gloves. It was the least he could do for her after getting her yanked into Alrujah against her will. It wasn't his fault, but it sure felt like it. Besides, finding gloves for her might win him some points.

Subtle blonde highlights ran through her brown hair. Parted down the middle of her scalp, it spilled over her ears and down her back. "Why in the world is my hair so long?" She sneered. "And brown?"

"We're in the game. You're exactly like Lauren drew you. She did all the character design and …"

"Lauren drew me this way? And now I look like some hippie flower girl with this stupid nightgown and gosh awful hair?"

"I think," Oliver said with a boldness that surprised him, "you're very pretty. You're pretty with black hair and with brown."

"Oh gag. Look, I really don't care what's going on here. I just want my gloves back." She lay down again and pulled the covers up to her slender neck.

"What are you doing?"

"Going back to sleep. Shut the door on your way out, would you?"

Oliver knelt next to her. The chill of the stone floor bit through his thick cotton robe. "You can't go back to sleep. We have to go. Like, now. We have to make it to Varuth before nightfall, and it's a long ride."

"I don't have to do anything. And if I don't have gloves, I intend to do exactly nothing. Now get out of here. You're messing up my hibernation plans."

Half of him wanted to pull her out of bed forcefully so she would understand the urgency of the situation. The other half wanted to kiss her cheek and watch her sleep. Neither of those were logical options, and he was, above all, a man of science and reason. The whole situation made him emotionally tired. He took a deep breath, pushed himself up with his prayer staff until he stood over her. "You have to come with us. There's going to be a war soon. If we don't get out of here right away, things could get pretty bad."

She sighed and opened her eyes. "I'm serious. I'm not doing anything unless I get some gloves."

If he remembered correctly, Lauren—Indigo—should have a pair in her room. With a few modifications, he could get them close to what Erica wore in North Chester. Sure, he couldn't change them from white to black, but she would have to deal with the color.

Dagger lay down and wrapped his tail around his legs.

The wolf gave him an idea—a way to get Erica some gloves and impress her at the same time. "There are some gloves in the castle. We might be able to save some time by having Dagger get them."

She sat back up. "Dagger is the wolf, right? How exactly do you suppose he can get some gloves?"

"You can tell him to. Your character, Lakia, is a summoner. A caller. She talks to animals is what I'm trying to say. Anyway, you can tell him to go to Indigo's room and grab some gloves. She normally keeps them on her dresser."

"Hold on. Who's Indigo?"

"Lauren."

"This makes no sense."

"You'll catch on soon enough."

She didn't answer. Wind whispered through the windows. She shook her head. "This is probably the dumbest thing I've ever done. Hey, Sparky."

The wolf stood up. Its head nearly came to Oliver's waist. It was a beast of a wolf, way too large to be a normal timber wolf, but Lauren had wanted it so. "His name is Dagger," Oliver said.

"No, I don't think so. I like Sparky better. Now, get fetching, Sparky."

* * *

When Lakia's timber wolf ran out of the room, Lauren fidgeted with her white velvet cape trimmed with fur from the notorious White Wolf. Aiden stared at her with his piercing blue eyes. She hadn't thought it possible for him to look better than he had in North Chester, but standing here in his silver battle armor, he was near irresistible. "What's taking them so long?" she wondered quietly, hoping Aiden would close his mouth and stop staring.

He didn't.

"What do you think is taking so long?"

His armor caught the light of the suns from the window and glinted. She blinked. "Say something."

"The door handle."

She frowned. "Does it freak you out?"

"It's a little weird." His right hand rested on the hilt of his sword.

Weird? Frustration and embarrassment rushed back to her like she was home again watching Bailey Renee leaf through her journal and laugh, or getting grounded by her mom for getting a C in chemistry.

After a moment's quiet, Aiden said, "I'm really surprised. This armor looks heavy, but it's not."

Lauren shrugged. Without thinking, she said, "It looks good on you."

He smiled. "Thanks. I like your cape. Very super-hero."

Her face flushed with heat in the cold air. She pulled the cape around her tightly and shivered.

The wolf rushed back down the hall with a pair of long white gloves in its mouth and disappeared into the deep room.

"Those were my gloves," Lauren said. Why hadn't she put them on? It only made sense to wear every scrap of clothing she could find in this cold. Stress must have made them slip her mind.

Aiden asked, "Why does that dog have your gloves?"

"It's a wolf. And it's probably bringing them to Erica. She's got this thing with her gloves."

He unsheathed his sword and peered down the sterling blade with one eye. "Is it a pet?"

"Kinda."

"Cool." Aiden held the blade gently, his cheek to the cold steel. "My dad's really into fantasy and all, but I'm not really into the whole video game thing. I'm more into sports—football and stuff. But I have to say, this is pretty cool. I mean, don't get me wrong, I want to get back to North Chester, but this sword is pretty sweet, m'lady."

Lauren grinned. "M'lady?"

He shrugged, stunning her eyes with the reflection of the suns. "I figure, when in Rome."

She rocked back and forth on her heels, tugging at the white ribbon in her long hair. If she'd been this pretty in North Chester, she'd have plans to ask Aiden to prom. She smiled with coquettish confidence. "I designed your sword."

Still holding it level with his eyes, Aiden pointed it down the hall, his eye glancing down the blade as if it were a compass giving him direction. "Beautiful job." He took two quick steps back and twirled it around him, first on either side, then over his head. "Feels good. Natural." He slipped it back in its sheath.

Lauren's heart jumped at his ease with the blade. She wanted to kiss him, but Indigo and Jaurru weren't supposed to kiss until much later in the game. But she wanted to go off script, live in the moment, enjoy every second of the bizarre situation. A quiet voice inside her, something coursing through her like her magic had warned her not to deviate from the script, as if disaster loomed like angry clouds waiting to strike out with brilliant flashes of lightning.

Lightning. She felt it now, a tingling like electricity, from her toenails to the tips of her flowing hair.

Aiden's face twisted in confusion and unease. "Lauren? Your hair is standing up."

Her hair rose from her shoulders like she was in space. Small purple sparks flashed from one strand to the next like a tiny thunderstorm.

Aiden looked at his silver armor and took a few steps back. "Bro, that is way freaky."

Bolt 1. She remembered the exact page she'd penned the words on in her journal. Six pages in, nearly fifteen lines down, she described the opening spell as a low-level electrical attack useful against armored opponents.

Like the ice spell, it manifested itself without her conscious will. Her powers simultaneously amazed and terrified her. If she couldn't control her magic, it could be disastrous for anyone nearby.

She closed her eyes. Her fingers crackled, and her feet rose an inch from the ground. Her eyes snapped open. "I have to let it out."

"Bad idea," Aiden said.

She moved to the window to release the energy into the sky. "You may want to move back." Aiden didn't argue. He moved to the opposite side of the room, pressed his back against the stone wall. Lauren stretched out her arms. The electricity focused in her chest before it flowed up her arms and shot into the sky. The few clouds glowed sapphire before they fizzled into gray.

Aiden's armor clanked behind her. He approached her slowly, cautiously. "I don't think I like it."

"Is everything okay out here?" The voice sounded a little deeper, grittier, than Lauren remembered, but she still recognized Oliver.

She turned around. "Fine, why?"

"I heard a huge crack."

"Bolt 1." She smiled. "You outdid yourself."

"Wait till you see Surge." He grinned.

Erica walked out a few minutes after Oliver, Dagger at her heels. She wore a green velvet, long sleeved dress with black stripes running down each arm. She'd torn the fingers from Lauren's gloves and somehow cut the elbow-length cloth down to her wrists. Other than the color, they could be the twin of the pair she wore in North Chester, loose threads and all.

Lauren tried not to be irritated. Would it be too much for her to wear them as they were, even if they didn't match exactly? For Erica, it probably would be. The fact Erica wore them at all, considering they weren't black, shocked Lauren.

Erica slipped her dagger in its sheath on her leather shoulder holster and smoothed her dress when she looked up and stared at Lauren. "Who are you?" she asked. One eyebrow raised.

Lauren closed her eyes in frustration. "It's me. Lauren."

"Maybe it's her dream," Erica said.

"Come on, girls," Oliver said. "Take it easy. We're going to have to work together if we're going to find a way home."

Ignoring his comment, Erica said, "This dress totally sucks. It's like, make-me-puke bad."

Lauren frowned. Softly, she said, "At least it has black on it."

The wolf rested against Erica's leg. "Geez, Sparky, get off me. You'll get hair on my dress."

Lauren sat on the windowsill. Dampness lined the air. Snow couldn't be far off. "His name is Dagger."

"She likes Sparky better," Oliver said.

Lauren rolled her eyes. "I didn't think you liked the dress."

She pushed the massive wolf with her leg. "I'd like it less if it was covered in dog hair."

"Wolf hair," Oliver corrected. He put his hands in the long sleeves of his robe.

"Whatever," Erica said. "Let's get out of here."

Oliver said, "Good idea. We have to follow the script. If we don't, we may never get home. You're going to have to trust me on this." He looked at Lauren. "Trust us. We know what we're doing."

Lauren said, "Speak for yourself."

Chapter Eight

They rule over their worshipers and receive power from their sinful prayers. They have turned their hearts from the service of Adonai. They serve themselves, and because of their atrocities and their love of evil, Adonai has declared them abominations.

—The Book of Things to Come

T HE LIGHT OF THE twin suns, high over Alrujah, diffused through a thin layer of gray clouds. The heavy drawbridge lowered with slow, agonizing clinks of thick chain and machinery. The four sat atop white steeds in the shadows of the broad castle walls as the bridge touched down on the opposite side of the moat. Oliver held his breath as he crossed. He didn't want to show fear, but beneath the rough oaken bridge swam parial-barbed vi-fish, alligators, and various water dragons. Most had been imported from surrounding territories, but some came from as far away as the lakes in the Callbred Mountains. Each had been specifically chosen for their ferocity and insatiable hunger.

With each hoof-fall, the bridge echoed. Water frothed on either side. The castle guards kept the vi-fish hungry, in case of invasion. But the moat fulfilled several purposes, not just defensive. A shorter drawbridge jutted out on the other side of the castle—one used like a pirate's plank. Criminals, capital offenders, and those labeled as traitors of the crown were forced at sword-point to walk to the edge where a black garbed man would push them into the deep. He'd put in the code because he thought, at the time, it would be cool. Now, seeing the back of the black-finned fish splitting the water, the long necks of the water dragons rising like miniature Loch-Ness monsters, and the slightly over-sized alligators swimming like ancient dinosaurs, "execution-by-moat" sounded far less cool.

"Pretty sick door," Erica said. Sparky matched her horse's steps and walked between her and Oliver.

Her green and black velvet dress made her look strangely different, but her dark eyes still locked up his heart. "Thanks," he said.

He pulled his hood off his head and felt the waning warmth of the dual suns on his face. The larger sun warmed the left side of his face more than the smaller warmed the front.

"Two suns? This whole place is weird," Erica said.

He said, "Yeah."

The soldiers stationed inside the castle tapped their spears in unison. Oliver nudged Aiden. "Turn around, face the guards, and hold your sword up."

Aiden complied. The suns glinted off the hardened steel, and the soldiers stepped out of view. A second later, the gate started to move up. Two blurs ascended the bridge and disappeared.

"What was that?" Aiden asked.

"The blurry people? Chameleon Soldiers. They wear light refracting chain mail so they seem to disappear."

"So they're like stealth soldiers?" Aiden asked.

"Pretty much," Oliver said.

"Bro, that's pretty sweet. Glad they're on our side."

Lauren fidgeted. She pushed her hair behind her ear, which meant something bugged her, and he'd probably end up getting an earful. "What's wrong?" he asked.

Lauren pointed to the drawbridge and frowned. "I don't remember them."

Oliver covered his hands in the long sleeves of his blue robe. The suns moved quickly across the sky. It would be dark soon. The warmth of the day would vanish, and the melting snow would refreeze. Traveling with a group of four took much longer than traveling with two. And with Aiden's heavy armor, no way they'd be able to make the same pace Oliver and the messenger had made riding from the monastery to Castle Alrujah. "We need to keep moving. We only have a few hours before we can make it to Varuth. Otherwise, we'll need to set up camp."

They rode west, away from the castle toward the monastery. Once they'd crossed the river Oliver and the messenger had crossed a few hours ago, they'd head north toward the Dragon's Back Mountains. They'd need to climb deep into them if they wanted any chance of getting to *The Book of Sealed Magic*, assuming it was even in the same place when they got there.

Lauren, who rode on the opposite side of Oliver, a formation designed to protect Erica and Aiden until they were more comfortable with their skills, crossed behind everyone until she rode beside Oliver.

"I thought we said nothing goes in unless we both approve it." Voice shaky, she sounded like her mother.

"I was going to show you in the Beta. If you didn't like them, I was going to take them out."

"But you put them in. You didn't tell me anything about them." She pushed her hair behind her ear. The horses shuffled through the hoof-deep snow.

Oliver remembered when he found her standing in the snow in her pajamas two short days and a lifetime ago. "It was a last minute add. Don't worry, they're cool. We probably won't see them at all."

"That's what I'm worried about," she whispered. The greater sun dropped toward the Dragon's Back Mountains. The air cooled almost immediately. The lesser sun would only be out for another hour and a half. "How do they work in the story?" she asked.

"They find the Mage Lord, report back to the king. The king contacts Indigo and warns her before the Mage Lord launches a complex ambush. They save our lives."

The river sparkled on the horizon. Lauren's eyes were blue, much bluer than they should be, like when she froze the handle off Erica's door. He sighed. As much as he liked her, she was, as Bailey Renee would say, prone to drama. He wished she would settle down and realize not everything was a matter of life and death. "Take it easy. You're going to go all magic again."

"Well, how am I supposed to feel?"

Oliver shivered, either because the greater sun was setting or because the cold, cold Lauren rode so close to him.

"I'm sorry, okay? I should have talked to you, and I didn't. Better?"

"It's a start," she said. Her eyes stopped glowing, but still shone a deep blue. "I don't know if I can trust you anymore. This was supposed to be *our* game."

Oliver shook his head. "It is. You're making too big a deal out of it."

"Am I? I mean, they may change other things in the game. What if they stumble across *The Book of Sealed Magic* and bring it back to my father?"

Oliver pulled the reins, commanded his steed to stop. Aiden and Erica, a few paces ahead, turned their horses around. Oliver looked hard at Lauren. "Your father? You know he's not real, right? I mean, you're not starting to think this whole thing is legit, are you? This is some bizarre aberration, an anomaly. We're going to get back. You may not want to, but the rest of us sure do."

Lauren stopped her horse and returned his stare. "What's that supposed to mean?"

He'd had his fill of her constant self-pity. Before he could stop himself, he said, "Well come on, Lauren. You're miserable in the real world, and you're miserable here. This is what you always wanted, and now you have it, and it's not good enough. If one little thing is wrong, you get all bent out of shape."

Lauren's blue eyes moistened. Her skin turned a pale blue. "Are you trying to hurt me? What's wrong with you?"

Fatigue robbed Oliver of whatever tact and patience he had left. The events of the day had left him drained of energy, and the group had a long ride ahead of them. "What's wrong with *you*?" A childish response, yes, but she questioned his motives, like he'd done something wrong, like he'd betrayed her. Her daddy issues had morphed into latent insecurities, made her think she couldn't trust anyone.

Lauren's jaw dropped. She heeled her horse, turned toward the Cerulean Woods, and rode quickly ahead. She passed Erica and Aiden at a pace just below a gallop. Sparky barked after her but remained obediently by Erica's horse.

When Oliver caught up with the other two, Aiden asked, "What was that all about?"

Oliver shrugged. "She gets like this sometimes." Annoyance and resentment seethed under his skin. He boiled in the cold air.

Erica sighed. "I guess I'll go talk to her."

Oliver and Aiden stared at Erica.

"What? I can't be nice all of a sudden?"

Oliver smiled. "It'd be good if someone were."

* * *

A horse trotted up behind her, but Lauren didn't slow down. She continued on over the Fellian River, ignoring the sound of hooves on the wooden bridge. The clear water shimmered in wild reds and oranges. During sunsdown, the river ran with liquid gold.

When the other horse finally caught up, Lauren turned. Her eyes warmed, and she wondered if she were going to cry. She tried to keep herself composed. She didn't want Aiden to see her cry, and she didn't want to give Oliver the satisfaction of knowing how much he'd hurt her.

But it wasn't either of them. Instead, Erica, with her long brown hair and dark eyes, rode beside her.

"You okay?" Erica asked. She sounded genuine, as if she really cared. Sparky circled once around Lauren's horse.

"Terrific."

"Sarcasm's more my color. You don't wear it well."

Lauren shrugged. "Don't even care right now."

The horses pressed on, beyond the bridge, toward the line of trees that marked the beginning of the Cerulean Woods. "Sure you do." Erica's horse stepped over a felled branch. "Look at you. You're about to cry."

Was it that obvious? Lauren sighed and wiped her eyes.

"You care about Oliver. You care what people say. And I'm guessing you're tired of being picked on. Me, I gave up caring a long time ago. Hurts a lot less."

The expansive harspus trees thickened around them. Their bare branches twisted around themselves. The ground peeked through the thin snow. Damp leaves gathered on the hooves of their horses. Lauren wondered how long it took Oliver to program this level of detail.

In the spring, the leaves of the harspus trees would turn blue, instead of green. They'd blend perfectly with the sky, and it would be hard to tell the two apart. Now, the blue leaves had turned orange and yellow and covered the dirt of the woods like tile.

Erica's sudden kindness put Lauren on her guard. She didn't want to reveal too much, even though she ached to tell someone, anyone really, how she felt—angry, sad, worried lightning or ice or fire might leap out of her and strike her friends at any moment. Oliver had attacked her so unexpectedly. Why had he acted as if she'd accused him of treason? She wanted a simple answer. She thought to say all this to Erica but remembered Erica probably hated her. Instead, she said, "People change."

Erica waved a hand at Lauren, from her head to her feet. "Yeah. Some of us get crazy skinny overnight. But most people don't change *that* much." She grabbed a leaf that clung stubbornly to an otherwise bare branch, examined both sides, and dropped it. Sparky sniffed it like it was food. "I'm going to tell you straight out what I think. You care too much. You're too sensitive because you've got a big heart."

At least she said "heart" and ignored the other big parts of her.

"It's cool, don't get me wrong. But it's dangerous, too. Means you get hurt easier."

"Don't try to make this my fault. Did you hear what he said?"

Erica put both her hands up in mock surrender. "Don't get all angry. It's no one's fault. You're not bad because of it or anything. Me, I don't care enough. It's like, nothing really matters to me. We each have our own set of problems."

Lauren imagined how uncomfortable the sharp-edged dry leaves would be if any got stuck in her boots. Thank goodness she'd thought to include horses in the game. "So why do you care if I'm angry or not? Don't you think I'm a witch?"

Erica ran her hand over the black bark of a harspus tree. Probably wishing her green nails were as black as the bark. She took her hand off the tree and shrugged. "Figured I should do something to help. We're all in this together. Witch or not."

Lauren's anger melted away. "Well, thanks, I guess."

"Just don't ask me to cheer you up or make you laugh. I kind of suck at that."

Lauren smiled. "Not as much as you think." She pulled the reins, and her horse stopped. They turned their steeds. Aiden and Oliver rode out of earshot. Aiden's helmet glinted in the light of the lesser sun. "I guess we should wait for the boys."

"Sure, why not."

When Oliver and Aiden caught up, Oliver asked, "Better?"

"A little," she said.

"Sorry I got all worked up back there."

"Water under the bridge," she said. And, for the most part, she believed it.

Oliver's hood shifted. "If we keep moving, we can make it to Varuth before sunsdown. Traveling at night isn't safe."

"Too dark?" Aiden asked.

"Too dangerous. Pretty soon, the days will be dangerous, too."

With disdain on her face, Erica said, "Let me guess—monsters?"

"Every game has enemies," Oliver said. "Alrujah has some pretty vicious ones. The scariest ones come out at night."

Chapter Nine

And the four shall move as fingers on a hand. They will work separately and together. And one shall come alongside as a thumb, and complete the Hand of Adonai. The five will break the six evil spirits, and they will crush the Great Deceiver.

—The Book of Things to Come

THE LESSER SUN HAD dropped behind the Dragon's Back Mountains only ten minutes before a low, earthy sound rumbled over them, as if, at any moment, the ground would ripple in waves like a great earthquake.

"I heard it, too." Oliver pulled his prayer staff from its holster on the side of his saddle. "Adonai save us."

Erica asked, "Adonai?"

"This isn't a good time." He dismounted and crouched down.

"What are you doing?" Aiden asked. Already, he'd pulled his sword and shield.

Lauren crossed her arms. Her eyes screamed with heat, and her skin crackled in the cold air. "Beresus," she said. "Think angry gorilla on steroids."

Aiden twisted his sword in a loop. "Nice, bro. This ought to be fun."

Sparky growled. His fur bristled, and he barked twice.

Something big, like the shadow of a garden shed, lumbered toward them. "There," Oliver whispered.

Aiden dismounted quickly. He shifted his weight to his back leg and pointed his sword to the shadow.

Erica dismounted, stared at the hulking beast. "We're supposed to kill this thing?"

Oliver knelt and mumbled something Lauren didn't understand. Heat welled inside her. She was sure if she sneezed, flames would shoot out her nose. She slid off her horse, put her hand on its neck to steady it.

Her fear manifested as heat. Fever hot, her fingertips burned like blisters.

The massive shadow sprang forward, and before she realized it, she'd extended both arms toward it. The blackness disappeared as the beresus lit up in orange flames. It slowed for a minute but still lumbered forward. The fire burnt itself out, and Lauren's breath caught in her throat. *Now what?*

Her horse whinnied and ran off into the woods. The other three followed after.

Aiden charged the beast, his sword outstretched. He leapt forward, sword and arms extended until the blade sank deep in the belly of the beast.

The beresus shrieked an awful, high-pitched squeal nine octaves higher than its low rumble minutes earlier. It raised its massive arms and smashed Aiden out of the way.

Aiden lay on the ground, moaning. He tried to get up but collapsed.

Heat rose again.

Erica stood slowly, brushed the leaves from her dress, and said to Sparky, "Don't just stand there!" The wolf rose off its haunches and bounded toward the smoldering animal.

The beresus pulled its arm back and made low grunting noises like a gorilla.

Sparky leapt toward its throat. The beresus caught him and threw him to the ground. Sparky yelped.

More mumbling from Oliver. On one knee, he'd dug the tip of the prayer staff an inch deep in the damp earth. He hung on to it with both hands, bowed his head until his forehead touched the staff. His face lit with blue light from beneath his cloak.

"Do something!" Lauren shouted.

Still kneeling, with his eyes closed, Oliver stretched his hands toward the night sky.

He was praying. Had to be. His prayers healed the wounded, made them stronger.

The beresus moved to Aiden and picked him up by the ankles.

Lauren put her hands together and pushed them toward the beast. Another explosion of flames, another yelp. It dropped Aiden.

Deftly, Aiden flipped in mid-air and landed on his feet. In the light of the flaming beresus, Aiden grabbed his shield. He rotated it quickly, so the pointed end faced the gorilla-like animal, and plunged it into its chest. While the beast screamed, Aiden wrenched his sword from the depths of the beast's belly. He jumped and slashed at the beresus's throat.

The colossal creature staggered backward and fell on its back. It rolled over as the flames dissipated, pulled its knees under it like a baby learning to crawl, then collapsed. The rising and falling of its back ceased.

Terrified and exhilarated, Lauren smiled. "We did it! Totally amazing!"

Oliver didn't look as excited. He looked tired. Erica stood over Sparky, running her hand over him. And, were those tears?

Aiden kicked the beresus over and pulled his shield out of the beast's chest. He pushed its chin up with the heel of his left foot and plunged his blade into the soft neck. He stood over it for a while and watched it bleed. "Any more of these things hanging around?" he asked, his voice deep and smooth like water carving a river in rock.

Lauren's excitement waned, and the freezing air chilled her. "We can't be sure until we get to Varuth. They'll have guards stationed outside the walls. Keeps monsters at bay."

Oliver moved behind Erica, touched Sparky, mumbled.

"What are you doing?" Erica asked.

"He's praying," Lauren said.

"I can't understand a word he's saying." She sounded irritated and a little sad.

"It's not English. It's in a language I made up." Suddenly, her cheeks heated with embarrassment instead of magic.

"Tell me what he's saying."

"I don't understand it. I can't remember it at all. I wrote it years ago."

Oliver continued his prayers. Sparky's feet twitched.

"How can you not remember a language you made?"

Aiden walked over to join the group.

Lauren shrugged. "The same way I can call fire from heaven, the same way you can talk to animals, the same way Aiden can stick a sword a foot deep in a beresus. We're becoming more like our characters. And my character doesn't speak the ancient tongue."

Aiden nodded. "For sure. I don't know how I did any of that, but it sure felt like I'd been doing it a long time."

"Vicmorn's prayer healed you, and his prayer will heal Sparky as well."

"Vicmorn?" Erica asked.

Aiden pointed to Oliver. "This guy here."

"You mean Oliver?"

Lauren closed her eyes. She hadn't even noticed she'd used Oliver's game name. Even more surprising, though, Aiden picked up on it.

Sparky stood up quickly and leaned against Erica's leg as if nothing had happened.

She petted the dog gently. "Listen, it's great you all can do that stuff, but I can't talk to animals."

Sparky howled.

"Sure about that?" Oliver asked.

"If I could, don't you think I'd call our horses back?"

"Give it time. You'll learn to talk to horses soon enough. For now, we can walk."

* * *

Humidity hung in the girls' locker room of North Chester like a wet blanket. The stench of sweat mingled with the sweetness of shampoos, soaps, and perfumes. Nearly everyone on the girls' basketball team had showered, dressed, and driven home.

Bailey Renee sat on the bench and leaned back against the wall of purple lockers. She had an iPod earbud in her left ear and her cell phone on the other. "Come on, Lauren. Stop pouting and pick up."

Autumn, the six-foot senior center, dried her hair in a purple towel. "Your sister picking you up?"

Bailey Renee hung up. "She's supposed to. But she's not here, and she's not answering her phone."

Autumn flipped on a blow dryer and spoke loudly over the whir of the motor. "Maybe she's outside."

"I've been checking. Her car's not here."

"So, what? You need a ride or something?"

"Yeah. I guess so. I could call my mom, but she'd get super mad. She hates us calling her at work. I'm telling you, I am so irritated with Lauren right now."

Autumn ran a brush through her thick blonde hair. "She must have a good reason for it. Maybe she's busy, or she won a million dollars but has to pick it up before seven."

"It's a good thing you can play basketball," Bailey Renee said. She took her backpack out and slung it over both shoulders. Her legs ached from all the running during practice. Her stomach growled, and she wanted McDonald's more than anything. She opened her locker and checked her makeup in the mirror for the third time. "I have homework to do. We're normally home by now. Honestly, I could probably walk the distance, but in this cold it'd be suicide."

Autumn turned off the hair dryer and wrapped the cord around the handle. "Well, I can give you a ride if you want."

Bailey Renee considered the offer. Her mother forbade her to ride home with anyone but Lauren. Sure, she'd let Franky give her a ride a couple times, but that was different. Franky was Franky. She never told her mom about those days. Come to think of it, Lauren never did either. So if Lauren didn't sell her out, why should Bailey throw her under the bus because she didn't pick her up one afternoon?

She shrugged. "Sure, if you don't mind."

* * *

The moon gleamed off the steel helmets of Varuth's City Guard. They patrolled the high walls while moonlight glinted off arrow tips. The smell of irises and honeysuckle—the famous Varuthian gardens, revered for their impressive array of colors year round—distracted Lauren. Unlike Castle Alrujah, no moat surrounded the city. Three-story tall walls, thick and granite, encompassed the people and buildings within. From far away, travelers often mistook the city for a small mountain. But up close, they marveled at the intricate designs wrought in the stone with chisel and hammer—battle sequences of meticulously etched dragons attacking ships on the high seas, soldiers locked in hand-to-hand combat or engaging in elaborate swordplay—became evident.

The snow hadn't come as Lauren thought it would. Instead of the spongy soil from earlier in the day, the frozen ground stiffened under her feet. She should be home now, picking up Bailey Renee, working on homework, playing video games. Instead, she traipsed through a too-cold evening toward a heavily guarded city.

Oliver took the lead. Aiden walked behind him, then Erica, and finally Lauren. Being in the back, a necessary evil, unsettled her. If any unsavory creatures—another beresus, or a fangand or arachand, or even an assassin hiding behind the trees—leapt out, she'd be the first one hit. The marching formation made sense, even though they'd not scripted it this way. Such a small change couldn't have any profound impact on the course of the game. She and Oliver, because they knew the game best, would be the most prepared. Still, after seeing Aiden in action, Lauren wondered if he should be in the lead. But Oliver knew the script best, and he should be the one to do the talking.

The trees behind Lauren rustled, and she spun around. Electricity tingled through her crackling fingertips. "We got company," she said.

In an instant, Aiden positioned himself next to her. His sword slid out of its sheath. "Now what?"

Lauren didn't have time to respond.

A whisper came from the bushes, smooth as the smell of honeysuckles. "Indigo?" The way it uttered her name, like the first secret spell whispered in a young mage's room, she knew she should recognize the voice, but she didn't. Strangely, though, it put her at ease. The crackling of electricity faded. Unlike the first time the magic came upon her, she felt more in control this time, able to harness the energy. Best she could tell, her magic and emotions were inextricably connected. Controlling her magic meant controlling her feelings—something she'd never been good at.

Aiden's voice came from behind her, even quieter than the strange whisper from the underbrush of the Cerulean Woods. "Who is it?"

She shrugged under the slight weight of her white cape. She pulled the edges around her arms and shivered. "I have no idea."

"Should we be worried?"

"No."

Aiden turned his attention to the walled city. "Bro, I think they know we're here. They've got arrows ready, and they're aiming right at us."

"Into the bushes," the voice whispered again. "Hurry."

An arrow shot past Lauren's ear, and she fell to the frozen soil. "Why are they shooting at us?" she asked Oliver.

Erica said, "I'm guessing this isn't in the script?"

A loud clang made Lauren spin around. An arrow glanced off Aiden's helmet.

"Not cool," he said.

They receded deeper into the woods, away from the city walls. Aiden followed Lauren to shield her from the barrage of arrows. A scream pierced the night, a loud mix of pain and anger.

Erica held her side. Oliver knelt over her. In an instant, Aiden held his shield between their group and Varuth.

Twangs of strings reverberated and melded with the thunking of arrows in the frozen turf. Arrows flew in both directions now.

She wondered, for an instant, who was shooting back at Varuth.

Hard hands yanked her shoulders. She couldn't hold her feet under her, and she fell back. The hands held her firmly, but softly, and dragged her to the woods. "Keep your head low," the voice said.

Two men dressed in black emerged from the woods. They grabbed Erica by her shoulders and pulled her back into the underbrush. Oliver went with her each step of the way. Aiden sneered on his way in.

Lauren finally saw the face of the voice. It looked familiar, something she'd drawn, but nothing she could remember exactly. Like déjà vu, only with the added frustration of a confused dream.

"There are those of us who cautioned me against contacting you. They wanted me to leave you to the marksmen of Varuth. And after what your father has done, I honestly thought about it," the voice said.

"You speak too freely. Guard your tongue. I am the daughter of King Ribillius, Princess Indigo. And I am not my father." She'd adopted the voice of her character, more on instinct than conscious will.

"It is as I told them," the man said.

She had trouble identifying his face in the dark, but he had a short, flat nose. He wore the same black leather as the other men. The Varuthian crest—a blood red dagger pointing down at a forty-five-degree angle, piercing the head of a serpent that moved up at an opposite angle, forming a macabre V—adorned his tunic.

Varuthian Elite. Her thoughts cleared like the mist rolling back over the ocean. Ullwen.

Before Lauren met Aiden, in the earliest version of the script, Ullwen played the role of Indigo's romantic counterpart. But Varuthian soldiers never attacked the travelers, in any version of the script. And the Elite would never be outside the walls of the city. They would guard the castle.

"Why are they shooting at us?" Lauren asked.

"Varuth has closed the city completely. Your father is convinced the Mage Lord is within our walls."

"Then why are you out here? Shouldn't you be inside with the others, hunting the Mage Lord?"

Ullwen grimaced. "We need to go. We need to keep moving. Varuth is no longer safe."

Did she even have a choice?

"Keep low." He pulled her to a stop by her arm. "We have horses on the edge of the woods."

"But it's night," she protested. "It's not safe to travel."

"It's not safe to stay," he said. "Varuth won't follow us into the woods."

"But there are fangands in the woods," Lauren said.

Ullwen didn't break stride. "Better to fight a mindless pack of animals than a mindful troop of trained soldiers."

Chapter Ten

But their ways were evil. They sought irresponsible power, subjugated their people to slavery, and ignored the well-being of the other races. They worshiped strange gods and fashioned for themselves idols to worship. They celebrated themselves instead of Adonai. The jealousy of Adonai burned against them, and upon them Adonai passed judgment. He placed a plague upon them and banished them from Alrujah. And the plague was called the nar'esh.

—The Book of the Ancients

OLIVER WAS A COMPUTER programmer, not a track star. But he wasn't even a little bit tired. His taut muscles showed no signs of weariness. In fact, drawing the cold air into his lungs, he felt more alive here than he ever did in North Chester. Every muscle in his body, every tendon, every cell, responded to his unconscious call for obedience.

Erica dropped to her knees, and Lauren looked like she might be next. "We've got to stop," Erica said. Her breath came in gasps, and her arms shook. "We've been running for an hour."

Ullwen stopped. The other Varuthian Elite, who had been running flank, knelt next to Erica to urge her up. She pushed their hands away and flopped on her back. "I can't run anymore."

Ullwen said, "The horses are near. You can rest when we reach them."

"This game is starting to suck pretty hard." Her words came through heavy gasps of air.

Oliver marveled at Aiden. Athletic and strong in North Chester, here he was freakishly conditioned. After an hour's run in hundred-pound barbed armor, he didn't even breathe hard.

"You okay?" he asked Erica.

"Never better." Sparky sniffed the air. His large ears perked up. "Something wrong, boy?" Sparky's hair bristled. "I'm guessing that's not a good thing," Erica said.

The Varuthian Elite drew their weapons. Oliver's hot blood raced through his veins in the wintry evening. His heart beat like a dwarven hammer on his chest.

Sparky growled.

Erica raised an eyebrow. "What in the world is a fangand?"

Ullwen answered as he moved, sword unsheathed, closer to Lauren. "Surely you jest. Have you never ventured into the forest?"

Oliver whispered to her, his staff at the ready. "Think werewolves, but without the sense of humor. They hunt in packs, often attack from the trees."

The leaves behind her exploded. Oliver and Erica spun around. Erica screamed and Sparky leapt at the dark beast.

Streams of moonlight illuminated the heavy black fur accented with red and silver. Larger and broader than a man, the fangand flexed his chest, near four feet across from shoulder to shoulder. The beast grabbed Sparky by the neck.

Erica screamed again, high-pitched and loud, but not a cry of terror or fear. Oliver turned to her, convinced a fangand had her arm firm in its crushing jaws. But he found no other fangands though he should have—no fangand hunted alone. There should be at least two more, maybe three.

A caw similar to Erica's echoed through the night before being drowned out by a new sound, the sound of a thousand beating wings. She'd called razorbeaks.

They blotted out what little moonlight filtered through the trees. The air hummed with the beating of wings and the angry caws. Oliver heard the fangand before he spotted it in the animalistic darkness. It roared—an angry, guttural growl.

Sparky's muzzle erupted in choked snarls and snaps.

The murder of razorbeaks tore ravenously at the fangand, which flailed its long, sinewy arms in the night air. Razorbeaks bounced off its paws, its elbows. Some crashed to the leaves below, but righted themselves and circled around again, darting past its waving arms. Sparky, now free, ran past Oliver and Erica toward the imposing shadow of another fangand.

Lightning split the sky. Heat flashed against the left side of Oliver's face. Electricity punched the ground under his feet. Lauren backed slowly away from a smoldering fangand. She looked haggard, as if she hadn't slept in weeks. Her eyes, sunken, glowed blue. Her hair snapped like synapses. Ullwen and the other Varuthian soldiers circled around the second fangand, swords swinging and glinting in the periodic moonlight.

With sharp, hungry claws and teeth, fangands were perhaps the fastest creatures in the woods. Oliver wanted to charge into the fray, and while he could hold his own against a human opponent, in a fight between a martial-arts monk without a bladed weapon and a fangand, the beast would easily have the upper paw. He might be able to serve as a distraction, but more than likely, without coordinating a battle plan, he'd be in the way of the highly trained soldiers.

Prayer presented itself as the best option. It took every ounce of willpower he had, but he closed his eyes and, with one hand on his amulet, lifted his prayer staff toward the sky. "Adonai!" he shouted.

The Ancient Language bubbled up in him. He felt it first in his chest, and it crawled like spiders up the inside of his neck until he opened his mouth and the ancient words spilled out. He had no idea what they meant but knew it was important.

All at once, his eyes snapped open. Instead of the sallow blue moonlight that diffused through the thick tangled branches of the harspus trees, Oliver saw everything in the woods as yellow, bright as day, as if both suns were at their zeniths.

Ullwen cried from Oliver's left. He'd been knocked down. The two Varuthian soldiers with him readied their bows. They fired a quick volley. Two arrows stuck in the angry black fangand. It roared, broke an arrow in each hand and leapt at the two archers. Oliver targeted the beast's chest and hurled his staff at the fangand.

It found its mark. The staff punched the fangand in the chest but served only as a distraction. Turning from the archers, it locked eyes with Oliver. Already, he sprinted toward the wolfish animal. He leapt higher than he thought possible. His cerulean robe trailed behind him and, for an instant, he felt like a superhero.

The fangand swung at him, but Oliver kicked its clawed hand away, landed at its feet, and spun around behind it before it could grab him. He somersaulted away and grabbed his staff in one fluid motion. When he came up, he brought the staff in front of him in time to deflect a swipe from the fangand. He followed the block with a crushing spin-stab with his staff. The end of the staff caught the animal in the stomach. Wind rushed from its lungs.

Oliver kept moving. He punched the staff up under the fangand's jaw and cracked it in half. Two spurts of blood sprayed his face. Startled, he staggered back a few steps. He hadn't cut the fangand, so the blood must be his. He steadied his vision and saw two arrow tips in the beast's chest.

The fangand used Oliver's distraction as an opportunity to swipe at him. The sledgehammer fist caught him on the shoulder, and Oliver felt it slip out of the socket. Gnarled roots tangled his feet, and he fell backward.

The creature dropped to its knees and its paws. It pulled itself toward Oliver slowly. Every muscle in his body tensed. *Run*, they said. *Kick, anything!* Instead, he petitioned Adonai on his behalf. "Save me," he whispered. "Save us." For the first time, he understood the words he said in the Ancient Language.

This must be what Lauren felt like when she used magic.

The fangand pulled itself closer. Blood ran down its chest and abdomen and matted the black and red and silver fur. The skin on its nose wrinkled back to its eyes, making ridges, making rippling waves of anger. Its lips pulled up to reveal finger-long fangs in a thin, evil grimace. Blood seeped out and pooled on the ground in front of them. The fangand brought its nose up to Oliver's, sniffed, and collapsed. Its arms twitched, its tail swept leaves. And then it stopped moving.

Oliver took shallow breaths. He thought, for sure, the fangand would leap up at any second, claws and fangs first. But it didn't. He measured the breathing of the fangand, which slowed quickly, and eventually ceased. Was it playing dead? No, he hadn't coded them to do so. It must be dead—too much lost blood, likely.

He steeled his heart, willed it to slow, and reached toward the beast. He lifted up its jaw. It took him a moment to find them in the matted fur, two pulsing gashes the size of dolphins' snouts. The blood soured his stomach.

His shoulder ached—like a fantastic pinch from a giant. The pain exploded in his brain, hurt so bad, he could feel it in his eyes.

Ullwen stood over him. "Fine staff-work, Sir Vicmorn."

"Thank Adonai," he said.

Ullwen said, "I do, every day."

"Little help!" Lauren called.

A smoldering fangand leapt at her. She collapsed into the leaves with surprising speed. The fangand flew over the top of her. She stood and stretched out her hand. Ullwen sprinted toward her, sword drawn, but Aiden beat him to it.

With jaw-dropping speed, Aiden brought his blade cleanly through the fangand's neck. It collapsed quickly, and Lauren brought her hand back. She shifted her attention to the fangand in the cloud of razorbeaks. She stretched out her hand, and fire burst from the feet of the fangand. Its howl split the sky. The cloud of purple birds scattered.

Oliver smelled burnt hair and boiling blood.

The two Varuthian soldiers stood up and joined the fight. They each nocked an arrow in their bows and let them fly. Another howl.

The fire subsided, and the fangand, bloodied and burnt, rolled on the ground. Aiden walked to it and stuck his sword deep into the beast.

The yellow tint left Oliver's eyes, and all returned to normal. He ran his hand over the prayer amulet his father had given him and said a silent "thank you."

"That's why we keep moving," Ullwen said, his long black hair damp with sweat despite the chill in the air. Blood spattered his face and hands.

Weakened with exhaustion, Oliver thanked God for his healthy rush of adrenaline. He rubbed his shoulder, hoped the adrenaline would dull the pain enough to make it to the horses.

"What's wrong with your shoulder?" Erica asked.

"Separated," he said quietly.

Ullwen nodded. "I wondered. Would you like me to fix it?"

Before Oliver could tell him no, Ullwen had grabbed the wrist of the sore arm and yanked hard.

The bone scraped back into the socket, snapping in with the tight pull of tendons and ligaments. Oliver dropped to his knees in pain. The solution hurt more than the problem. He held his shoulder harder now, eyes clamped shut, tears squeezing to his cheeks.

Ullwen clapped him on the back. "The pain subsides quickly. We must move."

* * *

Autumn dropped off Bailey Renee and drove down the long, winding driveway before Bailey even had her keys out. She fumbled through her backpack in the dark and wondered why no one left the lights on for her. Lauren must be pouting still, but she'd never taken it to this level, never sat alone in a dark house. Maybe Mom was right. Maybe she did need counseling.

Mom would be home in another hour. Still, Bailey couldn't shake the feeling that something bad may have happened. This wasn't like Lauren at all. This wasn't how she sulked. Bailey used her irritation to quell her rising apprehension, found the keys in her backpack, and let herself in.

She flipped on the light in the great room, a combined living and dining room. The television wasn't on. Aside from the ticking of the grandfather clock in the corner of the room, the house was quiet. By now, she should have heard video games blaring from Lauren's room or some sulky music. Anything.

Something was wrong. Fear washed her irritation away completely. "Lauren?" she called gently.

No answer. The still, calm house worried her. The icemaker rumbled like some dumb beast.

Bailey Renee walked directly to Lauren's room. She knocked hard with numb arms. Too many push-ups after practice and too many free-throws before. Her shoulders, fatigued from carrying the weight of literature novels and calculus texts, protested the force of her knocking.

In the kitchen, the refrigerator hummed. The pendulum groaned while the clock ticked. Chimes signaled the late afternoon hour.

Bailey Renee tried the door knob. Locked.

She told herself not to panic. Lauren must have gone to Oliver's house and accidentally locked her door before she left. Or she did it on purpose, to keep Bailey Renee out, away from her precious journal.

But why didn't Lauren answer her phone? "Lauren! Answer the door! You're starting to freak me out!" She dialed Lauren's number again. The phone rang on the other side of the door.

She went to her mother's door. The key to all the interior doors lay on top of the jamb. Bailey Renee took the dusty key and unlocked Lauren's door. Her mind invented terrible explanations and images, things she feared finding on the other side of the door—Lauren unconscious, passed out drunk, or overdosed on drugs, her dead body with bloody wrists.

But she found none of these. The room was empty. On the shelf closest to her bed sat Lauren's customary water glass, her keys, and her cell phone, flashing a notice: 13 missed calls. Those were Bailey's calls. Before school, during school, at lunch, after school.

Thirteen times she'd called Lauren, and Lauren never left without her cell. Until now, Bailey assumed Lauren had simply been ignoring her. Now, her worry kicked into high gear. If Lauren were in trouble, if she'd simply gotten lost or forgot her phone, why wouldn't she call Bailey from a pay phone? From Oliver's house?

Something was very wrong.

Bailey Renee scrolled through Lauren's contacts until she found Oliver's number. She punched the number into her phone and sat on the foot of Lauren's bed while Oliver's ring back tone hummed unconcernedly. *Mozart—really?* "Pick up, please. Come on, pick up and tell me she's over at your house."

No one answered.

She tried the home number. A female voice answered quickly. "Mrs. Shaw? This is Bailey Renee. Is Lauren over there?"

"No, she's not. I thought she and Oliver were at your house."

She set her backpack down at the foot of the bed. "He's not, and Lauren left her cell here. Did they say anything to you about doing something today?"

Mrs. Shaw's voice trembled with a wave of worry. "I don't remember Oliver saying anything. He's been working on that game of theirs non-stop for the last few weeks. I don't think he'd stop working on it for anything in the world. He said he was really close to finishing it."

Bailey's brain whirred. She had a flimsy thought, but one she wanted to cling to because it was optimistic and hopeful, and far better than the alternative. "Do you think they finished it? Maybe they're playing it for the first time at the computer lab? Or they went out to celebrate?"

"Could be. Let me ask his father." Mrs. Shaw got quiet for a minute. Muffled voices filtered through the phone. "He says Oliver was up late working on the game, and he hasn't seen or heard from him at all today."

Bailey didn't say anything. *Think.* The thought did little to motivate her mind to move. Fear had set in and halted every idea.

Mrs. Shaw was quiet, too. The sound of her breathing came through the cell. She spoke softly. "Do you think we should be worried?"

Chapter Eleven

They lived in peace in those days, the elves and dwarves and humans. They lived among each other, shared land and livestock. They traded wheat with honest scales. They took wives from other races. And Adonai walked among them.

—The Book of the Ancients

THEY REACHED THE HORSES a half-hour later, still in the dark, and Lauren wanted nothing more than to curl up in her bed at home. The chill in the air pinched her skin in a million places. Slightly pointed ears freezing, she pulled her hood over her head. She'd suggested stopping and making camp—really she wanted to build a fire—but Ullwen insisted they keep moving, no matter how much she or anyone else protested. She'd even tried commanding him as the Princess of Alrujah. He'd simply stared at her.

"It is precisely your position that urges us forward. Your safety is more important than your comfort. We can purchase warmer clothes when we get further along."

Though he'd come in and immediately taken control, having Ullwen along comforted Lauren. She didn't appreciate having to walk so far for so long, but it felt nice to have someone pushing them, someone urging them forward in a land that seemed stranger by the second.

Speaking of stranger, Ullwen's two companions stayed eerily quiet. NPCs were a lot creepier in person. Hardly seemed like real people at all. Still, they moved with the same fluid grace as Ullwen. Their hair, though not as wavy as his, had the same sheen of midnight black. If she'd met these two on the streets of Alrujah or Varuth, she'd assume they were twins—the annoying kind that insisted on dressing alike, speaking alike, and finishing each other's sentences. But these two spoke so seldom, she wondered if they could complete a sentence between them.

The harspus trees thinned, and the group came to a clearing where seven horses were tied to seven trees. They neighed, pulling their lips back and showing their white teeth and pink gums. Varuthians prided themselves on their meticulous care of their horses.

The well-combed manes nearly sparkled in the moonlight. Each hoof was properly shod with a solid iron horseshoe, which dug into the freezing soil. The horses' tails, long and flowing and free of knots, whipped around them. Their restlessness marked them as riding horses. They did not like being tethered. Their powerful legs worked ceaselessly, eager to run.

Erica stopped walking and wrinkled her brow. "Hang on a second, Skippy," she said.

Ullwen turned, his eyebrows slanted down toward his nose. "My name is Ullwen."

Erica sighed and shook her head. "How'd you know to bring horses? And how'd you know to bring them here. Smells a little fishy to me."

Ullwen sniffed. "I smell no fish."

Oliver said, "She means it seems odd. And I agree. You're not telling us everything. If you had horses available for us, why not have them at the edge of the Cerulean Woods? Why make us trek through dangerous land to get to a convenience that would have been more effective closer to Varuth?"

Lauren stood next to Ullwen. He set his jaw tight and he ground his teeth.

"Need I remind you," he said, "I helped save your lives? Twice. Why do you distrust me now?"

"Bro, you got to earn our trust," Aiden said as he stepped forward, hand on the hilt of his sword.

Lauren moved alongside Aiden, both to show her support and to subtly hint at her interest in him.

Ullwen's soldiers stood by either of his shoulders, their hands on their bows.

Not good. The last thing they needed was to fight Varuth's finest soldiers. She put a hand on Aiden's forearm to discourage him from drawing his sword. "Ullwen is right," she said. "Saving our lives twice should earn something."

"Could be a trap to get us to lower our defenses," Aiden said.

For the first time, he sounded paranoid. But, after waking up in some strange fantasy world, he had every right to be suspicious. "Ullwen would not raise a hand against me," she said, remembering the earliest version of the script as well as she could. She walked forward and touched Ullwen's cheek. "Two loves," she said.

Ullwen closed his eyes and touched her fingers. "Aye. Two loves."

Erica said, "Oh brother."

Ullwen said, "I have no brother."

"Would someone please get this guy to speak normally?"

"I do speak normally," he snapped. "But you speak like an Otherlander."

Oliver leaned against a harspus tree and said, "It's only getting later. We either need to make camp or move on. We need to rest, and if we have to ride to the monastery to do it, we should."

"I'm not moving until we get some answers from little mister hero," Erica said. "How'd you know there'd be four of us traveling? How'd you know Varuth would attack us?"

Lauren moved back to Aiden from Ullwen. He looked disappointed, or hurt, or jealous. The idea pleased her, and though she didn't want to, she smiled softly. "I think you better tell us," Lauren said to Ullwen. "No use having secrets, especially if you're planning on traveling with us."

Ullwen said to his soldiers, "Ride back to Varuth. Tell them you lost me in the Cerulean Woods, but you saw my tracks headed east, toward the sea."

Silently, the soldiers mounted two black horses and rode off into the night.

Ullwen continued and said simply, "King Ribillius is not the only one with spies. His Chameleon Soldiers may have better armor, but they're not as clever as Varuthian Infiltrators."

"Of course," Oliver said, gentle acceptance coming over him. He must have remembered the Infiltrators as she did.

"We learned of Ribillius's plan to root out the Mage Lord. Viceroy Thadeus did not appreciate the sentiment and ordered us to kill the Chameleon Soldiers if we found them. I urged him not to, but he was determined. The tension between our two cities alone could lead us directly into another civil war. He didn't care. No one cared. So I ran away, like a coward, but not before my spies reported you four were headed toward us. I knew my officers would accompany me, but I didn't want it to lead to their deaths, hence I prepared the seven steeds and brought them here, beyond where the Infiltrators would look for us."

Aiden dragged the tip of his sword through the fallen leaves at the edge of the Cerulean Woods. "And where will these steeds carry us?"

"Tonight, they'll take us to Harland or Orensdale. Which city depends on where you want to go next."

"We'd have to ride through the night to make it by sunrise," Oliver said.

Without hesitation, Lauren said, "West. Yeval Forest."

Ullwen laughed. "The Bleeding Lands? It would take us days to ride to it. And once there, what would we do? Hope to die quickly? No, I have no interest in going to Yeval Forest."

"Those are all myths," Oliver said, then whispered, "Sort of."

Ullwen rubbed the muzzle of the remaining black horse. "Do as you please. But don't expect me to ride with you. I'll keep my stay in Harland. My actions here tonight have left me without a home. If I return to Varuth, I will be executed."

Cold air pressed in on her, as if she were standing at the cliff overlooking North Chester. And, as much as she enjoyed being in the game, the memory of her pajamas and her slippers would not leave her alone. She was tired. She was sad. She was scared.

Dark, thick clouds obscured the stars overhead. The moon diffused into a silver disk. "We're sorry, Ullwen. I'm sorry."

Ullwen stared at Lauren. "Apologies cannot clear the bounty on my head, Indigo. I made a vow long ago, and I intend to keep it, whatever the price."

Lauren said, "I cannot hold you to your vow. So much has changed."

Aiden flipped a leaf in the air and sliced it in two. "Enough. If we're going, let's get moving." No question; he was jealous. Her cheeks heated against the cold air. Would anyone see her blushing in the dark? She hoped not, but guessed they would. She'd never had the attention of one man, much less two. It felt—nice.

"Tell me about it," Erica said. "This whole Romeo and Juliet thing's getting a little stale."

Oliver said, "The monastery isn't much farther. We can stable our horses, get a night's rest and some food, figure out where to go, and press on in the morning."

Ullwen began untying horses from trees. "The monk is wise. We should do as he says."

"Not sure I got all that, but if you guys are good with tall, dark, and creepy, I might as well come along for the ride." Erica hoisted herself onto the largest, thickest black horse. Sparky leapt up behind her and balanced himself on the flank of the steed. "Let's roll."

"That," Ullwen said, drawing his sword, "is my horse. I suggest you dismount immediately."

"Don't blame me. Midnight wants me to ride him."

Ullwen's face grew so pale, it nearly glowed. "How did you know his name?"

"Same way I know he hates carrots. Now hop on Blaze. He says he's faster than Midnight anyway."

Ullwen reached for Midnight's reins, but the horse reeled back, nearly tossing Sparky off.

Erica patted the beast and said, "Easy, big boy. We got a long night ahead of us."

"This is an outrage," Ullwen said.

Lauren laughed. "Lakia is a summoner. When it comes to animals, it's best to listen to her."

"But Blaze is not a warhorse," Ullwen countered.

Erica said, "Give him a shot. You may find you actually like him. Last one to the monastery has beresus breath!"

* * *

Less than an hour before sunrise, Oliver and the others rode up to several buildings that composed the monastery in the Cerulean Woods. The conglomeration of mismatched, roughly built stone structures, little more than different sized rocks hastily thrown together with mortar, spread across the span of several acres. The Monks of the Cerulean Order focused on three things: prayers, studies, and self-defense. They'd taken enough time to construct something that would stand and keep them out of the rain and snow, but did little else.

Even at this early hour, the monks worked diligently. Several men in robes identical to Oliver's pruned the broad bushes on the grounds with steel shears. Others stood with bowed heads at the doors of each of the buildings. The first building, the largest by far, had a door flanked by two large monks. This building consisted of the main worship center and the library. Monks moved in and out of the building, greeting each other wordlessly with nods of their heads.

The horses' hooves clopped on the frozen soil. One of the taller monks approached them. Oliver dismounted. They each bowed their heads slightly as a sign of respect. Each removed the hood pulled over his head. The man's appearance startled Oliver.

His head lacked all traces of hair, and, even in the faint light of the moon, Oliver could tell the man had no pigmentation. More than pale, his skin was swan-feather white. It shone brightly and reflected the ethereal blue light of the moon.

Oliver had no idea how he'd missed the red eyes under the hood. An albino, no doubt, but Oliver hadn't coded an albino, hadn't even allowed for something like that to occur at random.

A familiar fear settled in Oliver's chest. They were so far off the script, they had little chance of ever getting back on track. But the constant changes of the game, new apparitions, new motivations, unsettled him greatly. It seemed the game had decided not to play by the rules he'd established using *Deep Red*.

"Welcome back, Father Vicmorn," the man said in a soft, smooth voice.

Oliver's throat tightened. He'd not intended for any of the monks to speak, other than Eljah and Vicmorn. He wanted to ask who this man was, but, if he were truly Vicmorn, he should know. If he admitted his ignorance, they might suspect something.

"Thank you. Where is my father?"

"The library. Shall I notify him of your arrival?"

Oliver's mind assembled each bit of information. Vicmorn had been elevated from Brother to Father in the Cerulean Order when he'd received the prayer amulet. That gave him authority over every monk on the grounds, except for Eljah, a power which might allow him to avoid making simple mistakes. "Please do. I wish to speak to him before we sleep. My friends and I require rooms and beds, and our horses stables. We've traveled far and need rest and food."

Aiden muttered, "Yeah we do. I'm starving."

"Very well," the man said. He whispered to a monk pruning hedges and pointed to the stables. To Oliver, he said, "You may wait for your father in the dining hall. I will have food prepared for you and your guests."

"Thank you," he said, wishing he could thank the man by name. Oliver led the others to an octagonal building behind the main chapel. Glassless windows lined the walls. Inside, a long table stretched out across the center of the room, flanked by two smaller tables. The four sat at the table closest to the kitchen.

"So this is where you grew up?" Aiden asked.

"Vicmorn, yes." Being back in the monastery brought back strong memories, but not Oliver's. Vicmorn's memory floated up from dark waters like a drowned body.

He remembered being a child, no older than seven. A strong hand squeezed the back of his neck until he was sure his spine would snap. The hot metal of a Blood Monk's curved blade pushed under his chin. Outside, crops and trees and bushes exploded in flames. Monks in flowing blue robes defended themselves against men with long, flat sabers. Eljah stood before him while a trickle of Oliver's blood ran down the blade of the black-robed monk.

Give me the books or this one dies.

It wasn't real, only an echo of a memory, but it felt real, as if Alrujah was truth and North Chester the dream. Oliver put a hand under his chin and felt the slight rise of a pale scar.

Erica tugged at her gloves as she surveyed the room. "Think the walls will stay up long enough for us to eat?"

"They haven't fallen in over a hundred years. They may not be pretty, but they're effective." The conversation mercifully pushed the memory from his mind.

Ullwen paced the room, inspecting the walls and the plain harspus wood furniture. "I've always longed to come to the monastery of the Cerulean Woods. The dedication of the monks has been fabled for generations."

The door to the kitchen swung open, and Eljah emerged holding a wooden tray filled with vegetables and fruits—beets and broccoli, carrots and celery, persimmons and pears, all of which had been meticulously groomed by the monks to resist cold temperatures.

"No meat?" Aiden whispered. "Bro, I could full-on use a hamburger right about now."

"Welcome travelers," Eljah said. His smile curled one corner of his mouth and suggested he knew something, some secret he shouldn't know.

Ullwen said, "We are greatly honored. Thank you for your hospitality, Father." The term was not one of a familial relationship, as Oliver had with Eljah, but the proper title for Eljah, who was both a monk and an ordained minister of Alrujah.

Eljah set the tray on the table. "You must be hungry. Please, eat your fill. Adonai is good. We have a plentiful bounty this winter."

Erica took a carrot, leaned to Oliver and whispered, "When are you going to explain who this Adonai guy is?"

"Essentially, He's God," Oliver replied.

"Okay, and that would have taken too long to say while we were in the woods?"

"There were fangands coming after us," he said.

"Lame excuse."

Oliver sat at the table and took a stalk of celery. It was the first food he'd had in Alrujah. The stalk was crisp and tasted exactly like celery should. He shouldn't be surprised, but he was.

Lauren sat between Ullwen and Aiden and bit into a pear. Her eyes closed. She looked as exhausted as Oliver felt.

Despite the late hour, he pressed on. When he finished his celery and some carrots, and complemented them with some of the fruit, he asked Eljah, "What books were the Blood Monks looking for?"

Eljah's eyes flitted about the room quickly. "Blood Monks?" His feigned ignorance meant he knew something Oliver didn't. Likely, Eljah did not trust everyone in the room. Perhaps he knew more about Ullwen than Oliver did.

"What are you talking about, Vicmorn?" Lauren asked.

He shook his head. "Never mind. I had a nightmare last night is all." He stared hard at Eljah and hoped to convey a simple message. *We need to talk.*

Chapter Twelve

Humans were not as skilled as the dwarves in masonry and smithing, nor were they as skilled in the physical arts as the elves, but Adonai loved them above the other races. To them He entrusted righteous ambition, determination, and perseverance. These qualities served the race well. And Adonai established the throne and the blood of kings through the humans.

—The Book of the Ancients

BAILEY RENEE PULLED AT her bottom lip—a nervous habit she'd picked up from Lauren—while a Minnesota State Trooper filtered through her sister's things. Slightly shorter than her, he looked just as young. How long had this guy even been a cop?

Her mother crossed her arms and rubbed the skin on her elbows.

Detective Joseph Parker, a head taller than the trooper and thicker in the chest and shoulders, worked next to him. Worry lined his face. He looked no older than her mother.

Both wore gloves while they picked up her pillows and searched her sheets. They rifled through the books on her shelves, the video games, and strategy walkthroughs. They even checked her piggy bank. But Detective Parker spent most of the time at the window. He ran a finger along the weather stripping like an Army Sergeant going over new recruits' bunks. "You say the door was locked from the inside?" The smell of him and the sound of his coarse voice said he'd been a smoker for years.

"Yes," Bailey Renee said. Her mother took her hand. How long had it been since they'd held hands? She'd been four, maybe, crossing the street.

"Window doesn't look like it's been opened. Where does Dad live?"

Ms. Knowles cleared her throat. With one hand she touched the front of her neck, as if she had a necklace to play with. "He moved to California twelve years ago."

Detective Parker pulled off his latex gloves and shoved them in the pockets of his black coat. With a raspy, "Excuse me," he pressed past Bailey Renee and Ms. Knowles and headed toward the living room. "I have to ask the reason for separation. I don't mean to pry, but it is important."

"Divorce," she said. "He had a job in California. And another woman. A whole new life he liked better than what we had here."

Her mother had never said that out loud, and Bailey had never been brave enough to ask. While she was disappointed in her father, she didn't much resent him. Not as much as she should.

"Lauren was what, four?"

Ms. Knowles nodded. Bailey Renee moved to the couch and sat down. "You think he did it, don't you?"

Reaching into his coat's inside pocket, Detective Parker took a cigarette from a box and put it between his lips.

"I'd prefer you not smoke in my house, Detective."

"I'm not smoking. I'm thinking." He stared out the kitchen window to the frozen pond in the back yard. He'd stared at it a lot since he showed up an hour ago. "I'm trying to replay the scene in my mind. We haven't found any signs of forcible entry. You say she was gone this morning before school?"

Bailey nodded.

Parker reached a hand in the pockets of his slacks and pulled it out again, empty. He mimed lighting the cigarette, then proceeded to suck on it as if it were lit. "You're way up on this hill. Lots of ground to cover. Snow's too muddied to get much information. Her car's still here, so maybe someone picked her up. No signs of a struggle, so we can assume it was someone she knew."

"I didn't see or hear anyone last night," Ms. Knowles said. Anyone else might have thought her voice steady, but Bailey heard the weakness in it. Soon, it would crack completely. She was like this in emotionally stressful situations—all business, all calm resolve until she felt she had a moment to breathe. Then, her tears would come, and come hard. She'd done it when she rushed Lauren to the hospital two years ago after a near-fatal episode of anaphylactic shock from a bee-sting, and she did it again now.

Parker leaned against the counter and called to the officer in Lauren's room. "Any prints yet?"

"Just hers," the officer said.

Parker crossed his legs at the ankle. He took the cigarette from his mouth, pretended to exhale smoke, and put it back in. He looked hard at Ms. Knowles for a minute. "I'm quitting. If I die, it's not going to be from these things. Having some trouble letting go completely."

Ms. Knowles nodded. "I quit six years ago."

Parker closed his eyes for a moment, more in thought than fatigue. Without opening his eyes, he spoke to Ms. Knowles. "I know how this is going to sound, but I mean no disrespect. I have to ask. How were things here at home? There's a big difference between an abduction case and a runaway. Either way, Brandon's Law is still in effect, but knowing the case better will help us find her faster. So, if my questions seem too direct, I apologize."

"They were fine," Ms. Knowles said, but her voice rose sharply at the end. She sounded like a child caught cheating on a test.

Bailey's stomach soured. Why had she never considered Lauren running away? She'd never do anything like that. But the possibility remained, and she couldn't let her mother tell half-truths to protect her fragile ego. The stakes were far too high. "No, they weren't," she whispered.

Parker asked, "What was that?"

"They weren't fine," Bailey Renee repeated.

"She wasn't happy here?"

"Of course she was," Ms. Knowles said. She stood up from the couch quickly, touched her throat and started to pace. "Why wouldn't she be happy? She's got a beautiful home, three good meals a day, a loving family."

"Stop, Mom. She wasn't happy, and you know it."

Detective Parker flicked imaginary ash off the end of his unsmoked cigarette into the sink. He opened the fridge, stood stooped over with his face in the door for a minute before pulling out a container of water. "Where do you keep your glasses?"

"Real glasses or imaginary?"

"I'm not trying to quit water, Ms. Knowles."

Bailey Renee pointed to the cupboard above the sink.

He poured a glass and looked hard at Ms. Knowles. "I know how you feel," he said, decades of smoke choking each word to a pinch. "I'm not here to judge your parenting. Raising a teenager's one of the toughest things anyone can do. I get that. But if you want your daughter back, you have to be completely honest with me. I need all the information we can scrape together. Doesn't matter how insignificant it feels, how unrelated. And you can't worry about how it makes you feel or look. You're not on trial here."

The speech sounded rehearsed and stiff. He'd probably worked tons of cases like Lauren's.

Parker put the water back in the fridge. "Please continue, Bailey." The cigarette stood at attention between his fingers while he sipped the water.

Bailey took a deep breath. If Lauren had done something to hurt herself, Bailey would at least be partially to blame. And she couldn't live with that. "I should have been nicer to her," she said.

"You were mean?"

"Sweetie, please. Families fight sometimes. Her life was no worse than anyone else's." Ms. Knowles put a gentle hand on Bailey's shoulder.

Bailey Renee stood up and walked to the kitchen. She leaned on the opposite counter and stared Parker in the eye. "I wasn't very nice to her. I teased her about her weight. I teased her about the game she was making. It may not sound like a big deal, but I'm sure she got teased at school, too. A home should be a safe place. A place where you don't have to worry about ridicule and yelling or fighting."

Parker drained the last drop of water from his glass, set it on the counter, and put the cigarette between his lips. If he had lit it when he pretended to, the thing would have been smoked out long ago. "How old are you?"

"Fourteen."

He pushed his lips out. The cigarette pointed at her. "You sound older."

"Thanks?"

Ms. Knowles came into the kitchen. Fear broke her voice, and her eyes turned gray, the color of cement glazed with rainwater. "Detective Parker, I never did anything to hurt Lauren. I never laid a hand on her."

Hands in his pockets, Parker said, "That may have been the problem."

"I beg your pardon?"

"Ever hug her? Put your arm around her?"

Her hand went back to her neck, and Bailey looked at her feet.

Parker grimaced, the cigarette bowing. "Forgive me if I'm too forward. My ex complained a lot about my lack of tact."

"I don't blame her," Ms. Knowles whispered.

"Can I assume, then, that there were few signs of affection?"

Bailey nodded.

"You think she felt isolated?"

"Are you interrogating me?" Ms. Knowles snapped.

Parker took the cigarette from his mouth and replaced it in the box. "No ma'am. Just trying to get a picture that will help me find your daughter."

"I didn't call you here to accuse me of being a bad mother." Anger replaced the fear in her throat and made her voice tiger strong.

"We're on the same side, here, Ms. Knowles," Parker said.

"Everything we can tell him will help him find her, Mom."

Parker's cell phone rang. He answered. "Got it. We'll be over soon." He hung up. "You said she was friends with Oliver Shaw?"

Bailey nodded.

"I'll head over there and ask a few questions, see if they know anything." He replaced his phone in his pocket. "She had journals in her room. A lot of them. May we take them? Scan through them? See if we can find anything?"

"You won't," Bailey Renee said. "They're all filled with stuff about her game."

Parker nodded. "I'd still like to see them if that's alright."

Her voice wilting, fingers pressed to the small of her neck, Ms. Knowles said, "That's fine."

Parker called after the other officer. "Wrap it up fast. Grab the journals. We have to make a stop on the way back to the station."

* * *

After the meal, Eljah had a few monks escort the travelers to the guest quarters in the south building. Oliver's quarters, though, were above the main chapel next to Eljah's. So when he followed Eljah out of the dining room, he expected to turn left, but Eljah turned right.

Slender silvery light split the dark night sky. In the space of an hour, the lesser sun would rise over the Dragon's Back Mountains. Eyes heavy, he followed the taller monk with the understanding he had something in mind, something important, to talk about.

Even with Ullwen bedding down in a different building, Eljah acted cautious as if someone watched them. Ullwen must not be the one Eljah didn't trust. In the distance, Oliver's eyes caught a faint silver shimmering in the trees, like light filtering through water. Chameleon Soldiers.

Surely Ribillius trusted the monks. Why would Korodeth waste his resources spying on monks?

The shimmering disappeared.

The vanishing act unsettled Oliver. He leaned heavily on his prayer staff, thankful that the pain in his shoulder dissipated. The weapon gave him a small measure of comfort, but against an invisible opponent, it wouldn't be much use.

Eljah moved to the library. At this hour, few monks studied. These rose early to spend a few silent hours delving into the depths of ancient texts. Strangely, he still remembered the scheduling of the brothers. The albino monk sat at the middle table. He stood and acknowledged Eljah and Oliver with a slight bow. "Good morrow, Fathers."

"Good morrow, Brother Dillard," Eljah said. Oliver made a note of the man's name. To the other monks gathered in the library, Eljah said, "Please, Brothers. Continue your studies in your quarters."

They gathered their books and, wordlessly, shuffled out of the room. When the door closed behind them, Eljah grabbed Oliver's prayer staff from his hands. Before Oliver reacted, Eljah swung it toward Dillard's head.

The albino monk ducked, but a sickening crack reverberated through the room. Dillard spun around, bent over, straightened again. A chair skittered across the floor, seemingly of its own accord.

Dillard punched air. With a deft motion, he yanked the space in front of his fisted hand. As if by some trick of stage magic, a disembodied head appeared floating over Dillard's grasp.

Chameleon Soldier. Of course. "How did you know?" Oliver asked.

Eljah said, "They've been here since shortly after you left. We anticipated they would watch us until your return, and perhaps even beyond. But we must move quickly." He hurried to the east wall, which, like the others, was lined with shelving of harspus wood. Books, all bound in red and gold covers, filled the shelves. Several blue-bound books, however, sat scattered throughout the shelves from the lowest levels near their feet, to the upper levels near the extent of Eljah's reach, and everywhere in between. The spines read *History of the Cerulean Woods*. Each had a volume number ranging from 1 to 12. Aside from the uniformity of the color of the books, the room reminded Oliver of Lauren's. All those shelves, all those books. How she had time to read them all and do all of the writing for the game, and stay up with her homework, baffled Oliver.

Eljah tilted volumes three, seven, and twelve. A sound, like a latch falling open, broke the otherwise still room.

Dillard pulled the center table from the middle of the room and lifted a piece of the stone floor beneath it. The stone had to be at least a hundred pounds, but the muscular monk lifted it as if it were a baby. He set it down gently, grabbed on to the sides, and dropped down into the dark hole. His fingers disappeared silently.

"Quickly," Eljah said again. "Every moment counts. We only have a few hours." He pulled a torch from the wall and followed Dillard into the black hole.

Oliver's blood pulsed in his forehead. Each beat of his heart made his head feel like it might burst into flames. None of this was in the script. He'd never designed a passageway like this, or the blue bound books for that matter. Chameleon Soldiers should never spy on monks. And monks would never attack, not without good cause.

He rubbed the back of his neck, slowed his breathing, remembered how much he trusted Eljah and wondered if that trust had been misplaced. Still, he could not ignore the compulsion to follow him.

Chapter Thirteen

They will come in a time of darkness, and their coming will herald disaster. Kings shall die. Cities will be ravaged. Abominations will again walk Alrujah. But the Hand of Adonai will restore order to His creation.
—The Book of Things to Come

BECAUSE THE MONASTERY DIDN'T often house female visitors, only the occasional traveler, Lauren and Erica had to share a tiny upstairs room in the south building. The moonlight through the two glassless windows provided the only light in the store room. The monks apparently used the lower floor to store gardening equipment. Hedge clippers hung suspended on the uneven stone wall. Racks of hoes and rakes, shovels and pick axes lined the walls. An innocent enough room, but Lauren knew the Monks of the Cerulean Order could use any of these as weapons with deadly efficiency, though they would never kill a man if they could avoid it. Fangands, however, and beresus and sasquatch, were a different story.

Lauren followed Erica up the dark, irregular steps. Her legs shook and ached, like she'd just run the mile in PE. In truth, she'd probably run much further than that, then rode a few extra miles on the back of a stocky war horse. She wanted to collapse into a bed and sleep for three and a half weeks.

A single bed had been pushed up against the windowless wall opposite the door. Stitched animal skins composed a simple mattress, more a sleeping bag than anything else, really.

Eyeing the bed, Erica said, "Awkward."

Lauren wanted to curl up on it, no matter how uncomfortable it might be. Lying was better than standing. Even the rock floor looked good to her. But, no matter how much her bones ached, she couldn't put the memory of what Erica had said to her as they rode away from the castle out of her mind. When push came to shove, and Lauren needed a friend, it'd been Erica who'd stepped up. Not Oliver or Aiden. How easy would it have been for Erica to ignore Lauren? Instead, she went out of her way to be kind, something Lauren had never done for her. "You can have the bed," Lauren said.

Sparky leaned against Erica's leg, and she scratched behind his ear. "No way. You're the princess. You take the bed. Unless you're afraid there might be a pea under the mattress."

"Very funny." Lauren closed the door and sat in the corner of the room. She leaned her head back against the wall and crossed her arms over her chest. Closing her eyes, Lauren said, "It's my fault you're here. The least I can do is let you have the bed."

Erica rolled her neck from side to side. She rubbed her shoulders and tugged at her gloves. "I don't know whose fault it is. Not sure I really care, either. But I'm pretty sure it's not yours. Anyway, I don't mind the floor. Trust me. I've slept in worse conditions than this."

Lauren opened her eyes. "Really?"

Erica was quiet for a minute. Moonlight poured in through the windows. She ran a gloved hand through the shimmering blue brilliance and stared at the shadow of her hand. "Did a lot of traveling a few years ago. Bad motels, you know?"

Lauren laughed. "Right now, I'd probably take a rat-infested interstate dive over this."

Erica pulled the extra skins from the foot of the bed and tossed them to Lauren.

She caught them. Wolf pelts, mainly, but one had belonged to a bear. Though thin, the skins worked well to keep her warm. She sat on one to keep the chill of the stone floor from creeping up her back. The bear skin she wrapped around herself, snug under her neck.

How many winter nights had she spent at home, tucked under her down comforter, a good book and a dim reading lamp beside her bed. It was those novels, she thought, that caused her first to dream about Alrujah. It was Tolkien's *Lord of the Rings* that prompted her to begin writing her dreams down.

Alrujah had been clear in her dreams, had seemed real, but not like this. Now, Lauren longed for those books, for her warm bed, and for the safety of dreams.

Erica rolled a skin into a rustic pillow. She lay down on the bed, pulled a massive skin over herself, and closed her eyes.

The skin she'd used as a blanket covered her completely, even wrapped around her a couple times and tucked under her feet. Oblivious to the implications—monsters big enough to make humans look like action figures roamed Alrujah—Erica pulled the pelt close to her chest. "Keep her warm, Sparky."

The dog obeyed, lying down beside Lauren. Its massive chest expanded with each breath, and the stench of dog breath soured Lauren's stomach. But she'd take it if it meant a warmer night.

What worried Lauren now was the pelt Erica used as a blanket. The predominantly gray and black pelt had six brown stripes running down it diagonally like a spiral staircase. Sasquatch skin. A year ago, in her journal, Lauren penned the description of the beast. *Nine feet tall, strong as twenty men, hunt at sunrise, hunt alone, resistant to physical attacks and magic.*

Hadn't she wanted to live in Alrujah? Hadn't she thought it would be preferable to being fat and unloved? Here, she was beautiful. Here, people loved her. Here, people listened to her.

But here, she might be pounded into a purple pulp by scary strong beasts.

* * *

Oliver followed Eljah down the cold damp corridor. Eljah lit several torches, each spaced about thirty feet apart, along the rough hewn walls. Each illuminated about ten feet on either side, leaving periodic spaces of shadows.

Dillard's fist held the Chameleon Soldier by the light refracting chainmail. The man's invisible feet scraped across the floor.

"What is this place?" Oliver asked.

"This is the study. We built it shortly after the Blood Monks raided us," Eljah said. "This is where the work of Adonai is done."

Oliver had no desire to know the details of such work.

Eventually, the walls spread out into a single rectangular room. Like the library above, shelves lined each wall. Unlike the library, however, these books were bound in hard white covers, not red or gold. A table and chair, fashioned from the black wood of the harspus tree, sat in the center of the room. One particularly large book rested open on the table.

Dillard began stripping the armor off the soldier until he wore only his leather undershirt and pants. Dillard took the gold rope from around his waist and tied the soldier's hands to the chair. He tied the knot with all the speed and skill of a sailor.

Eljah already had his rope belt off, too. He knelt down and bound the soldier's feet to the chair. "Your rope, Vicmorn. Quickly."

Oliver complied. Eljah used it to tie both his rope and Dillard's rope together behind the chair. Completely bound, the soldier's hands and feet began to turn red and swell. "How long are you going to keep him like that?"

"Until he can answer our questions," Dillard said.

The soldier's head lolled forward.

"It doesn't look like he's going to wake up anytime soon."

"We have a matter of hours, son. Dillard, tell him."

The albino's red eyes flickered in the torch light. He touched the book on the table. "This is *The Book of the Ancients.* You know it well. But there are other books of great value and importance in Alrujah. Books that can change the course of our world forever."

Oliver leaned heavily on his prayer staff. The way Dillard had said, "our world," made it sound as if he knew Oliver came from a different one. Or, at least that other worlds existed.

The soldier's head started swelling where the staff had hit him. It looked like a second head.

Dillard moved to the shelves and began pulling books out. He took three and set them on the table. "These are books of history, of language, and of communication. Contained here are the languages of the world—of the dwarves, the elves, the different dialects of the humans. They are powerful books, but they are nothing compared to the four books of power."

The soldier moaned and tried to pull his head up, but it fell forward again and nodded.

Oliver looked at Eljah as if to question the sanity of the albino. Eljah simply nodded. "He has made the books of power his life's study. His knowledge of these books is one reason he did not take the vow of silence. He has proven his trustworthiness several times over. In many cases, he knows more than I do."

"What are these books of power?"

"Each of the four books contains vast power. *The Book of the Ancients* details the history of Alrujah. There is great knowledge and wisdom in it. Because of this, it is widely available throughout our world."

Again, he'd said, "our world." Oliver swallowed past an apple-sized lump in his throat.

"*The Book of Sealed Magic* is an ancient book, nearly as old as *The*

Book of the Ancients. The spells contained within that book hold the power to rend our world. Shortly after the War of the Suns, King Solous hid the book so the powers would never again threaten Alrujah. Its story has been told and retold. It has become legend, and while nearly any Alrujahn can tell you of the book's existence, none can tell you where it is.

"But few know of *The Book of Things to Come.* Only one copy remains. The Monks of the Cerulean Order have been entrusted with the location of this book. Not even the Council of Yeval know where it is.

"Contained within its pages are prophesies that chronicle the coming of the Hand of Adonai. It is very specific in what it reveals. If the Mage Lord, or any one of the Shedoahn Order were to find it, it could mean a dramatic shift in the balance of power, and evil would reign over Alrujah."

Oliver needed to sit down. Exhausted from the ride, from the battles, from the emotional turmoil of being yanked into another world, he wanted to sit and rest his legs. He hurt in places he didn't know he had places. Absentmindedly, he took the prayer amulet in his hand and ran his thumb over it.

The sudden barrage of rapid-fire information, some he knew and some he didn't, baffled him. His brain didn't work as quickly when his body hurt so much. He felt like Aiden, listening to Lauren prattle on about the proper way to begin a literary analysis essay. "Slow down, Dillard."

Eljah said, "There is no time to slow down."

Dillard spoke softly, a whisper of a promise, a sacred secret. "The Hand of Adonai has arrived. The book speaks of a monk, a caller, a mage, and a knight."

The soldier moaned. His eyes fluttered.

Oliver knelt down. He put his prayer staff in front of him and bent over to touch his forehead to the cold stone floor.

"There is more, my son," Eljah said. He extended a hand to Oliver.

"No. No more. I can't … not now. I need to rest. I need to sleep. I need to wake up. I need something."

Eljah knelt next to him. He put a hand on his shoulder. "Dillard has studied the book his entire life. If we called him to, he could record every detail, produce a word-for-word copy."

Oliver shook his head. He'd not coded a *Book of Things to Come.* But he did know it. He remembered it. He remembered the location with perfect clarity. "Margwar," he said.

Dillard spoke. "You have learned much, and you do need rest. Go to your quarters. Sleep. We will wake you in one hour. You must go then. We must separate for the sake of safety."

Oliver rolled on his back. He put his hands on the top of his head and took slow deep breaths. Uneven rocks pressed into his back, along his spine, under his ribs, the base of his neck. "This isn't real."

"It is," Eljah said. He took a book from the table and gave it to him. "Have faith, son. Adonai will guide your steps. These books are your compass, Vicmorn." He put his hand on his shoulder and stared intently at him. "It's still hard to believe. Why is it we pray for a miracle and are surprised when Adonai answers?"

Oliver sat up. "What miracle?"

"You are the miracle. The answer to prayer. The Hand of Adonai is among us."

"Read the books," Dillard said. "They will answer your questions."

The white bound book Eljah handed him was titled *The Language of Adonai*. He opened it and instantly recognized the words. It was in English, for one, which surprised him, since the other books were all composed in Lauren's fictional language. And it was typed, not like the handwritten copy with words like black animals slanting toward prey.

It began with a title page: *Deep Red User's Manual*

Oliver's stomach cramped.

Chapter Fourteen

But jealousy for Adonai's favor wrought war among the races. Elves sought to assert themselves over the humans. But the heart of Adonai rested with King Solous, and the elves did not prevail against them.

—The Book of the Ancients

LAUREN WOKE UP TO the sound of sharp, fast knocking. "Get up, girls. We have to go."

Sleep crusted her eyelids. She rubbed them and blinked twice. She half-expected to open her eyes and be back in her room. The voice, she thought, must be her mother rushing them out the door for school. But her mother didn't chase them out anymore, and besides, she'd never had a voice deep as the Grand Canyon.

"Oliver?" she asked.

"Oh come on," Erica mumbled. "We just went to sleep. The suns are barely up."

"You've been out for at least an hour, maybe more. But we have to go. Get your things. I mean it."

Lauren stretched. "Why the rush?"

"I'll explain on the way. I have to get Aiden. I'll meet you in front of the main chapel in five minutes."

Erica sat up and rubbed her neck. She arched her back and a report of quick cracks zipped through the room. She stood up, stretched her arms, yawned, and bent over to touch her toes.

Lauren put her white fur-trimmed cloak back on and pulled the hood over her head. She wasn't excited about heading back out into Alrujah yet. She wanted some breakfast first. In fact, staying in the monastery until they found a way home sounded pretty good.

She wondered again about home. How much time had passed? Had any? The days in Alrujah only spanned fourteen hours. Yesterday moved faster than a normal day, but she was as exhausted at the end as she would have been if it had been a full twenty-four hour day. And it wasn't like Alrujah had a clock on every wall.

"Let me guess," Erica said. "No showers in Alrujah?"

"Not in the monastery. Most inns in the different towns have bath houses."

"Figures." She sniffed her armpits. "Ugh. Going to be an ugly day."

For the first time since she woke up in Alrujah, Lauren laughed. "Somehow, I don't think anyone's going to mind, so long as you can still call down swarms of razorbeaks."

"I don't suppose you can conjure up some deodorant or something?" She continued stretching, twisting from side to side, her arms in a hoop.

Lauren ran her hands up and down her arms, then her legs, hoping to stimulate some blood flow. It was cold, and her blood felt thick.

Erica cracked her knuckles, rubbed her hands together. "What do you think is so important?"

"I have no idea."

"Didn't you make this whole game?"

"Most of it, but it's not the same. Things that are supposed to happen aren't. Things that weren't supposed to did. I don't really know anything anymore."

Erica tried to pull her hair back. "I *really* hate my hair."

"Sorry."

"Whatever. Let's just go before Oliver the cryptic monk leaves without us."

* * *

Oliver's eyes felt as dry and hot as deserts. His entire body ached. He leaned against a tree next to Aiden outside the main chapel. Where Oliver was stiff, Aiden was limber. He threw his armor on in about half the time it took him yesterday. He learned quickly.

The lesser sun had barely cleared the Dragon's Back Mountains. The chill in the air stabbed through Oliver's robe. Monks loaded several carts with wooden crates filled with books and food. They worked in silence, with Dillard and Eljah directing them with nods and gestures.

"Bro, I'm totally confused right now. We just got here. Why are we taking off?"

"It's not safe here. When Korodeth realizes his Chameleon Soldier never reported, he'll send his troops out in full force." He scanned the south building. Erica and Lauren should arrive soon.

"Why would he? Isn't he on our side?"

"Tensions are too high right now. He wouldn't have had a man here if he trusted the monks. So, he wouldn't think twice about razing the place."

Aiden bit into an apple. He chewed it loudly. "Would Ribillius really let him do that?"

"Ordinarily, I'd say no way. But the way things have played out so far, anything's possible. And Eljah sure thinks Korodeth would do it, with or without Ribillius's blessing."

Three monks led the five horses to Oliver. With a nod, they tied them to five separate trees. Each was saddled, and each saddle had two bags filled with fruits and vegetables, breads and cheeses. Oliver's, however, bursted with books.

Ullwen emerged from his quarters, his curly black hair pulled back behind his shoulders. His beard had grown thicker.

Oliver ran his fingers over the stubble on his chin and wondered if Erica liked facial hair or not.

Behind Ullwen, Lauren and Erica emerged. They came up to him quickly. "So what's the rush?" Erica asked.

"Long story short, we're not safe. The monks are disbanding and heading to different chapels throughout Alrujah. We're going to Margwar." He mounted the golden steed. "Food's in the saddlebags."

Ullwen unhitched the horses and leapt on to Blaze's back.

Aiden deftly climbed on his horse and began rummaging through the packs of food. "Cheese? You kidding me? Finally, some protein!"

Erica put a hand on Midnight's black neck. "Missed you, too," she whispered. She climbed on his back and ran her fingers through his mane.

"Hold on a minute," Lauren said. "Margwar is abandoned. Why would we go there?"

"To get *The Book of Things to Come*. Its prophecies should point us to *The Book of Sealed Magic*. If we can find that, we can likely find our way home and save Alrujah in the process."

* * *

Bailey had been asleep for an hour when her alarm went off. The sun wasn't up, and she shouldn't be either. She'd made up her mind not to go to school today. She wanted a day to figure things out. She'd go back tomorrow. She turned the alarm off and closed her eyes.

Another alarm went off. She sat up. The faint sound carried through thin doors. Lauren's alarm.

Bailey looked around her room. Hot tears surrounded her eyes. She kicked the covers off, chastised herself for not turning Lauren's alarm off last night. Thank God her mom's room was on the other side of the house. If Mom heard Lauren's alarm, her tears would never end.

She shuffled into Lauren's room, banished the horrendous images her mind had conjured last night and hit the snooze button with sluggish fingers. Eyes half-shut, she fiddled with the clock until she'd found the switch to turn the alarm off completely.

4:30 AM.

She didn't know why she stood in the room for so long, couldn't explain it if she tried. She took in the shelves and shelves of books and video games, the tiny television and Xbox 360 balanced on her desk. Her bedspread was rumpled, sheets askew. Homework littered the floor. Every detail insisted Lauren was there, or had been there recently.

Lauren didn't have to get up early. She could sleep in an extra hour, easy, if she wanted to. But she got up early every morning to take Bailey Renee to school so she could watch current events in her Honors Social Science class. Had Bailey ever thanked her?

She probably hadn't.

Bailey Renee wiped her cheeks with the sleeves of her flannel pajamas. She stepped over the scattered paperwork, slid into Lauren's bed, and pulled the covers over herself. She closed her eyes, smelled Lauren's Mountain Breeze shampoo on the pillowcase, and fell asleep quickly.

* * *

Black rock jutted up from the otherwise flat expanse of the Harland Plains like a wall of fractured marble. Beyond it lay the western fork of the Fellian River. More than hills, but less than mountains, the rock formation defied labeling, and didn't even appear on the map of Alrujah. Oliver must have pulled the information from Vicmorn's memory. Lauren sighed.

Within the black rock, a series of caves ran together. Most didn't extend very deep but provided enough room for ancient travelers to find shelter from storms, a place to stay warm through blizzards and the like. However, most travelers used the shoddy roads between cities now and avoided these caves.

But within the series of caves, two ran very deep. Carved by the dwarves, these were used as escape routes during the Plague of the Nar'esh. Few survived long enough to make it through them. Still, Lauren and her friends should be able to make it to Margwar through these, if they could survive the nar'esh.

It took most of the day to reach the caves. Along the way, Oliver explained the details of why they needed to hurry, and why they had to leave at all. While Dillard could repeat the entire book, several portions were indiscernible. Mystery veiled the prophecies. Several portions of it were in the language of Adonai. And while Dillard and several of the monks were well versed in various languages, none comprehended the language of Adonai. It wasn't for men to know the tongue of Adonai.

"And Adonai is God, right?" Erica asked.

Ullwen chuckled. "You speak as if you don't know Adonai."

"Maybe I don't."

Ullwen spoke harshly. "Careful. You border on blasphemy."

"On what?"

Oliver broke in. "Forget it. We need to think about how we're getting down to Margwar. It's going to be pretty tough."

They slowed when they reached the rocks. The horses climbed the steady sloping path gingerly; making sure each step was solid. The narrow path had only enough room for one horse to pass at a time, and while not high enough for a fall to be fatal, such an accident would hurt for days.

Oliver led the group, and Ullwen took up the rear. The horses plodded along, their hoof-falls echoing over the valley below. Oliver liked the sound. Unlike the horse he rode to Castle Alrujah, this was a war horse. Erica had told him the horse's name was Wrath. Far too harsh a name for such a wondrous animal. Thick with muscle, it responded so quickly to the slightest nudges, Oliver felt as if he, not Erica, was the summoner.

He slowed to a stop as all of the horses made it to the upper ledge. They looked over the valley of plains spread out beneath them. Far to the west, the torches of Harland's eastern wall flickered.

Aiden pointed to the dancing orange glow in the distance. "They always lit up?"

"Aye," Ullwen said. A simple answer to a simple question.

Oliver leaned to Erica. He swore he could still smell her perfume, a delicate waft of earthy oleander, a faint woodsy smell. Had his memory conjured the scent to trick his mind, or had she picked up the scent of the harspus trees in the Cerulean Woods? It made no difference. His enjoyment of the aroma was not dependent on his understanding of its origin.

He nudged her with his elbow. He wanted to get her attention, but he also wanted to test the waters of physical contact. Would she recoil? Would she say something so derisive he'd want to hide under Wrath? She did neither. "You okay? You've been quiet."

"Trying to take it all in," she said. "So this place is dangerous?"

Oliver brought Wrath around to the opening of the cave. "Yes."

"How bad? On a scale of rabbits to beresus?"

"You'd need a different scale."

"Fantastic," she muttered.

Aiden said, "Nice, bro. I could use a challenge."

"What do you call the fangands?" Lauren asked him.

He grinned. "A warm up."

Erica pulled her white gloves tighter. Sparky jumped down onto the ledge, which was much wider than the path leading to it. Erica followed suit and dismounted. "We can walk the horses to the caves. They're pretty tired."

Oliver smiled. "You're really getting the hang of this calling thing."

"Guess it doesn't suck as much as I thought." Her brown hair caught puddles of moonlight. She'd never been more beautiful.

Ullwen slid off his horse. "I think we're all tired."

Horses in hand, the five walked the few feet to the correct cave. From the outside, it looked like all the others, which was why so many overlooked it. Oliver walked inside. "About fifty yards in there's an offshoot to the left. The dwarves used it for their horses when they carved this place up. It'll be a little shorter than the stables these horses are used to, but it should suffice. It's warm and dry, which is more than I can say about the outside."

Snow fell and stuck to the black ledge.

Oliver kept moving. "Beyond is a central room with eight offshoots. The central room has a venting system, so we'll be able to have a fire there."

"How exactly does a cave get a venting system?" Erica asked.

"Dwarves are handy like that," Lauren said.

Ullwen and Aiden stabled the horses while Erica followed Oliver and Lauren to the central room. The walls of the room sloped upward until it seemed as if there were no ceiling at all. What little light filtered in from outside dissipated on the black floor until it was tar dark.

As the day pushed on, the strangeness of Alrujah—Lauren wielding magic, the familiarity of riding horses, two suns crawling across the sky—became seamless, normal. Even the immensity of the cave didn't astound him, not like it did the others.

Lauren's eyes widened, and Erica craned her neck back. "I can't see a thing."

"Me either," said Lauren.

"How about some light?" Oliver asked.

Lauren shrugged. "Don't know. I mean, sure I throw fire, but not sure I can control the intensity or size."

Erica said, "Give it a shot, girly. What's the worst that can happen?"

It got quiet. Oliver strained his eyes against the dark. He imagined his nose wrinkling as he squinted. Best he could tell, Lauren held her hand in front of her as if there were a bird in it.

Lauren breathed slowly. Oliver walked a little closer, Erica by his side, and squinted a bit more. Lauren's eyes clamped shut. Her hand started to glow until a little flame, about the size of a chicken egg, rose from her cupped palm. Shadows danced on the walls, big and black. The chicken egg flame grew to the size of an ostrich egg. Lauren had to hold it away from her body. "This thing's hot," she said. "I'm burning my face. Let's get wherever we're going quick."

Oliver raised an eyebrow. "You're pretty amazing, Lauren."

Erica grabbed his elbow. "You heard the lady. Let's hustle."

Before long, they'd reached a small circular pit in the ground. "Careful with the flame," Oliver said. "There's an enchantment here that lets you have fire without wood, but I'd suggest turning the flame down a bit."

Lauren's hand glowed orange. She nodded and closed her eyes again. In a minute, the ostrich egg flame shrank to the size of a skink. She knelt down and waved her hand over the pit. The lizard flame jumped and swelled into a camp fire. Lauren jumped back, and Erica snickered.

"It's not funny," Lauren snapped. "You put your face in it and try not to jump."

Erica pulled her gloves up and scratched Sparky behind the ear. "Relax. It was cute."

"Cute?" Lauren's eyes reflected the fire cruelly.

Oliver sat down cross-legged and warmed his hands by the fire. "Thanks, Lauren." The cold of the cave retreated. His numb cheeks tingled.

Erica sat a few feet back from the fire. Sparky put his head in her lap. "Your whole magic thing is pretty awesome, I guess."

Lauren sat on the opposite side of the fire from Oliver and Erica. She smiled. "Thanks. You don't suck either."

Oliver laughed. "You girls are something else."

Ullwen and Aiden sauntered in—slightly favoring one leg or the other, Aiden's hand on his neck, each with a grimace. Guilt stabbed Oliver. No matter how much he tried to convince himself it wasn't his fault they'd been miraculously pulled into Alrujah, his heart disbelieved his mind.

He compiled the code, scripted the game from beginning to end, and modeled the characters after Aiden and Erica. And though they'd adjusted well, better than he expected, he knew they'd be happier back in North Chester.

Hunger gnawed at his stomach. Fatigue wearied his muscles. He remembered shouting at Lauren yesterday, and guilt punched him again. He closed his eyes, ignored the gnawing pangs of hunger, and prayed Adonai—God—would work His magic.

Magic. The thought made him smile. Lauren's magic awed him. Erica called birds from the sky. Aiden slayed beasts as if he'd been born with a broadsword in his hand and a dagger in his teeth. Comparatively, prayer seemed pretty weak. But without his support, the others would be dead already.

"Let's rest for tonight," Ullwen said. He and Aiden had each brought a saddlebag with the remaining food. "We should eat and sleep. We will need our strength for tomorrow."

"For sure," Aiden said.

Oliver leaned back on his elbows. *Adonai*, he prayed, *let me wake up in my own bed. Let us all get back home quickly and safely.*

Chapter Fifteen

Shedoah sought to unseat Adonai from His celestial throne. His pride angered Adonai, and Adonai cast him and his wicked spirits from the seven skies to the barren earth below.

—The Book of the Ancients

BAILEY STOOD QUIETLY IN the space Detective Parker worked in. She didn't want to call it an office. More like a lumbermill's graveyard. Paperwork lay scattered about his desk. Seven file cabinets lined the side wall. A wall of windows separated his space from the beat cops. Parker had opened the white blinds. Two chairs sat in front of the cornice of paperwork. Relatively free of personal touches, the only thing that spoke of Parker's life outside of the department was a row of framed sketches of a young girl, probably a daughter, lining the top of the filing cabinets.

Detective Parker sat in the chair on the other side, the phone pushed against one ear, an unlit cigarette behind the other. He nodded and made agreeing noises—more grunts in the affirmative than actual words. He'd slicked his black hair back. It didn't appear he'd shaved since last night. His peppery stubble lined his jowls. He motioned for Bailey and her mom to sit in the unoccupied chairs.

They did, and he hung up. He patted his chest with both hands and did a quick inspection of his jacket pockets, before finally finding the cigarette behind his ear. He slipped it between his lips for a second before pulling it out again. He leaned back in his chair, studied the sundry case files spilling over the sides of his desk, and said, "What the department needs is a maid."

Or he needed to be less sloppy.

Ms. Knowles fished in her purse for a stick of watermelon gum. She handed one to Bailey and offered another to Detective Parker.

Parker busied himself reorganizing the papers into manila folders and never noticed the gum. He cleared his throat, put the cigarette behind his ear, and leaned forward. "How you guys holding up?"

"We're fine," Ms. Knowles said with all the conviction of a faithless minister.

Parker looked at Bailey.

"Fine, I guess," she said.

"Right. Good as can be expected. So here's what happens over the next few days in cases like Lauren's. First, we get on the talk box and rustle up as many officers as we can. We get everyone's eyes and ears going. We put notices up on electronic billboards. You've seen them, I'm sure. We shoot out text messages to all cell phones capable of getting emergency alerts. All of Minnesota's going to be looking for her. We've got Amber Alerts in California, Minnesota, and every state in between."

"You really think it's him?" Ms. Knowles asked. She worked the clasp on her purse—opened, closed, opened, closed.

"It's the best possibility we've got right now. But here's the thing— we got eyes all over the place. But some other things have come to our attention. I got three more phone calls last night, all for missing teens, all the same age. Seems a little fishy to me, so I thought I'd ask all the families a quick set of questions, see if I can find any commonalities between the cases."

"Three other missing kids?" Ms. Knowles said.

"Oliver," Bailey Renee whispered.

Parker looked at her, suspicion lining his bleary eyes. It'd been a long night for him, by the look of it. "How'd you know?"

"He was Lauren's best friend. I called his family yesterday. They said they hadn't seen him. And if Lauren's gone, Oliver's probably with her."

"They romantic?" He put the cigarette in his mouth, mimed taking a drag.

"Gosh no," Bailey said. "At least, I don't think so." She hoped not. A few years ago, she'd developed something like a crush on Oliver. Her crush eventually mellowed into a quiet respect, but she'd always remember him as her first crush.

"Could they have been secretly romantic?"

Sun poured in through the window behind him. Bailey scrunched up her nose and squinted.

"No, I don't think so," Ms. Knowles said. She sounded too eager to answer, as if she wanted Parker to think she was an involved mother. "More like business partners. They were working on some video game together."

Detective Parker pushed his lips together as if he were kissing the damp end of the unlit cigarette. He made a note on a pad of yellow paper. "How much do you know about this game?"

"Not much," she said softly. "She wrote everything in her journal. Never let me near it. Didn't talk to me much about it."

"Me either," Bailey said.

He jerked the cigarette out of his mouth and stabbed it toward Bailey. "You know what kind of game?"

"Role playing," Bailey said.

Parker nodded. "Knights and dragons and princesses and all that?"

"I guess so."

He looked over the cigarette. "I could use a smoke about now."

"How long have you been quitting?" Ms. Knowles asked.

"Two days. You said you quit, right?"

"Several years ago."

"We'll have to compare notes sometime. Do either of you know an Erica Hall or Aiden Price?"

Ms. Knowles shook her head. "No, I'm sorry. We don't."

"Not Erica, but I know Aiden," Bailey said. "He's not missing, is he?"

He leaned back and crossed his legs. "It would appear so. Can you tell me how you know him?"

"Everyone knows him," she said. "He's on the football team. Helped us win league this year. Got State Finals coming up soon."

"Yeah, I heard about that. How did Lauren know him?"

"She started tutoring him in English a couple days ago, but nothing before then."

"She tell you that?"

"Franky did. My boyfriend. He's on the team with Aiden."

Parker scribbled in his pad. "Has she changed her group of friends lately? Shown an interest in spiritual leaders or cults?"

"Cults?" Ms. Knowles asked. "No. Absolutely not."

"How about you, Bailey? You hear her talking about anything like that?"

"I doubt she'd tell me if she did. But I don't think she would. Oliver talks about God a lot, but I think it was normal church stuff. Nothing super crazy. Definitely not cult-worthy."

"Got it. One more question. Do you know a Sarah?"

"Sarah what?"

"I don't know."

Bailey nodded. "We have a Sarah in our chemistry class."

"Would Lauren have her number in her phone?"

Ms. Knowles said, "Possibly. They worked in the same group on a project earlier this year. I helped them put together the presentation board."

Parker found a filthy ashtray under the papers. He pantomimed knocking ash from the end of the wet cigarette. "They get along?"

"I don't think so."

He opened Lauren's cell phone. "Not much on here to point us in any directions. Mainly stuff to Oliver, but nothing to go on. Only other thing is a text from Sarah." He showed Bailey and Ms. Knowles the text. "Look familiar?"

"Oh, poor Lauren," Ms. Knowles said. "What a little bully!"

If I wuz as fat as u I'd kill myself.

Sarah Skeleton wrote that. Bailey stared at the message, then flipped the phone closed. She'd go to school tomorrow, long enough to see Sarah Skeleton, long enough to get herself suspended.

* * *

Lauren had no idea what time she woke up. Near the entrance to the central chamber, light crawled along the floor. The greater sun must be up, or at least on its way.

Lauren sat up and studied the slick black walls. She didn't remember the cave, which didn't surprise her. Oliver had put plenty of personal touches on the game they were supposed to be creating *together*.

Irritation warmed her from the inside out. She'd not slept for anything more than fifteen minutes at a time. Her entire body knotted, and bruises lined her limbs. Her temper stretched like old, frayed elastic.

Erica grumbled and rolled over. Sparky pulled double-duty as a pillow through the night. His skin twitched and Erica sat up. "Alright, alright. I'm up already. Geez."

Aiden, Ullwen, and Oliver all slept with their heads on the saddlebags. Only Erica refused, and only because she had a better offer from Sparky. But Lauren still wondered if it would have been better to sleep on the backs of the horses.

Lauren stood up, took a few deep breaths, and walked to where the sun crept in. She pulled her fur-lined hood over her head to warm her ears and stood in the sunlight.

Erica joined her and started stretching again. She bent over and touched her toes, then went further and put her hands flat on the ground. How long had it been since Lauren had touched her toes? She followed Erica's lead, bent over, and touched them with ease. She reminded herself she could only touch her toes because of her digital body, and all her self-loathing worked its way back into her heart. She stood up straight, folded her arms, and tried to slow her breathing.

"Since we're all up, let's get a little breakfast in us," Oliver said. "There's some bread and cheese left, a couple things of fruit. Go light, though. There's not much to eat further on in the cave, and we may have to be there for a night. Two if we're not careful. After we eat, we'll head to the deeper caves."

The deeper caves. The caves Oliver hadn't bothered to explain to her.

She had no interest in fighting this battle with Oliver again. So when he suggested plumbing the depths of the mystery dwarf cave, she hardly batted an eyelash. Her frown may have betrayed her disapproval. If it did, Oliver was too hung up on Erica to notice.

Maybe that's what this all boiled down to—Oliver's need to impress Erica. Maybe that's why he put in the Chameleon Soldiers and the mystery dwarf cave, and why he cut the fingers off Lauren's gloves.

When Oliver so boldly dictated their plan, without room for discussion, Lauren unfolded her arms. She squashed the urge to argue with him because he was probably right. They needed the book. Too much of the game had already changed.

She'd learned to use her fire spell effectively, and, with a little more practice, she'd do the same with her ice and lightning spells. But those spells wouldn't do a thing against the Mage Lord. They needed guidance. They needed to use their skills and get stronger to defeat the Mage Lord, to get home.

"I suppose," she said as she folded her hands behind her, "you'll want me to light the way?"

"I can make some torches," Ullwen said.

"Well, that'd be handy *and* dandy," Erica said.

"I'm not sure we want torches," Oliver said.

"This is no time to show off, Oliver." All the work Lauren had done to suppress her anger was undone. In a flash of heat, her patience evaporated, and she tore into Oliver the way she tore into Bailey Renee, the way her mother tore into her nearly every night. "Hooray for you:

You know your way through this cave in the dark. But not all of us do."

Oliver sighed. "Don't get all sore again, Lauren. That's not what I mean."

Her temper snapped. She was tired of being the victim, tired of people calling her fat and ugly, tired of people insulting her ideas and calling her an overly sensitive drama queen. She was tired of her mom suggesting she needed counseling, that something was wrong with her. Lauren had a point, whether or not Oliver wanted to admit it, and she wasn't about to let him turn this against her, like she was the one making the scene. "Why don't you tell us exactly what you had in mind? Why not actually tell us the whole truth for once."

Oliver put his hands up. "Look, I'm not trying to upset you. This isn't about you or me. It's about finding the book, okay?"

"Don't you dare twist my words. I never said this was about me. This is about all of us. We deserve honest answers."

"He's just trying to help," Erica said.

"I don't see the problem," Ullwen said. "We need *The Book of Things to Come*, and Vicmorn says he can find it. He is a monk, after all. Perhaps he knows more than we can see."

"He's a lying monk, is what he is. And of course he knows more than we can see. He created this whole stupid world *by himself.*"

"What aren't you telling me?" Ullwen asked. "Indigo, you can tell me anything." He took her hand. "I'm here for you. I would leave these three if not for you."

Lauren put her hand over her heart. "So terribly sweet of you. But you don't exist!"

"What?"

Oliver shook his head. "Indigo."

"I am *not* Indigo!" Control slipped away, and anger flashed fever hot in her forehead and cheeks. The fire in the pit roared.

Sparky leapt back and bared his fangs. Erica gasped. She stared with wide eyes at the fire. Sparky ran to her heels, away from the fire. She put a hand on his neck.

Lauren pointed at Ullwen like her finger was a knife. Her voice echoed off the black stone walls. Without thought, words rushed out of her mouth like water over a cliff. She could stop them as much as a twig could dam a river. "This whole thing is a stupid game. You don't exist. You're nothing but a bunch of ones and zeros, some stupidly complex computer code."

Ullwen didn't move. He set his jaw tight. His chest inflated with a deep breath. He let her finger stab him. "I don't understand."

Lauren turned to Oliver. Her eyes reflected the flickering light of the fire. "You made him pretty dense, didn't you?"

"Lauren," Oliver said. He extended a hand toward her gently as if he were trying to calm a rabid animal.

"Don't you *Lauren* me."

Aiden grinned. "Haven't seen this side of you. Kinda feisty."

Lauren glared at Aiden. "Don't flatter yourself." To Oliver, "I am so sick of your lying."

He's not lying, she thought. But she couldn't stop. She thought of her dad, her real dad in North Chester. "I'll be back in a day or two. Won't even know I'm gone," he'd said. Weeks later he insisted he'd come home soon, eventually, after he found himself. He promised to show up for her birthday.

Now, Oliver was lying. Worse, he wanted her to lie. For the good of the game, he'd say. But lying was lying, and it sickened her. "I think it's high time you start doing some explaining to Ullwen. It's a little discourteous to drag him into this, even if he doesn't exist."

Oliver shook his head. "He wouldn't understand."

"Don't speak about me as if I were not here," Ullwen snapped. In one fluid motion, he hung an arrow on his bowstring and pulled the feathered end back to his ear. The flint tip pointed at Oliver's chest.

Moving equally as fast, Aiden snapped his sword from its sheath and pressed the point under Ullwen's chin. "Easy, bro. I can't let you kill our best chance at getting home."

Ullwen whispered. Aiden's blade pressed into his skin with each word. "I deserve answers."

Oliver turned slowly to stare down the shaft of the arrow. His breath slowed.

The fire dimmed dramatically. Sparky barked. The echo exploded through the eight caverns. He leaned back on his haunches and bared his teeth at Ullwen. Erica said, "You may want to drop the arrow, Skippy. Otherwise, it's going to get very messy in here."

"I have no quarrel with you four, but I deserve answers."

"You do," Oliver agreed. "Of course you do."

"You say I won't understand. You underestimate me."

Ullwen's fingers trembled. The feathers of his arrow quivered. How in the world did it come to this? How could Lauren have let herself get so out of control? She took a few deep breaths. The fire under her skin ran cold. The tips of her fingers turned blue and ivory. "I think we better tell him."

"Put the arrow down," Oliver said. "I'll tell you everything you want to know. You have my word as a Monk of the Cerulean Order."

Ullwen's lip twitched. He dropped the arrow. "Make it good."

Chapter Sixteen

And she shall see the face of Adonai and the robe of the Lord, but she will not understand it. She will not understand the light and will fail to describe His beauty. She will speak of it as a vision, and few will believe her, but she will speak the truth of what she has seen.

—The Book of Things to Come

SITTING AT HOME DROVE Bailey Renee crazy. She got so tired of being consistently reminded of Lauren's absence. She couldn't even turn on the television to take her mind off it. Every time she did, a news break about one of the four missing teens interrupted whatever mindless show she'd hoped to watch. Never new information—just another interview with one of the family members.

Several news stations had already called her mother, but Ms. Knowles wouldn't have them, wouldn't talk to them. Bailey had even gotten a call from them on her cell phone. She hung up on them, but not before she told them to leave her alone. Of course, her choice of words had been much more abrasive than her mother's.

She sighed. *No news is good news. Or really, really bad news.* She couldn't stop the same thoughts from punishing her brain. Lauren went for a late night walk and got lost, or broke a leg and was stuck in the cold. The other two teens kidnapped her and Oliver for some secret underground slave trade, or a crazy cult, or a gang initiation. She holed herself up in some underground bunker anticipating the end of the world, while Bailey Renee sat at home and anticipated the end of her family. Without Lauren, her family wouldn't work. Her mother may be strong enough to survive an unfaithful husband, may be strong enough to be a single mother and work extra hours to provide for her daughters, but if Lauren vanished, it'd crack what little strength her mother had left. Bailey knew that as much as she knew the sun would rise each morning.

But Bailey wouldn't let that happen. Though the police had already tried contacting her dad, and her mom had, too, both unsuccessfully, she wondered if she might be able to find him. She went to her room and tried not to look through Lauren's open door. She grabbed her cell phone from her desk. Turned on her laptop and called her father's cell phone. He didn't answer. He didn't answer his home line or his work line. She did talk to his manager, who said the same thing he'd told the police: Mr. Knowles was on vacation and wasn't due back for another week. Camping in the Sierras, he said, with his wife.

Detective Parker had said it was awful convenient that Mr. Knowles's vacation started the same night Lauren disappeared. Still, though the timing worked out, it didn't feel right. Why would a man who hadn't contacted his daughters or ex-wife in over seven years decide to kidnap one of his daughters all of a sudden? Her father may be a deadbeat dad, but he was not a kidnapper.

Undeterred, she dialed Oliver's number. Mrs. Shaw answered. Bailey Renee kicked her shoes off, spun around in her chair, and put her feet up on her bed. "Mrs. Shaw, this is Bailey Renee."

"Hi, hon. How are you?" Her feathered voice suggested she needed comforting as much as Bailey.

"Up and down. Can you talk for a minute?"

"Of course."

"Did Oliver know either of the other two kids?"

Mrs. Shaw swallowed. She took a deep breath and exhaled slowly. "He knew Erica. They had a few classes together. But I don't think he knew Aiden. Aiden wasn't really the kind of kid Oliver would hang out with."

"But Erica was? What was she like?"

"I guess she wasn't the kind I thought Oliver would hang out with, either. She was pretty gothic—all black all the time. She didn't smile a lot."

"Doesn't sound like Lauren's type of friend either."

"Hon, have you heard anything else about them? Has Detective Parker told you anything else? Or asked you anything? Maybe if we work together ..."

Bailey Renee thought of the text from Sarah Skeleton. "Not much."

"Have you heard from your father?"

"Nope. He's about as deadbeat as they come."

"I'm so sorry, hon."

"Me, too," she said. After they said their goodbyes and hung up, Bailey turned around. She launched her browser and navigated to

Google. She typed in "missing teens common answers," but nothing useful came up. Everything was too specific to other cases. She tried other combinations but never found anything worthwhile.

The edge of frustration pressed against her chest like a knife point. She wouldn't give up, not this easily. Not ever. She decided to change her tactics. She dialed Franky's number on her phone and pulled up yellowpages.com. *Price.* Her fingers moved quickly. Franky picked up. "Can you come get me?" she asked.

"Sure, from where?" he said.

"Home." She typed in Hall next. Selected the addresses.

"You sound upset. Are you mad at me?"

"Of course I'm upset, stupid. But, not everything's about you."

"Sorry," he said. "Don't get all bent out of shape, though. It's not my fault she's gone."

She printed the list of addresses on her computer. Instead of pressing the argument further, she decided to let it go. He may be dumb, but at least he loved her. "How much free time do you have this afternoon?"

"I've got a project for Econ due tomorrow."

"And you haven't started it yet, right? You're not going to do it, are you? I mean, you never have before."

"Senior year, baby. I got to make sure I pass this class."

She checked her clock. After two. No stupid economics project was more important than what she had to do. "Come get me. I only need a few hours. We'll be done by dinner. Then I'll do your project for you."

Franky cleared his throat. "You mean we'll work on it together?"

He was so cute when he tried to act smart. "That's what we'll tell your teacher and our parents. Now hurry."

"Alright. Fine. Relax. Man, you're kind of pushy today."

"Don't even start with me, Franky Myers. Get here in fifteen minutes or you can find yourself another girlfriend." She hung up and printed out a map of North Chester. By the time Franky pulled up in his parents' Jeep Grand Cherokee, she'd already planned the route they would take to visit every Hall and Price house listed.

* * *

It may have been thirty degrees in the cave, but Oliver sweat under his thick cotton robe. Ullwen eyed him like he might decide, at any moment, to restring the arrow and loose it at Oliver's neck.

Oliver spoke quietly and slowly. "We're not exactly from around here."

"Given," Ullwen said.

"We're from," he paused, realizing exactly how stupid their story would sound. He thought, for a moment, about Jesus. When He explained to the world who He was, they called him crazy and hung Him on a cross. Oliver hoped this story would have a happier ending. "We're from another world. One outside your own. We," he motioned to Lauren and himself, "designed this world. Everything you see, from Castle Alrujah to the Otherlands."

"More you than me," Lauren muttered.

"What do you mean, 'designed'?"

Oliver hesitated. He wanted to say "created," but that would make him like God. But wasn't he like Him? Wasn't he created in God's image? Hadn't he created this world and come physically into it to save it? He thought of Jesus, who was both God and Man, and of his ultimate sacrifice to wipe out sin and death, to restore eternity.

Oliver didn't like thinking of himself as a deity. There was one God, one God alone. Regardless, they shared unshakable similarities. He proceeded cautiously.

"What I mean is that we created this world."

"Adonai?" Ullwen asked, a tremble in his voice. He looked at Oliver with reverence and fear. "You are Adonai?"

"Not even close," Lauren said.

According to the religion of Alrujah, Adonai created the world. For Oliver, it was an extension of faith—Adonai was simply the Hebrew name for God. So, to Oliver, Adonai was God. But to Ullwen, maybe Oliver was Adonai—the creator of Alrujah.

"Not in the sense you're thinking." Oliver sighed. Too complex and too long. He wanted to move, to put the last five minutes behind them and proceed with their lives, their pursuit to return to their normal existence in North Chester. "The world we're from was created as well."

"By Adonai?" Ullwen asked.

Sword still ready and poised, Aiden listened intently to Oliver. Lauren's anger and angst vanished. Even Erica seemed interested. So what agitated him so much? No one pressured him, and no one tried to shut him up. Why did he feel like he was stepping on toes? Was it because the other three weren't Christians?

Or because he was afraid the others would find out he was a

Christian?

Oliver's throat knotted up. His stomach cramped like he was hungry, or like the bread and cheese had gone bad in his bowels. "By God. The one true God. Adonai is one of His names. He created the heavens and the earth." Oliver had no idea what to say next. He prayed for wisdom. He prayed the others would understand, no matter what he said or how poorly he said it. "It's a really long story. But he created us, and we created you."

Ullwen asked Lauren. "Is this true?"

Lauren whispered. "Yes."

Ullwen collapsed to his knees. "God has come to dwell among us. I am undone."

Aiden spoke first. "We are not gods."

"Speak for yourself," Erica said. She whipped her hair over her shoulder and smiled. After several lengthy moments of silence, she said, "Kidding."

"But, if what you say is true, you created us, and you have come to save us from the evil of the Mage Lord. Yet you say you are not gods?"

"It's a bit of a mind-freak, isn't it?" Erica said. "We didn't really expect you to get it, but I'll try to break it down and make it all real for you. We're not from here, but we are here now. We breathe, and we bleed. And we'd really like to not bleed anymore. Think of us as lost travelers. Call us Otherlanders, call us elves or dwarves or dragons or fairies or sprites or whatever else you crazy medieval castle-building types have running around your mountains and forests."

"And you can stand up," Oliver said. "You never need to bow to us."

"The four in the world, but not of it, and the one called alongside. The Hand of Adonai," Ullwen said. His eyes flitted up to the ceiling. "I have read portions of *The Book of Things to Come*."

Oliver didn't like the sound of that.

Erica said, "Okay, care to elaborate, Oliver? He's speaking gibberish."

"One of the books of power," Oliver said. "How did you come to read it, Ullwen?"

"As a child, my mother used to read me portions of the book. I learned early that to speak of the book was to take your life into your hands. This was before the Shedoahn Order collected and burned every copy of it. They took my mother from me."

Suddenly weak, Oliver said, "I swear, Lauren, I didn't put that in here."

Aiden's voice was deep and quiet. "Who did?"

Lauren crossed her arms. She didn't look irritated, she looked scared.

Erica cleared her throat, pulled her gloves up, and said, "Well, are we going to sit here all day and pout, or are we going to go get the book? Sunslight is burning here, people. Let's get the lead out."

Ullwen stood slowly. He stared at Oliver with such reverence, Oliver thought he might sacrifice a cow to him.

"Yeah, about the book," Oliver said.

Lauren rolled her eyes. "What now?"

"It'll take some doing to get it, from what I understand."

"How so?" Aiden asked, his voice smooth and dark as the marble walls of the cave.

"There are eight passages. Most of them are dead ends, but a few have switches that unlock other parts of the cave. Some of these switches have to be activated at the same time for us to get to the ruins."

"What ruins?" Erica asked.

"The ruins of Margwar," Oliver said. "The great dwarven city."

"Margwar was destroyed nearly a century ago," Ullwen said. He slipped his bow back over his shoulder. "The dwarves went missing soon after."

Oliver leaned against a wall. "Anyhow, long story short, we'll need to break into two teams. We'll each cover two passages. Some are longer than others. But once we're done, we'll meet back here, head down to Margwar together, grab the book, and be back here in time for dinner."

"Sounds simple enough," Erica said. "Let's get moving." She folded her gloved hands. Sparky alternated between sitting and standing.

"What about the nar'esh?" Ullwen asked.

Lauren glared at Oliver. "Tell me you took the nar'esh out. They're not still here, right? *Oliver, right?*"

Oliver didn't know what to say. Though Lauren wrote the history, the specifics of the nar'esh were his idea—inspired by a nightmare. They'd eventually agreed to take them out of the game, but their presence sure wouldn't be the first anomaly. "They're a residual code is all."

He wondered how much time he'd spend fighting enemies and how much time he'd spend apologizing to Lauren. Likely, it'd be equal.

"Nar'esh? I'm guessing those are the bad guys," Erica said.

"They're the reason the dwarves disappeared," Ullwen said.

Aiden stared at Oliver. "Bro, you gotta give us more than that. What are we up against?"

"Cave beasts. Imagine a bat cross-breeding with a spider and a human."

"Gross," Erica said.

"So we have to fight them?" Lauren asked.

"A lot of them."

"Isn't separating kind of a bad idea?"

Aiden said, "So long as I have my steel, I will fear no nar'esh."

Erica grinned impishly. "He's really into this now, isn't he?"

"We should be able to handle it," Oliver said.

"*Should*?" Lauren asked.

"We don't really have a choice, do we? But there's a ton of spells in it for you," Oliver said.

Lauren folded her arms disapprovingly.

"Good spells, too. Quake, Plague, Petrify, Sleep."

Lauren's eyes brightened.

Erica asked, "So where are we going, and who's going with me?"

"Lauren and Ullwen can take the east passage," Oliver said. "Aiden, Erica, and I can take the west."

Ullwen smiled. "Very well. I shall defend her with my life."

Aiden slipped his helmet on and drew his sword. "Show me the nar'esh," he growled.

Chapter Seventeen

The humans of Alrujah cried out for Solous to punish the elves, to banish them from Alrujah, to put them to the sword. But Adonai softened Solous's heart. With great wisdom, Solous established Harael, the island nation, for the elves to rule.

—The Book of the Ancients

FRANKY HONKED TWICE ABOUT fifteen minutes after Bailey Renee printed up the list of addresses. She already had directions scrawled out and a map printed. She grabbed her cell phone, shoved it in the pocket of her pink parka. She pulled a pink beanie down over her ears and headed to the door.

Her mother scrubbed the kitchen counter. A nervous cleaner, she scoured until water and cleanser wrinkled her hands. "Are you going out?"

Bailey zipped up her jacket. She'd only be outside for a minute, but the cold would make the short walk from the door to the car unbearable. And once the sun dropped behind the mountains in the next few hours, the temperature would sink like a three-pointer off Kobe's fingers. "For a bit. I'll be home for dinner."

Ms. Knowles meticulously scrubbed the grout behind the coffeepot with a blue toothbrush. "I'm not sure I'm comfortable with you going anywhere tonight. It's too cold."

"I'm going with Franky. We've got to work on a project tonight. We're going to go do some research."

"Sweetie, I'm serious. Please don't go. You need to stay here. Tonight of all nights, you need to stay here. What if we hear something from Detective Parker?"

"I have my phone, Mom." She pulled it from her pocket and waved it at her mother. "A couple hours. Promise." She turned back to the door, unlatched the lock, and opened it. The quick blast of afternoon cold scratched at her cheeks and made her eyes water.

"Bailey Renee Knowles. Don't you dare step out that door."

Had her mother ever used her full name before? She turned back around. "Are you saying I can't go?"

"You're darn right I am. You never asked me if you could go, for one. And for two, it's way too cold outside to be running around town." She drummed the toothbrush on the tile counter. "And lastly you have to stay home. You have to."

Bailey spoke gently. "You never made me check with you before."

"Things are different now."

"What if I said I was going to look for Lauren?"

Ms. Knowles's eyes reddened. "Sweetie—don't do this, okay? Please. It's hard enough without her here, hard enough to think I may have driven her to do something crazy."

"You didn't, Mom. She's fine, wherever she is."

"How do you know?"

Bailey shrugged. Her eyes got hot, and her cheeks flushed against the cold of the outside air.

"You know what Detective Parker told me this morning? He told me they were dragging the lake for her body." Each word came out more slowly than the last. Her mouth opened at the end as if there were more to say, but what could someone say after something like that?

Bailey could hardly listen to it. How much harder would it have been to actually say it?

"So no, you don't get to go out tonight. Close the door. Call Franky and tell him he can work inside. But you're not leaving this house." She put both hands flat on the counter and leaned over. Her elbows locked with scary intensity.

"I have to go, Mom. I have to find out what happened to her." She fought to suppress the looming storm cloud of tears. She pulled her hood up.

"I'm serious, young lady. Don't you dare step outside. You let the police do their job. Our job is to wait here at the house in case she comes back."

"She's not coming back!" Bailey shouted. "Don't you get it? She's gone, and unless we find her, she's not coming back! She didn't run away, no matter how much you think she might have. Someone took her, and I'm going to find out who."

"Where are you getting these ideas?" Ms. Knowles asked. "Honestly, it's like you're a completely different person. The Bailey I know would never have argued with me like this."

Bailey pulled a Kleenex from her jacket pocket and dabbed at her eyes. As gently as possible, she said. "The Bailey you know would never leave against her mother's wishes, either." She set her jaw tight and pointed to her chest. "But this Bailey would. This Bailey is going to find her sister."

Ms. Knowles grabbed a pair of unused yellow rubber gloves and balled them up in her fist. "Don't do it, Bailey. I'm serious right now. Don't you dare leave me." Tears marred her perfect makeup. They ran in heavy drops to her chin.

"I love you, Mom." She turned back to the door.

"Don't you do it! Don't you do it! If you walk out that door, don't bother coming back! You're no daughter of mine if you leave me. Don't you leave me like your daddy left me! I mean it, Bailey. If you walk out, don't bother coming back!"

Bailey closed her eyes. Tears froze to her cheeks. She closed the door behind her and walked to Franky's Jeep.

* * *

The cave grew colder the further in they went. Aiden's steel greaves clacked on the rock floor as they pressed on.

Oliver held a torch Ullwen had fashioned for them. Lauren had won that battle, and he was glad. The torch may alert the nar'esh to their presence, but it gave them a fighting chance to survive an onslaught. He guessed they only had a few more feet before the nar'esh would climb down the walls and attack.

He remembered the night he designed them in three dimensions. He was not eager to see what they looked like life-size.

Something moved up ahead. "Did you see it?" he asked quietly.

"Yup," said Aiden. He tightened his grip on the hilt of his silver sword.

Erica whispered. "So, what now?"

Oliver searched the rest of the cave with the dim torchlight. "Keep walking. Go slow. Keep your eyes open and be ready."

Erica held the daggers Ullwen had given her before they separated—one in each hand—one curved, the other straight. She held them upside down, as Oliver had designed her to. She wasn't supposed to wield two daggers until much later in the game, but her other abilities advanced so quickly, he had no doubt she'd handle herself with them.

Oliver switched the torch from his right hand to his left, and his staff from the left to the right. Almost as an afterthought, he said, "And whatever you do, don't let them touch you."

* * *

Ullwen had an arrow on the string of his bow. Lauren plodded forward with a tiny ball of fire in her palm, hoping against hope Ullwen remembered Oliver's instructions. Her heart pounded much too fast for her to remember anything. She'd never seen the nar'esh—just come up with some vague notion that some creature had obliterated the dwarves—but Oliver loved challenges. The nar'esh would not be pleasant.

Something caught her eye, a movement, something subtle, hardly noticeable. Ullwen's hair? Yes, over his left shoulder, his black curly hair feathered over his back. How could there be wind in the cave?

"Did you feel it?" Ullwen asked.

"I felt something."

He lowered his voice to a whisper. "They're here."

A twang echoed off the slick walls, the whiz of an arrow splitting air. A high-pitched squeal echoed from the distance of the cave. Something vaguely human fell and crumpled on the rock floor. She squinted, but the dark obscured all detail. "Nar'esh?"

He nodded. "Aye. And where there's one, there are ten."

The fire in her palm snapped out. Cold ran from her core to her fingertips.

"The fire," Ullwen said.

"I don't know," she whispered. Her voice cracked. Blood-numbing fear made her voice shake.

"We need the fire," Ullwen whispered with urgency.

Something touched her shoulder, something soft and slimy. The coldness of it chilled her even more. "Ullwen?"

The touch became a grasp of long, thin fingers. They must have been twice the size of human fingers, and they came to a point. Four sharp nails dug into the front of her shoulder, and one more on the back—five "fingers" in all. "Ullwen," she said again.

Another twang, but no zipping of arrow this time, only a nearby thunk and another screech.

The hand on her shoulder pulled her to the ground, and her head cracked on the rock floor. She screamed.

"The fire!"

But the fire didn't come. The chill of fear mounted, grew to bursting within her. It crept in through the back of her eyes, and icy numbness spread through her neck and lips until shards of ice sprouted out of her like thorns on a rosebush. She shrieked, stood up, and flailed her arms.

Shrieks echoed from all directions. The sound of scraping like nail files surrounded her. Something touched her arm, then on her other arm. She spun around. The icy spikes hit something like a mattress, again, and again. More shrieks.

She was going to kill Oliver. If she lived through this, she would kill him.

The weight on her arms slid off. Skittering, like mice racing over tile floors, replaced the sound of shrieking. All sound ceased, save her shallow breath.

"What in the world was that?" she asked as she shook.

"Those," Ullwen said, "were the nar'esh."

* * *

Franky shifted into reverse and started to pull out of Bailey's driveway. "What was that all about?"

Bailey didn't answer.

"Hey," he said. He took her hand in his and squeezed. "You okay?"

Laughter split her sobs. "Franky Myers, that may be the dumbest thing I've heard you say. And you've said a lot of dumb things." She wiped her eyes, opened his glove box, found some Kleenex, and blew her nose.

"Nice, babe. Real attractive."

Bailey took a few deep breaths and concentrated on slowing her ragged gasps. "Shut up." She gave him the directions she'd printed out.

"What are all these?"

She cleared her throat and buckled her seatbelt. "The addresses of every Hall and Price in North Chester."

Franky turned south on Grove Street. He glanced over the paper quickly. Franky took a minute to put all the pieces together. Finally, he said, "You're looking for Aiden and Erica's families?"

"I have to talk to them."

Franky drove carefully over the icy roads. "Didn't the police already do that?"

The Jeep warmed quickly. Bailey struggled out of her parka and put it in the back seat. She didn't want to remember what had happened—didn't want to think she might not be able to go back to her house. "Yes, but I haven't."

"What are you going to ask them?"

She thought for a minute. "I don't know."

"Well, I can save you some time. I know where Aiden lives."

Why hadn't she thought of that before? They were friends and teammates. Just because she didn't know him didn't mean Franky didn't. "Okay. We'll go there last. Let's see if we can find Erica's family first."

Clouds gathered above the river to the west and rippled out like an upside down ocean. "Storm's a-brewin', Marge," Franky said.

She didn't want to, but she smiled. "You're such a goof."

"A hot goof."

He had a point. He turned west on Pine Avenue, toward the lake. Bailey wanted to start as close to the lake as possible and move east. That way, they could avoid traffic and end up close to her house when done. "Am I doing the right thing? Am I being stupid?"

"Baby, you're never stupid." He ran his fingers over her cheek.

Bailey closed her eyes. "I keep hoping I'll wake up and Lauren will be here. She'll be back, or better yet, it'll be like she was never gone, like I dreamed the whole thing."

He said, "Doesn't even seem real."

"It doesn't, does it?"

"A bad movie."

"A bad dream."

He turned onto Elm Street, drove almost down to the bank of the river until he found a long, stretching driveway. A house the size of a hotel stood at the end of the driveway, beyond a brick wall and an open iron gate. Franky drove slowly to the home. "This Erica chick must be loaded. Maybe it's a ransom thing?"

"No one's asked us for money," Bailey said. She unbuckled and slipped into her jacket.

"Not yet, you mean."

"Would you please shut up, Franky?"

"What? I'm saying maybe …"

Bailey got out, slammed the door and walked to the house.

Chapter Eighteen

And the world shall twist around them. It will form itself to them; it will resist them. And they shall bend the earth around them, the water and the skies, even the air and the trees. They have known the world, but will not know the world.

—The Book of Things to Come

O LIVER'S AMULET GLOWED. THE faint light diffused through his blue cotton robe. And, strangely, it warmed him. The heat from the metal, warm as blood, melted through his body. It reminded him that God's limitless power had no boundaries. God, the true God, still reigned supreme, even in this world. But, admittedly, he struggled to believe with much conviction. Nothing in his Christian upbringing prepared him for jumping from one world into another.

Enoch had done it. Enoch walked with God and was no more. And a chariot of fire carried Elijah away. Neither died, but both disappeared forever. Is that what had happened to him and his friends? Did God make a habit of snatching people from Earth and thrusting them into other worlds?

An ear-splitting scream made him close his eyes. He snapped them open again and held the torch higher, hoping to better illuminate the narrow passageway. He needed to see the nar'esh, needed to see what the dark imaginings of his mind created.

True to their design, six moved in front of them. Likely, the same number flanked them. Most of them sat like frogs on the floor, knees bent at awkward angles, arms straight from their shoulders to the ground, their palms flat on the rock floor. Two, though, crawled on the walls on either side of the passage. One crawled on the ceiling, staring down at him with its tarantula-like eyes. He tucked his staff under his arm and readied himself.

The nar'esh were long, tall, and sinewy. Loosely human in their musculature, their limbs stretched out like elastic. "They're about to attack," he whispered. He tried to keep his voice steady, but had little luck. He cursed himself for programming Erica's digital counterpart with only daggers. What good was a dagger against the likes of the nar'esh, with arms as long as logs?

"There's more, above and behind us," Aiden said.

Erica spun her daggers. "Good job with the monsters, genius boy. Nothing like being outnumbered three-to-one."

"I wasn't planning on having to fight them for real," he whispered.

"Anyone ever tell you you're too smart for your own good?" Erica asked.

"Quite often, unfortunately."

"Don't listen to her, bro. The numbers of the dead can only bring us gory glory."

A squeal—so high Oliver's brain shook—shattered the stillness of the cave. His head hurt, and pain stabbed behind his eyes. The nar'esh hunting tactic—shriek and strike. It left their prey disoriented and clamoring, giving the near-blind beasts an advantage.

Erica covered her ears, the daggers pointing out like a gruesome set of headphones. She pinched her eyes closed. In the dim light of the torch, he could see the wrinkles of her face, her grimace, as if someone had stabbed her.

Unfazed, Aiden moved fast again, thrusting his sword in front of him, pulling it from the black, shadowy nar'esh and spinning around to separate another from its head.

The nar'esh bled a lot. Dark liquid spilled on the rock floor like viscous tar. Something spattered on Oliver's face. Aiden had thrust his blade into another.

Four more nar'esh leapt toward them. Closing his eyes, he took two steps back and pointed the torch at them. Two, directly in front of him, backed away. Two more flanked him. He held his ground, steadied his breathing, and waited. He tried to block out the sounds of shrieking and stabbings, tried to hear the faint click and clack of nar'esh nails on rock walls. But he couldn't. He'd have to rely on the instincts of Vicmorn.

Moving with practiced form, Oliver spread his arms out to his sides. The torch on his left swung close to the nar'esh. The black beast leapt back into the shadows.

On his right side, Oliver's staff hit something soft, like tree branches wrapped in towels.

He didn't stop. He turned on his heels, bringing the torch to the nar'esh he'd hit with his staff. Its skin lit quickly and burned like a match.

The resulting screech rattled his ears.

He used the distraction, and the new light, to bring the tip of his staff into the chest of the nar'esh behind him. He shoved it into a wall and felt the creature's sternum crack. Its long arms wrapped around the staff. Oliver drove again, and it went limp.

Another shriek, but this time it sounded more like a chirp. Erica.

Shadows descended from the ceiling. It was like a tornado, a black wind swirling in the dancing orange light of the torch and the still blazing nar'esh.

Bats. They called back to Erica. They swarmed the ink-dark monsters. The nar'esh turned their attention from the team to the bats.

"Now," Oliver said.

Aiden raced ahead of him, slicing and cutting with swift motions. Never had Oliver imagined such high-caliber swordplay. Aiden must be adapting the standard set of moves in new combinations to better complement his arsenal of attacks.

The narrow passageway ignited in screeches and squeals, shrieks and screams. Erica moved with surprising grace, stabbing and slashing with her daggers. Several nar'esh reached for her, but most pulled their arms away after a quick slash. Her flashy attacks kept the nar'esh back but did little to provide a permanent end to the wave of monsters.

Aiden laughed. "These things are a trip!"

From the ceiling, the black stick shadow of a nar'esh fell on Aiden. His shield slid off his arm, and the feet of the nar'esh pinned his sword to his chest.

Oliver spun, his staff outstretched, and crushed the nar'esh's skull.

Another dropped from the ceiling. Aiden held his sword up, and the beast impaled itself on his blade.

Erica kicked one back and followed with a swift attack. She sank both blades in its chest, then pulled away before it could grab her.

Another monster clicked its tongue four times, alternating pitches.

Erica cocked her head to one side and stared at the nar'esh. "They talk?"

More clicks of tongues, and the final three ran under the cloud of bats and away from the torch light. They disappeared into the darkness.

"That was creepy," Erica said. She slipped her daggers back into the leather sheathes Ullwen had given her.

Aiden kept his sword out but balanced it on his hand and his shoulder. "Bro, that was wicked sick."

Oliver shook his head. This was too real. He touched Erica's elbow gently. "They didn't touch you, did they?"

She shook her head. "I don't think so." She didn't pull her arm away. "You'd know it if they had. How about you, Aiden?"

"I'm good. A little messy. Those things bleed like leeches."

The simile didn't really work. Must be why he needed an English tutor.

"You never told us what happens when they touch you," Erica said.

"I didn't want to scare you," he said. "I figure we can cross that bridge if we come to it."

"I'm guessing Ullwen already knows what happens?" Aiden said.

"If he knew about the nar'esh, he should know about the dangers of their touch."

"What if he doesn't?"

"If he doesn't," Oliver paused, allowing the hypothetical situation to play through his mind, studying each outcome with slightly different variables. And then it hit him—Lauren.

* * *

Lauren's chest tightened. In her ears, Ullwen's words jumped together and back, skipped like a scratched CD. "Indigo, are you alright … alright Indigo? Are you?"

The pain, like being squeezed to death by a beresus, came after the pinching in her neck. Her insides smoldered, not like the burning that preceded her bursts of magic—more like swallowing battery acid. Her shoulders burned, too. She tried to call for help, but couldn't speak.

"Lauren, we need fire … fire need, Lauren." Ullwen spoke slowly, soothingly.

Her legs numbed. Dizziness seized her as if she'd just gotten off a tilt-a-whirl. Even splayed on the cold stone floor, her world didn't stop spinning.

"Lauren?" Ullwen's voice sounded as if it had been carried over tin cans and string.

She wanted to throw up. She was going to die. The pain, the searing pain spread like octopus tentacles through her. She couldn't breathe. How long could she live without air? She was drowning, and there was no water.

The little she could see in the dark looked fluid and runny. It rippled like a lake in the rain. She closed her eyes. Compared to the persistent pain, death sounded appealing.

But what happened beyond death? Would she end up back in North Chester? No. Death in Alrujah was as real as death in North Chester.

God, she thought, pushing her mind past the pain. *God, please.*

Images stretched out in her mind. Oliver at his computer, clacking on his keyboard. The cliff outside her house in the snow. Oliver's arm around her as she stood in her pajamas. Her sister and her mother. Her father. She loved them all.

She saw Oliver's face again, his dopey sideburns down to his jaw, his silly hood covering his head. Then, she saw nothing.

* * *

Oliver's chest burned as if a freshly forged ring had slipped down his cloak and seared itself into his sternum. The amulet. He tucked his staff under his arm, reached under his robe and clasped it in his hand. The burning ceased, but an image of Lauren formed in his mind.

She looked different. Spines of ice stuck out of her gray skin. He recognized the dullness of her pallor—she'd been touched by a nar'esh.

Immediately, he dropped to his knees.

Erica's laughter erupted sharply. "What'd you do, trip or something? How graceful."

Oliver clamped his eyes shut and prayed. The amulet burned for Lauren. She needed his prayers.

"Oliver," Erica said, concern replacing the humor in her voice. "What are you doing?"

Oliver ignored her. He focused on the image of Lauren. Holding the amulet, he saw her in the east passage. Ullwen had his hand on her forehead as if checking for a fever. Not good.

"It's Lauren," he whispered.

"What about her?" Aiden asked.

Oliver prayed for her, prayed God would heal her. He wondered how God worked here, why He would even put them here. Anger scorched his chest. Home may not have been perfect, but at least they didn't have to fight for their lives.

"What's wrong?" Aiden demanded again. His steel armor clanked as he plodded over to Oliver. He readied his bloodied sword.

"Lauren's been touched," Oliver said.

Aiden's voice came quickly and firmly. "I think it's time you tell us what happens."

He said, "It's poison. Wicked fast and fatal." He said the final word with surprising ease, which startled him, and made the anger well up again. Not at God, but himself. Hot guilt kicked him. If he hadn't programmed the nar'esh, or this cave, Lauren wouldn't be in this situation.

"You should hope, for your sake," Aiden said, "that it's not."

The stench of nar'esh blood, some combination of rotten grapefruit and vomit, distracted Oliver as he prayed. He choked back a gag and remembered something from the code—a residual combination he'd put in shortly after designing the nar'esh. "We have to find her. Fast. Aiden, bring your sword. Erica, I need you to keep an eye out for a green mushroom. It should be glowing. It'll be near a wall."

"I hope you're not planning to make Lauren eat a glowing mushroom," she said.

"Not for eating." He stood up and ran toward the east passage.

Chapter Nineteen

The Great Evil that brought humans from Alrujah into slavery will rise again. His power will rend the earth, bring fire from mountains and stones from the sky. Alrujah will cry out, as a mother in labor. And the Hand of Adonai will close like a fist around the Evil.

—The Book of Things to Come

O LIVER KNEW THE RUSH to Lauren's side wouldn't take long, but every second counted. He ran like he'd never run before—not like his life depended on it, but like Lauren's did. In the frantic race, Erica snatched the first mushroom they passed and a couple more for good measure. She slipped them in the sleeve of her dress and matched the hectic pace Oliver set.

Oliver found Ullwen, exactly as he'd seen him when he touched the amulet, holding Lauren's head in his lap, his hand on her forehead.

"The nar'esh," Ullwen said.

"We know." Oliver dropped to his knees and put his fingers on her neck, just under her jaw line. No pulse. His throat knotted up. "Mushrooms," he squeaked.

Erica gave him the four she'd grabbed.

"Get me a rock," he said to Aiden.

The clanging of Aiden's armor echoed down the corridor, but no more nar'esh would come. They would amass deeper within the caves, waiting for the travelers to venture further into the depths.

Aiden came back with a small black rock the exact color of the wall. "Will this work?"

Though small, the rock had a long, flat surface. "I'll make do. I need your sword."

Aiden presented the blade to Oliver, who mopped up the blood with the mushrooms and laid them on the cold black floor. He kneaded the flesh of the mushroom with the black blood and glowing liquid until it became a paste. "Where did it touch her?"

"I didn't see," Ullwen said. "Her fire went out."

Oliver handed the torch to Aiden. Welts rose up from Lauren's skin like ulcers. The red circles of raw flesh on her neck plunged under the neckline of her dress. He untied her cloak and carefully pulled the shoulder of her dress away from her neck. "Here," he said, indicating the scarring. Within the larger red circles, four round, black stains marred her clammy skin, like acid burns. He recognized them—something else that seemed cool when he coded it.

He smeared the paste over the raised sores on Lauren's shoulder and neck. She didn't move. "Come on," he whispered. Nothing happened.

"Will this work?" Aiden asked. "This better work."

"It should," he said. "Why isn't it working?" He needed help. He needed a miracle.

His amulet burned his chest again. *Of course*, he thought, and put it in his palm. He closed his eyes and put his hand on Lauren's sore shoulder. He prayed in a language that still sounded foreign to him. At times, he had no idea what he said. Other times, he knew exactly what the words meant.

Rich and full in his mouth, they marched up from his stomach, balled up like fists, and shot out. They came fast in places, punctuated with hard consonants and softened by long strings of vowels. His tongue rolled; it pressed his teeth and his lips; it clicked on the roof of his mouth.

The more he prayed, the more the words made sense. He distinguished a pattern, a long, repeated phrase. "A miracle, a healing, Your power, Your glory."

Lauren shrugged, her head snapped back on her long, thin neck. The red sores turned black. The welts of raw flesh began to close. "Lauren," Oliver said. "Can you hear me?"

Aiden handed the torch to Erica and knelt beside Lauren. He took off his steel gauntlet and stroked her cheek with the back of his fingers. "I'm here," he said. "I'm right here, Lauren."

* * *

Lauren felt as if she floated in a tub of used motor oil. She tried to stretch out her arms and legs, but they hit an invisible wall. A black thought hit her hard, punched her like a fist—*a coffin*. She was dead and in a coffin. No doubt.

Someone pulled the drain in the motor oil. It slid down over her skin, emptying from the space around her. The heaviness of her body returned, and immediately an invisible force pressed on her chest and her stomach. It pushed so hard, she wanted to throw up.

The oil evacuated her coffin, but she was afraid to open her eyes, afraid if she did, she'd see nothing. But with the oil out of her ears, she heard chanting, some gibberish.

I'm not dead, she thought. *I'm crazy.*

Another voice, distant and echoing, clear as static, but familiar. She wanted to latch onto it like a rope and hope it would pull her home. "Lauren. Can you hear me?"

A voice from the dark, "I'm here. I'm right here, Lauren."

She hardly recognized the word "Lauren" as her name. It sounded foreign, some strange adjective from a land far away or long ago.

The pressing weight on her chest and stomach pushed harder, and she wanted to scream. Her head snapped back, but she would not open her mouth. The oil might return at any time.

Harder, still harder it pushed. She would be crushed under something. She forced her eyes open, first, a little, a sliver of a slit between the lids. No oil. She opened a bit more. Darkness. Helpless against the urge to scream, she opened her mouth and screeched. The weight crushed her completely, and she fell. She arched her back, threw her head back until she thought she might tear the skin on her neck. She flailed her arms. The invisible walls dissipated, and she kicked her legs.

Something clamped her ankles and wrists, pressed her shoulders down hard. Hands. Fingers. On her ankles and wrists and shoulders.

The nar'esh? She remembered their long, sharp fingers, and she screeched like a bat. Her call echoed, came back to her again and again.

Another noise over the ring of terror—her name. "Lauren." She recognized it now.

She screamed. She kicked and flailed.

"Lauren!" A strong voice like deep water over a cliff. "Lauren, stop! You're going to be okay, but we need you to stop struggling."

She didn't trust the voice, didn't believe it. But no matter how hard she tried to ignore it, the voice compelled her to comply. She ceased her flailing and kicking and let the weight of her body settle her on the cold rock beneath.

A dull orange glow in the shape of a halo spread out like sunsdown over a river.

* * *

The Halls who lived in the mansion near the lake were not the ones missing their daughter. Neither were the Halls who lived in the suburban development behind the Supervalu. The Halls who rented the dilapidated three-bedroom home on Shimmer Ave. hadn't even heard of the missing girl. The Halls in the apartments east of North Chester High had only been married for a year and had no children at all. Bailey Renee liked them.

She slid back into the Jeep and closed the door quickly. She rubbed her arms and shivered. "It's starting to snow," she said, brushing a few stray flakes from her hood and jeans.

"Where to next?" Franky asked her.

The afternoon sky grew dark with tenebrous clouds. Bailey Renee turned on the dome light and checked the list. She unzipped her parka, folded up the list, and put it in her pocket. "That's it. No more Halls."

Franky didn't start the car. "No more Halls in North Chester?"

She shrugged. "None listed."

"So what's that mean?" He started the Jeep and let it idle for a minute before shifting into gear.

"It means Erica's family isn't listed, or they don't live in North Chester, or someone lied to us." Her tears threatened to return, but she was tired of crying, especially in front of Franky. A senior football star, he could have any too-pretty cheerleader he wanted. But he'd chosen her, a freshman, as his girlfriend. If she broke down and sobbed like a baby, it'd freak him out for sure. Why hang on to a freshman drama queen?

"Hey," Franky said, pulling her chin toward him. "You're going to cry."

"No I'm not," she said. Crying twice in one day might stab their new relationship.

"Yes you are. You need to, anyway. Mom says it's healthy. She cries all the time."

Bailey laughed a little.

"You can laugh, or you can cry. It's okay either way."

Though she wanted to choose laughter, crying won out. She reached out for him, hugged him hard.

He wrapped her up in his arms and held her tightly. "We'll find them," he said. She fisted the back of his jacket and let herself cry.

* * *

With Lauren on the mend, Oliver turned his attention to Erica's bleeding arm. She'd been standing too close to Lauren when Lauren started her convulsing and took one of the ice-spines in her shoulder. That's when Oliver pinned Lauren's shoulders to the rock. Aiden grabbed Lauren's wrists, and Ullwen restrained her ankles. Still, Lauren's knees pumped up and down.

The deep, jagged wound on Erica's shoulder made Oliver regret his decision to make the monk the only healer. Healing took time, took energy. And if anything ever happened to him, what would the others do?

"I'm fine," Erica said, holding her hand over the wound. Blood seeped from between her fingers.

Lauren opened her eyes. She opened her mouth to speak, but nothing came out.

Oliver released her shoulders and ran his hand over her forehead. Her skin had cooled to near normal temperatures. He felt for her pulse again. Faint, but there. He thanked God, and, in a flurry of emotions, kissed Lauren's forehead. He whispered, "Don't you ever do that again."

Lauren whispered, but it sounded like a squeak.

"Easy," Aiden said. His face twisted in concern. He took her hand. "Rest. I'm here."

Ullwen sneered at Aiden.

Oliver told Aiden to monitor her pulse. "She should be fine now, but we want to be sure." He walked to Erica and tried to swallow the knot of guilt that sat like an apple in his esophagus. "I can help," he said.

Erica shook her head. "It's not that bad. You need to watch Lauren."

"Lauren will be fine."

"It's that kind of thinking that just about killed her," she said. Her eyebrows shrank toward her nose. "Don't you get it? If you had told her to be careful not to be touched—"

"She would have panicked and never gone alone with Ullwen." Oliver didn't feel the conviction with which he spoke. He didn't believe what he said either, but he tried to. If he could believe it an accident, he could move on. If not, the guilt would crush him.

"Are you listening to yourself?" Erica asked. "You can be pretty dumb for a genius."

Oliver frowned, and guilt pushed up a geyser of nausea. "I didn't mean for this to happen. I only wanted to get us home."

Lauren coughed. "Oliver," she said.

He turned, at once grateful to hear her voice, and sickened at what she might say. "How are you feeling?" he asked.

"Like death," she whispered.

"You're not all that bad," he said with a smile. Less than a minute ago she had no pulse. A Lazarus-style miracle in any world.

"You're a liar," she whispered.

She had a right to be upset. "I didn't want this for us. You have to believe me."

"I'm the one who wanted it," she said, her hand firmly in Aiden's. "I was dead, wasn't I?"

Oliver didn't want to tell her the truth, but he nodded. His eyes tightened.

"I remember it," Lauren said. "I remember everything."

"What do you mean?" Aiden asked.

"Everything," she said. She spoke slowly and softly, taking big gulps of air. "If we die here, we are absolutely dead."

Chapter Twenty

He who is without a name shall proclaim the name of the One who saves. He shall be of them, but not with them. And they shall give him a new name, and he shall rule over them, and restore his people to the mercy of Adonai.

—The Book of Things to Come

AIDEN PRICE'S FAMILY LIVED on Riverwood Drive, about ten blocks north of North Chester High, in a house smaller than the first Hall home, but a good deal larger than the apartments. The lights outside the gray split-level house glowed warmly.

About fifteen minutes earlier, somewhere around four o'clock, the sun dropped behind the mountains. The snow clouds blocked what little light remained in the late afternoon. "Do you think anyone is home?" Bailey Renee asked.

"His mom stays home, so she should be here."

"But there are no lights inside."

"She may be upstairs. The light in the study is on in the back of the house."

Bailey nodded. She slipped her parka back on. "Will you come with me?" She shouldn't have to ask, but sometimes Franky needed a nudge.

"Sure. Yeah." Franky stepped out of the Jeep and Bailey followed him up to the front door, careful not to slip on the icy walkway. He knocked.

Bailey stood close to him and leaned her head on his shoulder. He put his arm around her and they shivered together. He hummed, and her heart warmed.

What a voice he had. Incredible warmth, a resonating vibrato. It was one of the things that had first made her notice him.

But when she started dating him two months ago, she hadn't figured it would last long. A senior and a freshman together just didn't happen. And what would her mom say when he turned eighteen in six months?

But it hadn't mattered to her then. She liked him, and he liked her.

Who cared about anything else? Now, though, here in his arms, his voice soothing her anxiety, she wanted it to last. "I like this." A solemn sorrow lined her voice.

"Me too."

The inside of the house lit up in yellow. The door swung open, and Mrs. Price stood at the threshold with mousy blonde hair askew. She'd not put on any makeup to disguise her red, swollen eyes. "Franky?"

"Hi, Mrs. Price. This is Bailey Renee. Lauren's sister."

Mrs. Price put a hand over her mouth. "Oh my."

"Can we talk for a bit?" Franky asked.

"Of course." She stepped out of the way and closed the door behind them.

The Prices had a nice home. The furniture all smelled fresh from the showroom, from the modern black leather couches (a terrible idea for Minnesota—too cold in the winter, too hot in the summer), to the big screen LED television. By the look of it, dust had never touched the place. The smell of pine said Mrs. Price spent a good amount of time keeping things tidy.

Two medieval swords hung above the fireplace. Paintings of fantasy scenes hung on the walls in rich, golden frames.

"You like fantasy?" Bailey asked.

"My husband," Mrs. Price said. "I've never really been into it, but he's a sucker for anything with dragons or swords." She moved to the kitchen and motioned them toward the living room. "Let me fix you something to drink. What would you like?"

"Nothing, thanks," Bailey said.

"I'll take a Coke, please."

"Absolutely." She sounded grateful for a distraction, for anything to take her mind off the tragedy of a missing son. "What are you guys doing for dinner? Do you want to stay here? Steven should be home in another thirty minutes or so. I have a roast in the crock pot, and there's plenty to go around."

She tried to sound nonchalant, but her offer came out more as a plea.

"I'm not sure what my mom has planned," Bailey said, though the offer sounded good. For now, she'd give her mom a little more time to cool down and then call her.

"So, what brings you two by?" Bailey understood the subtle, unspoken qualifier—*since Aiden isn't here.* She poured Coke from a two-liter bottle into a Miami University glass.

"We wanted to talk a bit, if that's okay," Franky said. "About Aiden."

Mrs. Price paused as she put the Coke back in the stainless steel fridge. "What do you want to talk about?"

Bailey Renee cleared her throat. She held Franky's hand and said, "Did he know any of the other three?"

She took the glass to Franky and sat on the arm of the couch. "I don't know. I think he knew your sister. He said something about her helping him with an essay a couple days ago. That was the last night I saw him." Her voice took on a slight accusatory tone.

"I remember. Franky had to give me a ride home after practice. Normally Lauren does. Did they know each other before then?"

"Not that I'm aware of."

"What about Erica or Oliver?" Franky spoke softly. The gentleness of his voice amazed Bailey.

"I don't know anything about them," she said. "I've already told the police all this. I'm sure they're doing a fine job of locating the kids."

"I know. I'm trying to put the pieces together in my mind, too. I want to be able to help them as much as possible. I get this feeling," Bailey said, "they're all related somehow. Like they're all together, and okay."

Mrs. Price stood up. She walked back to the kitchen to check on the roast. "A nice thought."

"You don't feel that way?" Franky asked.

She opened the lid of the crock pot, smelled the steam, poked at the roast, and replaced the glass lid. "What am I supposed to think, Franky? We haven't been out here more than six months and already my son is missing." She pointed out the sliding glass door to the small lake at the center of the residential area of North Chester. "For all I know he's in the bottom of the lake!"

Franky stood up. "I'm sorry, Mrs. Price. I don't mean to upset you. We can go if you'd like."

Mrs. Price shook her head. "No. Please stay." Her voice quavered, and she suddenly buried her face in her hands. She pounded a fist on the counter and cried in loud, quaking sobs. She turned her back to them, slid down to the floor, and cried and shook and cried and shook.

Franky walked to her. He sat beside her and put an arm around her. He sang to her, something soft, without words. And his voice, soft and light, a summer's breeze, elevated itself above her crying. She held on to him, and Bailey couldn't blame her. His voice had that effect on people, made them want to reach out to him, to hold on to him, to cling to the strength in that voice.

Bailey didn't recognize the song, but she didn't have to. The melody sounded like a father singing to a daughter. A church song, maybe? Bailey's lungs convulsed in spasms. She tried so hard not to cry, but watching Franky on the floor singing to Mrs. Price was too much.

After a few minutes, Mrs. Price finally started laughing. "Look at me," she said. She smiled and wiped the tears from her cheeks. "I'm such a mess. I'm sorry."

He helped her to her feet. "No apology needed."

Bailey stared at Franky's Coke. Condensation ran down the sides of the glass to the wooden coaster it rested on.

"You okay, Bailey?" Mrs. Price asked. She dabbed at her eyes with a Kleenex.

"I'm fine," she said and cleared her throat. "If you don't want to talk, I understand."

"I'm just so scared." She sat on the couch opposite Bailey.

Bailey Renee nodded. Franky sat next to her.

"I was so proud when Aiden made the football team, and to see how talented he was. And he made friends quickly here. I knew he would. But Aiden is …" She searched for the right word. "I tried to keep him out of trouble in Miami, you know? Tried to make sure he'd find good friends to help him make good choices. But he didn't. I thought the move back here would help. I grew up here and loved it. I thought he would, too. But he hated me for taking him away from Miami. And just when he started settling down, getting his grades back up a little, staying out of trouble in school, he vanishes."

Bailey Renee picked at her cuticle to keep from looking at Mrs. Price.

"North Chester's about as small as you can get in America. If we're not safe here, where can we be safe?"

Franky nodded. "I'm sure he's fine. I'm sure they just got lost or something."

What a stupid thing to say. Of course Aiden wasn't lost. If he'd gone somewhere with the others, one of them would have taken their phone. But none of them did. None of them took their cars, their keys, their phones, their iPods, or even a set of extra clothes. They hadn't brought jackets, so they weren't going for a walk. Even if they had, the Minnesota winter would have been enough to jeopardize their lives if they didn't have someplace warm to stay.

Her voice quavering, Mrs. Price whined, "I never should have moved us up here. This is all my fault."

If Bailey didn't say something fast, Mrs. Price would break down into tears again. And if she did, Bailey wouldn't be able to keep from joining her. She cleared her throat and asked, "Did Aiden belong to any groups? Like church groups or after-school clubs or anything?"

"Just football. We went to church in Miami. Had a nice church family and all, but haven't found one up here that's right for us." She sighed.

Bailey had hoped being in the house would help her think of questions she might ask. Maybe she'd notice something that would magically point a finger to where the four had gone. But she didn't see anything—nothing the police didn't already photograph as evidence last night.

But there was something about the pictures and the chess set. She'd just noticed it now, sitting on the kitchen counter, halfway through a game. The pieces looked like they'd been hand-carved from different types of wood. One side was an army of elves, the other humans.

Bailey tilted her head back and stared up at the ceiling. Something, some clue, some indicator to crack the case, hovered vaporously just out of reach. It was like having an itch in the middle of her back, a constant reminder she couldn't find relief.

She needed to go home. She stood up. "I'm going to make a call real quick," she said. She walked back to the den and dialed her home phone number. Her mom picked up on the second ring.

"Mom? This is Bailey. I'm really sorry. I know what you said, but do you think you'd let me come home now? I can bring us some dinner."

She didn't answer immediately. After a long pause, she said, "If you ever try a stunt like that again, Bailey Renee …"

"I won't, Mom. Trust me."

Chapter Twenty-One

And the agent of Adonai's creation brought forth the rivers and the seas, separated the land from the water, placed birds in the air, and moles in the dirt, fish in the sea, and trees in the fields. The strength of Adonai's agent established the very suns and the stars and the moon.

—The Book of the Ancients

WHEN LAUREN'S STRENGTH RETURNED enough for her to sit and stand on her own, Ullwen dragged Oliver toward the center chamber. The way Ullwen sneered at Oliver made her wonder if Oliver would come out of the conversation with all of his limbs and fingers intact.

Aiden said, "They'll be fine. They want to talk about where to go from here."

"How about home?" she said.

Aiden laughed, and for once, sounded like he had in North Chester. "Sounds good, doesn't it?"

Lauren shrugged. "If you asked me a couple hours ago, I'd have said no. But now ..."

Aiden sat next to her. "When I was a kid, my dad used to play a game with me. If I got irritated or upset, he'd ask me what my favorite part of the day was. Kind of helped me focus on the good things, instead of the bad. Sounds corny, but it helps."

"Not corny at all," Lauren said.

"It is a little," Erica said.

Aiden grinned. "So, what is your favorite part of this little journey of ours? Or, if you prefer, what's the thing you miss most about home? The good stuff."

Lauren pulled her knees up to her chest. She rested her chin on her knees, closed her eyes, and thought hard to remember something good about her home, her family in North Chester. Nothing came to mind immediately.

"I never really liked North Chester," Aiden said, his voice a little sad.

"I didn't want to leave Miami. I hated Minnesota when I got there."

"Is that why you got in that fight?" Erica asked.

Lauren had almost forgotten about the fight, about Aiden getting suspended early in the year. He had that bad-kid vibe early on, which only made him hotter.

Aiden shrugged. "More to it than that, but yeah. Anyway, now that I think back on it, I guess there are good things about North Chester." He looked to Lauren and smiled. "I miss college football with my dad on Saturday mornings," Aiden said. He sat next to Lauren, clinking and clanking with each movement. "We have this whole routine. We get up a bit early, make ourselves a big breakfast—the greasier, the better—pop some corn and put our feet up. We watch all morning and afternoon. All my chores and housework get put off until Sunday. Even if my mom grounds me for grades or whatever, he still lets me watch." His voice softened, and he rested his hand on the hilt of his sword, stared off at the wall. "He's a good dad."

"Sounds nice," Lauren said, and remembered her weekends filled with chores and homework. If she was really lucky, she got to drive Bailey Renee and her friends down to the mall.

"And chess," Aiden said. "My dad carved this chess set. Fantasy themes. Elves vs. humans. He's always the humans. Makes me be the elves, but that's cool. We'll play a game over a few days. One move at a time. I like it."

"Coffee." Erica leaned against the wall and held her hurt shoulder. She spoke softly. "I don't really have a dad, but my mom used to be cool. Used to leave me her leftover coffee in the fridge for when I got home from school."

Lauren wrinkled her nose. The thought of coffee made her stomach sick. Always had. Still, it never stopped her mom from compulsively brewing pot after pot. She even had to clean it every day after school. She sighed.

"Used to?" Aiden asked.

Erica was quiet for a minute. "She's worried about other things now."

Lauren considered asking what that meant, but Erica's tone warned her it was a bad idea, so she let it drop.

"So," Aiden prodded.

Lauren shrugged. "My sister, Bailey Renee, is kinda cool, I guess. She's way too popular for me, and I have to drive her around everywhere, but we have some good talks in the car before her friends get in. I sit at the mall and read for a few hours while they walk around. Those are the good Saturdays."

Aiden smiled. "See? Not that hard."

"What about your dress?" Erica said. "It's gorgeous. You get to prance around like a magical princess. That's gotta be pretty awesome."

Lauren smiled. "It doesn't suck."

She thought of the way Aiden looked at her when she froze the handle on Erica's room, and the way he sounded jealous when Ullwen showed up. Those times might be her favorites. But she dared not say so. Not here, not now.

Ullwen and Oliver stomped back. The padded skins of their shoes muted their footsteps, made them little more than soft slaps on the rock floor. Ullwen said, "We have an understanding."

Oliver nodded. "I'll be completely honest about all dangers that may or may not face us in the challenging days to come."

Lauren grinned. A well-scripted answer. She imagined Ullwen telling Oliver off at arrow point. If he did, it served Oliver right.

"No offense, bro, but how about I go with Lauren this time?" Aiden said.

"We will all proceed together. When we reach the switches, we'll devise a way to keep it levered open. From there, we'll move on to the east passage, which should be a little easier of a trek, and secure the second switch. We camp back here in the central chamber, where it's safe. Tomorrow morning, we'll journey to Margwar for the book."

Oliver asked Lauren, "Do you want to come, or do you want to wait here?"

Lauren didn't want to go, but she definitely didn't want to be left alone. "I'm fine," she said, conjuring a small flame in the palm of her hand as evidence. She smiled to further sell her consent, though she feared they'd easily see through the half-hearted grin.

Oliver plunged his hands into the sleeves of his robe. "The nar'esh hate fire. Their eyes are adjusted to the darkness of the caves, so any light hurts them and puts them at a huge disadvantage. Between your fire and the torch, we should be able to hold our own and give them a run for their money."

"The nar'esh have no money," Ullwen said.

"Is everyone in Alrujah as thick as him?" Erica asked with a sideways smile.

"You mean my broad chest, no doubt," Ullwen said.

"Oh, no doubt for sure."

"I don't think he's picking up on your sarcasm," Aiden said.

Oliver said, "Let's go. The sooner this is over, the better."

Lauren agreed. She cupped both her hands together, squinted her eyes tight, then opened her hands with a flame in each. The more she used her magic, the easier it became to control. Nice, yes, but she had a long way to go before she became an expert. She fought to bury her insecurity and move forward with the same boldness and confidence as Aiden, as Ullwen.

Oliver, torch firm in his left hand, staff firm in the right, led the group. Ullwen and Aiden each took a side of Lauren to protect her from any surprise attacks. Erica brought up the end of the group, a torch firm in her hand, her tongue clacking and clicking in her mouth.

Lauren tried to ignore the annoying sounds, but they echoed off the walls. "Think you could maybe not make that noise?"

Erica shrugged. "Whatever you say, princess."

They passed the bodies of the nar'esh Ullwen had slain, stepped over them like they were sleeping cats. Staring at them for the first time, Lauren gaped at their abnormally large black eyes, which took up most of their faces. The rest was a tiny mouth stretched thin. They had no noses, and their bat-like ears, thin as skin, sloped up to points. The small light of the torch shone through the thin membranes and illuminated the blood vessels. Her stomach soured, and she quickened her step.

The nar'esh shrieked from the darkness beyond Oliver's torchlight. He slowed.

"More?" Erica whispered.

"Sounds like it," Oliver said. "Hard to tell exactly where they are. The echoes bounce off the walls. Makes ten nar'esh sound like one hundred."

Erica said, "When we get home, remind me to slap you."

"I'll slap myself." He stopped. "There."

Lauren swallowed hard. She struggled to keep the flames steady in her hand. She concentrated on the light it brought. With inhuman strength, she fought to harness her fear and turn it into something stronger, something like magic.

"They're behind us, too," Aiden said, his bloody sword held straight up-and-down.

Lauren took a few breaths and tried to make herself hot inside, but, try as she might, her fear ran cold, from her heart to her lungs to her limbs. The fire flickered.

"Keep steady," Oliver said. "We need light. We need your fire. We need you."

"I can't," she said.

Erica spun around and stared hard at Lauren through the waning light of Lauren's fire. "You are such a whiner. No one wanted me to say anything, but we're all getting a little sick of your complaining." Unlike Oliver, Erica had given up on whispering.

Shock usurped the fear in Lauren's face, and her eyes widened. "Excuse me?"

Erica pointed her finger in Lauren's chest. "You heard me, *princess*. You're a dainty little flower, aren't you? And you like it. You play the damsel in distress so perfectly."

"Lakia," Ullwen whispered harshly. "Hold your tongue."

"I'll not hold my tongue until little miss princess hears what we have to say."

Lauren shot long past shock and well into rage. The fire burned hot in her hands. She wanted to incinerate Erica, to use her as a human torch. How dare Erica accuse her of being a whiner? She just died! Lauren seethed. "You wretched little …"

"We've got bigger problems," Oliver said.

Something moved above her. *Nar'esh*. Without thinking, she threw her hands over her head, and the fire she had cupped in her palms exploded into a pillar of flame that spread out over the ceiling, licking at crevices in the rock like rain slipping through a storm drain. Three nar'esh fell in flames and crashed around the group.

Four nar'esh in front of Oliver shielded their grotesquely large eyes. Oliver waved the torch at them, and Erica shrieked for the bats to join the fray from the outlying chambers.

A black cloud poured over them. The still air became a torrent of beating wings. The nar'esh shrieked and pawed at the bats.

Sparky leapt from his spot by Erica's side and took a nar'esh by the throat. It staggered back and grabbed at the wolf. Sparky released the beast and stumbled along the floor, then lay down, his chest heaving in quick, ragged gasps. The nar'esh collapsed.

Ullwen put three arrows in the back of the nar'esh for good measure. Aiden busied himself separating the nar'esh from their limbs and heads.

Lauren's stomach ached from the sour stench of nar'esh blood and nar'esh flambé. She harnessed the fire within her, glowing hot behind her eyes. Her veins burned like crevices of a volcano, directing flows of magma toward the sea.

She must have leveled up. *Beautiful, Oliver.*

Targeting the remaining three nar'esh, the ones nearest Sparky, she loosed another column of heat and flame. They recoiled, collapsed, and burned quickly. The fire extinguished itself, and Oliver rushed to Sparky. He smeared the mushroom-blood paste on the sores that ate at the wolf's skin, held his amulet, and repeated the ancient prayer that restored Lauren.

"Will he be alright?" Erica asked, dropping to her knees next to the oversized canine. She put her hand on Sparky's face.

Whiner, Lauren thought, but she had enough decency not to say it out loud.

"He'll be fine," Ullwen said. "Vicmorn worked a much greater miracle with Indigo. This should present little challenge."

When Ullwen had finished his statement, Sparky's breath slowed, and his eyes opened.

Erica wrapped her arms around Sparky and smiled. "Too close," she said, as the last of the bats emptied from the cave.

Oliver nodded further down the passage. "Shouldn't be much longer." To Lauren, "Fancy magic work. Remind me never to make you angry at me."

Lauren blushed. "You mean again?"

"Yes, again. If you go first, you might be able to clear out our passages, and keep the nar'esh at bay. With fire like that, we may not even have to fight them again."

"It's worth a shot," she said, but she doubted she had the strength. Using so much magic left her tired, and her whole body ached. She must have overdone it after the first initial surge of power. But she wouldn't whine, not after Erica's tirade. Lauren glared at Erica and hated her a little bit more—for being so snobbish, for taking Oliver's attention away, for being the funny one.

But then, Erica said something Lauren never would have imagined. "You alright?"

"Fine," Lauren said, confused at her concern, but still irritated. "Wouldn't want to whine or anything."

Erica held her wounded arm. Sparky walked around her ankles. "You know I didn't mean that." Lauren wondered why Erica didn't sound defensive. "I said it to get you all fired up. Pun intended."

Aiden groaned. "Terrible."

"These are the jokes, people."

Lauren didn't care why Erica had done it. Only that she had. "Easy to say now."

Oliver stopped as the passage came to an abrupt end. "This is it," he said. "There's a switch right around here somewhere."

Lauren sighed. She focused on the fire still cupped in her palms and made it grow to basketball size. She didn't feel right. Maintaining the fire through the passageway and battling the nar'esh had drained what little energy she had.

"Got it," Oliver said. "Erica, let me have a dagger."

Erica handed him the small straight blade, keeping the curved in its sheath.

He pushed on a slightly protruding rock. It clicked, and he tried unsuccessfully to wedge the dagger in to hold the switch down. "The dagger's too big," he conceded.

Lauren's energy drained fast. A chill slithered over her, like a cloud coming over the suns and blotting out the warmth on her skin. But the torches only gave marginal light. They needed her ball of fire to see the crevice in the switch. The torches had burned through most of their fuel and had darkened over the last few hours.

"Try an arrow," Ullwen said. "The tip should be smaller than a blade."

Oliver took it and tried again, unsuccessfully, to wedge it in.

Aiden moved forward. "Let me give it a shot." He took the dagger, raised it to his ear, and sunk it a quarter inch deep into the tiny space between the wall and the switch.

"Okay, that was impressive," Erica said.

The last of Lauren's power slipped from her fingers. Her flame went out, and she sat down. She didn't want to cry, but the tears paid no attention and came anyway. It took what little strength she had left not to start sobbing. She would have to be content to sit quietly and cry in the dark.

Oliver spun around with the dwindling torch. "Lauren. What's wrong?"

Lauren lacked the strength and the ability to say exactly what bothered her. She was so very tired. "Need a little break." She tried to say this assertively, in hopes she'd dissuade anyone from overreacting, but her words came out in a hushed whisper, like a sensitive secret around overactive ears.

"Her magic resource must be exhausted," Oliver said. He waved the torch in front of her face. "You look pale."

Mercifully, he didn't mention her tears. "I'll be fine in a minute," she said breathlessly.

"I have something that may help," Ullwen said. He pulled a small wineskin from his tunic.

As Oliver moved the torch toward Ullwen, Lauren took the momentary darkness as an opportunity to wipe the tears from her eyes with the sleeve of her dress.

"Drink this," Ullwen said. He bent close to Lauren and put his hand on her cheek. "This will help."

Even if he did smell like dead nar'esh, his touch was soft and warming. She uncorked the wineskin and drank its contents. The cough-syrup thick liquid tasted like orange juice.

"Sap from the harspus tree," Ullwen said.

Oliver nodded. "Of course. It replenishes your magic reserves."

Lauren had forgotten the limits of her magic supply. She would have remembered if she had used more magic before battling the nar'esh, but she'd had little need to use much magic beyond the encounters with the beresus and the fangands.

The warm harspus sap coated her throat. The sweetness reminded her of when she was eight and had strep throat. She had to take penicillin for a few days. Each night, before bed, her mother would give her the syrupy medicine and kiss her forehead. Then, her mother would sing her to sleep. She heard her mother's voice again—wretchedly off-key, but Lauren had never cared. Two years later, her mom went back to work and forgot about her.

"Better?" Oliver asked. "You look better."

"Maybe she should sit out the next passage," Erica said.

"I'm fine." Lauren stood up, steadied herself, and held out her hand. "Want to see a magic trick?" She blew Ullwen a kiss, and fire sprang from her palm.

Ullwen's face split in a wide grin.

"Someone's feeling better," Erica said, "and I don't mean Lauren. Let's go before they start kissing for real."

Chapter Twenty-Two

The nar'esh eradicated the dwarves. They swarmed over them like wasps over a carcass. But Gilbur cried out to Adonai to save his people. And Adonai heard his cry and allowed a remnant to persevere the plague. These that survived left Alrujah and fled to the Otherlands.

—The Book of the Ancients

THE WEST PASSAGE WENT much faster than the east. Likely because he, Erica, and Aiden had already made it most of the way down when they realized Lauren was hurt. Also, he moved with increased strength and speed, which must be tied to an incremental improvement, like a level-up. Judging by the way Aiden's movements became more intricate and involved, the way he strung his combos together, Aiden benefited from the same evolvement. Erica and Lauren, too.

The intensity of Lauren's flames burned Oliver's face as they shot by. The cold cave heated fast when she started launching fireballs and crafting flame-whips. Instead of iceboxes, the narrow passageways became microwaves.

And Erica. She moved with the fluidity of a ballerina. Except most ballerinas didn't dance with a dagger and didn't splatter nar'esh blood on cave walls. Still, her wounded shoulder made her graceful movements choppy. She held her left arm close to her as she spun and ducked, kicked and stabbed. Aided by the dense cloud of bats for distraction, she moved like a deadly shadow.

But even with their enhanced skills, they struggled against the constant waves of nar'esh. With every spidery beast that fell, two took its place. The creatures gave them no time to think, and they became more aggressive the longer the battle in the west passage progressed. They moved closer to the torches. They did not scurry away from Lauren's flames or Aiden's sword. They met them straight on.

"We're close now. We're almost done," Oliver said.

"Do these things ever stop coming?" Aiden asked. A nar'esh dropped on his back. He backed into a wall and crushed it between his armor and the slick black rock. He swung his right arm and sliced one in half. Another leapt at him. He had time enough to extend his barbed elbow. The dagger-like extension sank into the beast's stomach. Aiden pulled free and kicked its head into the wall next to the other smashed nar'esh.

Two nar'esh surrounded Oliver. He jabbed one end of his prayer staff into the chest of the one in front of him and the other in the chest of the one behind him. As both took a step back, he twirled the staff around and cracked the first on the head, then brought it low and took the back creature's legs out from beneath it. He finished it off with a quick smash of the end of his staff in the face of each nar'esh.

He didn't like killing, but he didn't have much choice.

Ullwen had no problem killing the nar'esh. He fired arrows so fast it was like he was using an automatic bow. A split second after an arrow twanged off his string, he'd strung another. "I'm running low on arrows," he said.

Erica grunted, swiped at the extended arm of a nar'esh. "I'm guessing the sterling sword on your hip isn't for show."

"Aye, but I prefer my bow."

"You're not exactly in a position to pick and choose," Lauren said. She twirled a thin stream of fire around her head like a whirlpool. Several nar'esh moved back. They leaned in and out, timing their movements, waiting for her to falter to make their attack.

"Bro, these guys are getting way old," Aiden said.

The nar'esh shrieked and squealed, clicked and clacked. "Chatty, aren't they?" Erica said.

Ullwen shouted, "Stay strong! Their numbers are thinning!" He switched from bow to sword as quickly as changing a channel. The long blade sliced through the air with startling speed. Ullwen used the blade not to dismember, but for quick, precise strikes, as if he'd written the manual on tactical defense against cave-dwelling monsters. Fast stabs to bellies, to chests and eyes, and remarkably, even to armpits. Each creature staggered back before collapsing, their chests heaving slightly and arrhythmically.

Oliver had to be careful not to tangle his robe in the corpses falling around them. He spun, searching for his next target. Only one nar'esh stood. The rest lay collapsed in heaps around the corridor. Apparently mesmerized by Lauren's spinning flame whip, the final nar'esh took a few moments before it realized its pack had been cut down. Its tarantulan eyes surveyed the carnage in the slim passageway, and it turned to run.

Erica didn't hesitate. She squeaked a few times and sent the bats after the monster. While its progress slowed, she flipped her remaining dagger, caught the blade, and hurled it at the beast. The resulting thunk echoed down the corridor.

"Wow," Lauren said.

"Fine blade work," Ullwen said. "I may have misjudged you, m'lady. You may speak as an Otherlander, but you fight as an Alrujahn."

"You're not so bad yourself," she said.

Oliver wanted to sit down, but the corpses of nar'esh covered near every inch of the floor. "Let's keep going. We're close to the switch." His voice sounded strained, as if he'd just come back from an amusement park. "Anyone touched?"

Amazingly, no one was. Weary and bloodied, he stepped over the sinewy remains and various disembodied appendages until they cleared. The flickering light of the torch fell on something semi-rectangular and wooden.

The treasure chest. "You kidding me?" He remembered putting it in the code but had forgotten about it until now.

"What's that?" Erica asked.

"A box of goodies," he said.

Lauren's eyes brightened. "Please tell me there's some water in there. I'm so thirsty."

"Better. Some pretty sweet equipment. Some scrolls, too."

Lauren suddenly smiled. "Yeah?"

"Good ones, too, if it's still the way I designed it."

Ullwen stepped over the last of the nar'esh. "Let us gather our treasure, engage the switch, and get back to the central chamber. I could use a rest."

"You said it, bro."

Oliver walked to the worn chest and hit the clasp with his staff. His arms shook up through his elbows and to his shoulders, but the lock snapped. He knelt down and opened the lid.

The inside smelled of dust and cedar shavings. The hard wood had been painstakingly fashioned from the rognak tree—a breed native to the highlands of the Dragon's Back Mountains that eventually fell prey to disease when the dwarves moved underground and failed to cultivate them. The hearty trees weathered several decades of the tree disease that nearly destroyed the Cerulean Woods. Only the meticulous care of the Monks of the Cerulean Order had saved the harspus trees.

The chest should have a dwarven prayer staff carved from rognak wood—fabled for its lightness and resiliency. Nearly hard as steel, no wood proved more durable. The dwarves made a living out of crafting furniture, wagons, yokes, and other goods from it. Their craftsmanship lasted for centuries. The creations of the dwarves, ironically, outlasted the creators themselves. He hoped the same would not be true for all of Alrujah.

"Any goodies for me?" Erica asked.

"Yes," Oliver said, distracted by the absence of his staff. Far too big to fit in the trunk, it had to be nearby. He held the torch up a bit and checked the corner of the passageway. Sure enough, it stood upright resting against the wall.

How many years had it stood untouched by the nar'esh? It didn't make much sense, but he didn't question it. Right now, he just thanked God he found it. He snatched it up, thought about dropping his other staff, but decided against it. It might be better to have a backup. Part of him wondered if he could use both at the same time, but their length, six feet each, made it an impractical thought.

"So?" Erica prompted.

Oliver reached into the trunk. Several scrolls of rolled parchment rested on top. He handed those to Lauren. "Let me know if you get anything good." He pulled two gold bracelets from the trunk and handed them to Erica. "Ma'att'tal bands—forged by the dwarves and enchanted by the elves. The thinner bracelet should increase how many animals respond to your calls. The thicker should increase the range in which you can call them."

"Sweet." She slipped them both on her left arm and ran her fingers over them. "They're cold."

"And beautiful," he said. He wanted to add, "like you," but decided against it. Too much, too soon.

"Do I get anything from the magic box, bro?" Aiden asked.

Again, Oliver reached in and extracted two gold items, but this time, instead of bracelets, he pulled out a sword and a shield. "Same deal as Erica's bracelets. Forged by dwarves, enchanted by elves."

Aiden took them. He sneered at the sword. "What is this, a toy? It's like half the size of my silver sword."

"Stick it in a nar'esh," Oliver said.

"Wow. Rude," Erica said.

"No, seriously. Stick it in a nar'esh."

Aiden shrugged, walked the few feet back to the pile of carnage, and sank the blade into the flesh of a dead creature. Instantly, it caught fire. He pulled the blade away quickly, but the blood on the sword continued to burn. "Sick."

Lauren asked, "Sick as in gross, or as in cool?"

"Both."

Ullwen said, "Dwarves are short. They need shorter blades. If you are displeased, I would be honored to carry such a weapon."

Aiden thought about it for a minute. "I'll keep it."

"Then may I carry your Alrujahn blade?"

"It's a bit messy." He tossed it to Ullwen, who caught the handle deftly. He took Aiden's scabbard, slipped the blade in it, and fastened it around his waist.

Aiden surveyed the small round gold shield. "This thing is so tiny, it'd be like fighting with a dinner plate strapped to my arm."

Oliver stood up. He weighed his staffs, each in one hand. "What it lacks in size it makes up for in enchantments. It's resistant to elemental attacks, which is nice if we ever face a fire-breathing dragon."

Laruen rolled her eyes. "You didn't put that thing in the game."

Oliver shrugged. "Didn't you want me to?"

"When we were in North Chester. Now, I don't think I'd be too eager to see it."

"If we keep a low profile, we should be able to avoid it," he said.

Erica spun the bracelets around her thin forearm. "A dragon? For real? Please tell me I'll be able to call it to fight with us."

Oliver smiled. "That would be something else, wouldn't it?" He turned and took the last item out of the trunk—a black diamond-studded collar for Sparky. He handed it to Erica.

"Nice. My baby's got bling." She took Sparky's old black leather collar off and wrapped it around the same wrist she wore the Ma'att'tal bracelets. Classic Erica fashion. "Let me guess, forged by the dwarves and enchanted by the elves?"

"Enchanted by elves, yes. But the dwarves didn't make this."

Aiden asked, "Who did?"

"Me," Oliver said and shot Erica a wide grin.

"Is that everything?" Ullwen asked.

Oliver nodded. "Sorry, man, but I didn't program anything for you in here. You weren't supposed to be with us at this point."

He said, "I'm well with what I have. But we should return to the central chamber. We will need rest before going to Margwar. And I need some time to collect what arrows I can. I'll need to repair them for tomorrow."

Arrows. Oliver should have put some in the chest. He made a mental note. Even though none of the primary characters began the game with a bow, Erica's and Lauren's characters had skill with them. He'd make the revision once he got home, but it wouldn't do them much good now.

Erica snatched a torch from Ullwen. "Rest sounds good to me. I could go for a nap." On her way back down the corridor, she snatched the dagger from the dead nar'esh, wiped it on the thigh of her dress, sheathed it, and disappeared into the dark.

* * *

Though she'd pulled the covers up under her chin nearly an hour ago, Bailey Renee was no closer to sleep than she had been when she finished brushing her teeth and getting into her pajamas. Her mind would not shut up.

It had little to do with Franky's economics project, which Bailey finished just after nine. Granted, she could have finished much sooner if he hadn't insisted on helping. He stopped her every ten minutes to strum a few chords on his guitar and sing some stupid song about compound interest. But she figured he might as well learn something from his project, and if she had to pause long enough for him to put it to song for him to remember, she did so. Besides, it let her hear him sing, and that helped her forget, even for a minute at a time, the itching pain at the back of her brain.

Now, without his voice, staring up at the ceiling, the silver moonlight gliding over her skin, she jumped from one thought to the next—the economic downturn of 2008, four missing teenagers from North Chester, Sarah the Skeleton, going back to school the poor, wretched sister of a lost girl.

What would the other students think? Would they assume Lauren died and pity Bailey? Would they think Lauren ran away and pity Bailey for being related to a troubled teen? In the long run, she told herself, it didn't matter. She didn't want pity. She wanted Lauren back.

She rolled over in bed, turned the pillow to the cool side, and closed her eyes again.

Images marched in her mind: Franky gluing charts to a poster board, Lauren writing in her journal, Sarah the Skeleton's face laughing derisively, Oliver typing about a million words a minute in some stupendously complex code, her mom scrubbing grout with a blue toothbrush, Mrs. Price sobbing on the floor, Franky holding Mrs. Price like a son holds a mother, his voice soothing her with some church song she couldn't place, every face of every Hall she'd met that day, drawn up into frowns or contorted into clown-like caricatures.

She wanted to smack the sympathy right out of them.

Opening her eyes to escape the visions, she checked the clock. Midnight. She needed to be up in four and a half hours. She sighed, kicked the covers off, and went to the kitchen. She warmed up some water in the microwave and made another mug of honey chamomile tea. It helped to relax her on most nights, but her first mug, which she'd had about two hours ago, proved to be a complete waste of a tea bag. Hopefully this mug would be different.

She sat on the couch and pulled a blanket over her legs while she sipped the tea. Being in the living room made it a little easier for her, but, when she closed her eyes, her brain still exploded in images and memories.

She put the mug in the sink and resolved to try one last thing.

Standing outside Lauren's closed door, Bailey told herself she could do it. She could get to sleep in Lauren's bed. She could relax there. She had to. But opening the door felt a little like digging up a grave.

She turned the knob. No moonlight came in her window, but the light from the hallway showed scattered homework on the floor. She stepped over it, climbed into Lauren's bed, and closed her eyes again.

No images of Franky flashed in her mind. None of Mrs. Price or the Halls or of economics projects. Instead, she saw sweeping landscapes—vast expanses of plains and dense forests with blue-leaved trees. Horses galloping across the world on worn dusty trails. They carried knights and elves. Medieval weapons—bows and arrows, long swords and short swords, daggers and wooden staffs—dotted the tiny hands of the strange people.

She took a deep breath and smelled Lauren's shampoo, Mountain Breeze. She wrapped the covers around herself tightly, a Bailey Burrito, Lauren would say whenever she'd done it as a child.

Her hand slipped under Lauren's pillow and she felt something hard. She pulled it out and stared at Lauren's worn leather journal. On the cover, imprinted in gold letters, were the words *The Book of Things to Come.*

She didn't remember this journal. She opened to the first page and read about four weary world jumpers and their adventures journeying to a monastery in the middle of the Cerulean Woods.

She'd never bothered to read anything Lauren had written. She'd always dismissed it as childish fantasy, but Lauren's writing demonstrated control and subtlety. And Bailey couldn't shake the feeling that this journal may hold some clues.

She lay back down with a sigh. Of course she wouldn't find a clue. Unless Lauren broke story and wrote about running away, how could a work of fiction reveal any truth about the real world?

Bailey Renee closed her eyes and fell asleep within minutes.

In her dreams, she soared like a bird over a colorful fantasy landscape.

Like a bird.

Or like an angel.

Chapter Twenty-Three

In those days, Alrujah will forget the ways of the Ancients. They will cry out for relief, and they will find none until the final battle is done. "But my people should not be discouraged. They should not lose heart. Let them be encouraged and know their perseverance will be rewarded after the last days," declares Adonai.

—The Book of Things to Come

ULLWEN WOKE LAUREN AND the others early, and she liked him a little less for it. She wanted to go on sleeping. She wanted to be back in her bed. She wanted, amazingly enough, to see her mother and her sister again, to hug them both, and to spend a day at the mall with them. But she would have settled for twenty more minutes of sleep, even on a bone-cold stone floor.

It took her a few moments to shake the fog of sleep. When she did, Erica stood next to her, bending over, her legs as straight and thin as Oliver's two pipe-thick prayer staffs. Her palms halted halfway to the floor.

When Lauren bent over, her legs tightened. Her back hitched and she had to right herself and stretch up. Her back popped from tail bone to shoulder blades.

The pops echoed, and Oliver arched an eyebrow. "Sounds like you slept as comfortably as I did." He reached his hands high over his head.

Back cracked, she tried again to put palms on floor. She didn't make it, but she got close. At least her fingers still reached her toes.

Aiden and Ullwen continued the stretching trend. While not as flexible as Erica or Lauren, the two took their time. They stretched like athletes before a big game, focusing on each muscle group. She remembered Friday nights in North Chester, attending a game or two with Oliver. He hadn't wanted to go, but she'd made him. She didn't care much for the sport, but she loved to watch Aiden play.

Now, watching Aiden with one leg crooked over the other, used as a pivot to twist his back, she thought of pre-game warm-ups—him in his pads, helmet on, eyes blazing through the facemask. She'd memorized every lump of pads, every fold of fabric. He moved in Alrujah the way he moved in North Chester—fast and fluid, no matter how much heavy armor he wore.

"Are we ready?" Ullwen asked.

Aiden tilted his head to either side. His neck popped as loudly as Lauren's back. He slipped his steel helmet on and smacked it like it was a football helmet. "Let's do this."

* * *

In Bailey Renee's dream, she had wings. The tips of the feathered appendages stretched out beyond her peripheral vision. She felt the joints where they connected to her back, felt every muscle contract when they whipped down. The air pressed against her face, the currents rushed under her wings, lifted her higher. A sword, heavy and thick, sat in a holster on her hip, and the tip extended down past her knee.

She flew on some strange instinct. Experimentally, she shifted her body a bit and dove down to the left. She brought her wings down hard, then opened them wide. She flapped them up and down diagonally, holding herself upright, perpendicular to the ground. Like treading water, she thought. She moved herself forward, to the left and right.

She'd never smiled so broadly.

She worked her wings hard, catching the currents and using them to aid her lift. How high could she go? Flap after flap, she ascended in the strange two-sun sky. Beneath her, a massive medieval city spread out over hundreds of square miles. The more she ascended, the smaller it got, until, at last, it shrank to the size of a Lego brick. The thin air made breathing hard. Her back started to burn with the effort of flying. She'd not expected to feel fatigue in a dream.

Beneath the warm suns, hanging in the still cold air, Bailey folded her white-feathered wings around her and marveled at their warmth. Tilting forward, she fell, headlong, toward the ground. She freefell for nearly a minute, then snapped her wings open. Her descent slowed so rapidly she thought a bungee cord jerked her up. She tilted slightly, folded one wing, and barrel-rolled to her right. Finally, she flapped her wings twice and latched onto the golden spire atop the tallest tower of the castle of the city spread out under her.

Goose bumps tickled her skin. Aside from several well-worn paths, snow covered the ground. Several people gaped up at her. She smiled at them like a celebrity in a parade.

But terror marred their faces. They scurried indoors as several soldiers rushed out of the castle. Their steel helmets gleamed in the light of the setting suns. The sky turned the color of an Orange Julius—light orange and frothy with clouds.

Weirdest.

Dream.

Ever.

Soldiers in leather tunics pulled arrows from their backs and set them on the strings of their bows.

Bailey didn't have to stick around to figure out what they had in mind. She leapt off the spire, set her sights skyward, and flapped her wings furiously. Six arrows shot past her, but none touched her.

Time to find out how fast she could fly.

* * *

Oliver side-stepped the lunging nar'esh, bringing his rognak staff down across its outstretched arms. They snapped near the elbows, and he pivoted, brought the staff back up fast, catching the beast under the chin. Its neck snapped, and it crashed to the floor like a crushed aluminum can.

Erica ducked, grabbed both wrists of a nar'esh, and with a savage slash, cut both its hands off. It reeled back, holding its two bloody stumps to its tarantulan eyes. Erica took a few steps toward it and dropped both her daggers in its chest.

Even covered in rank nar'esh blood, she was beautiful. Lovely. Graceful in her savagery.

Lauren stretched out her hands and torched a nar'esh on either side of her. They lit up in flames, shriveled to the floor like slugs covered in salt.

"There are no more," Ullwen said. He almost sounded sad, bored.

The cloud of bats Erica summoned dispersed down the hallways, tiny shrieks bouncing off the rock walls. "Yup. All passages clear." She turned to the massive doors before them. "I'm guessing we made it to Margwar?"

With a snap of her finger, Lauren lit two torches on either side of the massive gold-gilded doors.

Oliver put his hands on the cold stone, traced the lines of gold with his fingers. "Very few people know this entrance to Margwar exists. They believe it to be destroyed or assume it never existed to begin with."

"Thank you, Professor Oliver," Erica said. She craned her neck back, taking in the twelve-foot high doors. "Aren't dwarves supposed to be small?"

Lauren nodded. "They liked to show off their masonry and smithing skills. They built things big because they could. It impressed visitors and earned the respect of foreign dignitaries."

"So they were compensating."

"I wouldn't say that," Lauren said.

Aiden said, "But Erica would."

Ullwen examined the door. "They do not appear easy to force open."

Aiden pushed the doors with a grunt. "Got to be a million pounds. What's the plan, bro? Secret knock?"

Oliver turned his new staff around in his hand. Several carved dwarvish characters ran up and down its length. "Secret knocks only help if someone opens it from the other side."

Erica said, "It'd be pretty bomb if we had some dynamite."

The worse the pun, the more Oliver loved Erica. "I think it has something to do with my staff, if I remember correctly. These runes are dwarvish. They must tell us how to get in."

"So get reading," Erica said.

"I can't."

"Excuse me?" Erica said.

Oliver tapped the point of the stick on the ground. "I can't read it."

Erica furrowed her brow. "Hold on a minute super genius. You can't read a language you put in the game?"

"I didn't bother memorizing the phonetic rules of every language I coded. I built in a translator from English to elvish or dwarvish. I'd type in what I wanted it to say in English, and it would come out in dwarvish."

"You're so weird," she said, but it sounded like a compliment.

"You don't remember what it said?" Lauren asked.

He frowned. "Kinda forgot about this place when I scrapped it from the main quest."

"I didn't think you forgot anything," Lauren said.

"You gotta think, bro. Our way home's on the other side of that door."

The books from the monastery. He dropped his staffs and rummaged through the saddlebags they'd brought along. Inside, he grabbed *The Language of Adonai*. He flipped through it for a bit until he found the section on running the translation subset concurrently with the physics engine. It didn't tell him exactly what he'd hoped it would, but it did give an example of a translation from English to dwarvish, which might be enough to extrapolate the phonetic relationship between the two languages.

Ullwen knelt next to Oliver. "What book do you read?"

"It's the instruction manual for the coding software I used to create Alrujah."

Ullwen stood up and took two steps back. "*The Language of Adonai*"?

"Yes."

"That is a holy book," he said in awe.

Oliver shook his head. "I appreciate your reverence, but I think we're a little past that." He flipped through the pages quickly until he found a spot near the middle of the book. As he hoped, he found the instructions and an example translation. But it did little to help. Primarily a fast substitution of letters and letter sounds, it would take too long to decode. But halfway down the second page, the manual showed the transcription of numbers. He recognized two of them: 3 and 20.

Revelation 3:20.

Here I am! I stand at the door and knock. If anyone hears my voice and opens the door, I will come in and eat with that person, and they with me.

Unbelievable. Aiden was right. A secret knock.

He knocked twice and recited the verse. A latch unhinged on the opposite side, and the two massive gold-gilded doors swung open.

* * *

Bailey remembered little of her dream when she woke up at 4:30 the next morning, only the sensation of flying, the fatigue in her back, the pressing of wind and pull of gravity as she barrel-rolled toward the earth. She spent the next thirty minutes staring at the ceiling trying to recapture the sensation of freedom and strength.

At 5:00, Bailey rolled out of Lauren's bed, grabbed the journal, stepped over the pile of clothes and books and walked to her room. She put the journal in her backpack—something for study hall if she lasted that long—and readied herself for the day.

While she showered, while she ate breakfast, while she should have been thinking about getting back into a routine and balancing her school work and sports schedule, thoughts of Sarah Skeleton distracted her. Bailey and Sarah had chemistry together third period, as did Oliver and Lauren. Two classes her first day back would be plenty.

Once she saw Sarah, she would go up to her and punch her straight in her too-pretty-for-you face.

Her heart twitched a bit with the thought. She shouldn't be this angry at someone who had no logical connection to Lauren's disappearance, but Bailey had read enough articles on cyber-bullying to understand its drastic effects. In all reality, hitting her wouldn't do any good. It wouldn't help find Lauren. Bailey would be suspended or kicked off the basketball team, or both.

But it would feel good. If nothing else, the punch would be a well-needed lesson in manners for Sarah.

She pulled her parka on, zipped it up, put the fur-lined hood over her head, and walked down to the bus stop.

* * *

Shortly after stepping into the ancient city of Margwar, Lauren and the rest of the group stopped. Her eyes widened to suns. Aiden whispered, "Whoa." Ullwen whispered something about clever dwarves. Even Erica stood silent, her head turning side to side, up and down, contemplating the immensity of the metropolis, the intricacies of the masonry and blacksmithing, the sheer complexity of an underground city.

Lauren breathed stale air and immediately recognized the smell. Old, dusty pages with a twist of citrus. She folded her arms for warmth and stepped closer to Aiden.

Oliver used the torch to light a trough of kerosene. Immediately, flames raced along the outlying walls of the city. Easily the size of North Chester, Margwar spread out before them like an unrolling map.

Arranged like a stadium, the city was tiered with the higher levels outside. Each inner level descended several feet. Buildings stretched out of the ground, complete with carved windows. Bridges sprang up from the upper levels like freeway off-ramps and ran down to the more central, lower levels. Black rock columns stretched up from the floor, thick as elephants. On the bottom level, constructed of equal parts gold and stone, stood a building of immense size.

Apparently unaffected, Oliver said, "Sure wish we knew where to find this book."

Aiden rested his hand on the hilt of his sword. "You don't know where to go?"

"We go here. But I don't know where in here exactly."

Erica said, "If I were a book of great power and importance, where would I hide?"

"A library," Ullwen said.

Oliver studied the carvings on his rognak prayer staff again. "No libraries to speak of, except in the palace. Dwarves aren't exactly big readers."

Lauren surveyed the city. The flickering light of the kerosene trench bathed Margwar, a city as large as any downtown in America, in a sheen of amber, illuminating its ornate carvings and gold work. Not content to simply make functional buildings, the dwarves had taken the time to decorate each window, each door, each wall with intricate designs—lines and curves flowing into and out of each other at impossible angles. The designs and uniformity of the structures impressed her.

Oliver squinted at his stick, running his fingers over the smooth grooves. Erica stood next to him, spinning her Ma'att'tal bracelets around her left arm. Aiden swished his sword through the air, apparently trying to become comfortable with the weight and length of the new blade. It glowed blue with electricity. Ullwen sheathed Aiden's old sword in an over-the-shoulder belt. The hilt of it tipped to the left of his neck.

Lauren had tucked her scrolls in the saddlebags. She didn't need them to use the spells. Once Oliver had helped her read them, they stayed with her. They remained in her, a source of power radiating an undulating energy.

The scrolls made her wonder. She'd read those, eventually, and they'd been written in dwarvish. She held her hand out to Oliver. "Let me try reading that thing."

He handed the staff to her. She didn't remember any sounds for the familiar characters. Some resembled inverted English characters, some upside down Spanish letters. The longer she stared at them, the more they flipped around and traded places.

Her eyes must be playing tricks on her. The characters jumped and spun, performing a dictionary circus. She rubbed her eyes to no effect. She held the staff toward Oliver. "Does this look the same to you?"

He tilted his head to one side like a curious mutt. "Yeah. Why?"

Sparky barked and rubbed against Erica's leg. "Hang on," she said and put her hand on his head.

"The words, I mean. Not the staff. Are they the same words?"

He held the staff up to the trench of kerosene and inspected it closely. "Think so. Why?"

Lauren shook her head. She took the staff back, squinted, and focused on the stick, but the harder she stared, the more the characters moved.

"Something wrong?" Oliver asked.

"The words," she said. They slowed, eventually stopped moving, reassembled themselves into something recognizable.

English.

She shouldn't be able to read it. Indigo never spoke dwarvish. But the words assembled themselves into English. The Lauren part of her twinkled inside. "I remember the language now. I can read it," she said.

Chapter Twenty-Four

Belphegor took for himself an abominable body, a twisting of bull and of man. Unto his likeness, the dwarves fashioned golden idols and stone idols. They honored him with wicked prayers and sacrifices which angered almighty Adonai.

—The Book of the Ancients

WHEN MR. COOPERSON, BAILEY Renee's English teacher, gave the class the last ten minutes to free-read, she pulled out the worn leather journal she'd taken from Lauren's room. She'd not remembered it being inscribed with *The Book of Things to Come*, but she never paid much attention to Lauren's and Oliver's game. Nothing more immature or childish than video games.

The scripting language Oliver designed interested her, though. He'd shown it to her once, and it made her head spin. She had no idea how he handled so many variables simultaneously, and how they worked together to solve minor bug issues. A self-correcting scripting language seemed like something more out of science-fiction than reality.

Bailey paid only enough attention to the story, the part Lauren made, to ridicule it. Now, she wanted to flip through the yellowing pages and find out what fantasies played through her sister's mind. With a little luck, she might even stumble across some clue, some small revelatory detail to balance the equation, to find out what happened to the missing kids—some thread to tie the game to the disappearances. Of course, that'd be about as likely as her winning the lottery. But if such a thread existed, she would find it.

She opened the journal, skimmed through the first few pages. Only a few pages had been written in. Not like Lauren at all. Lauren filled entire journals in a matter of weeks. In fact, over the years she'd been working on the game with Oliver, she'd filled forty-two journals with information and sketches about the game. They all sat on shelves in her room, conveniently numbered for easy reference.

So this must be the most recent. But why did it look so old? The thin, yellow pages crinkled under the slightest touch. Thick ink formed words on pages like dried leaves. She handled the journal with the utmost care and respect, terrified it might crumble to ash in her hands.

Too many words she didn't understand made the text hard to follow—Vicmorn, Indigo, Lakia, Jaurru, Ullwen. They all sounded like names, and all were capitalized, so she assumed they were characters. Context demystified other strange words. Fangands fit the description of werewolves. Ogres became beresus. And she understood what "abomination" meant, but the usage of it differed here. Instead of something hated, Lauren used it as a description of a race of monsters, super beings, or evil gods. Hard to say which one for sure.

The bell rang, and the class picked up their belongings. Bailey Renee slipped the journal carefully into her bag. She replaced her textbook and notebook on the shelf in their proper places, then headed to the stairs on the other side of the hall, toward the chemistry lab.

Sarah Skeleton would be upstairs.

Premature guilt twinged in her stomach. Bailey almost pitied prissy little Sarah. The prim little model wouldn't stand a chance against Bailey Renee. One punch, she told herself. Make it quick. In and out.

Students crowded the stairs. She made her way to the wall side and slipped past the mass of people filtering down, a salmon spawning.

At the computer lab, she set her bag down, nodded to Mrs. Diaz, then went back out to the hall in time to see Sarah Skeleton walking up in all her vanity. Her freshly curled long blonde hair fell around her face and shoulders. She'd applied her makeup with computer precision. She looked like someone cut her face out of a magazine and pasted it on her neck.

Bailey wanted to break Sarah's perfect little nose. She tightened her fist. Fingernails pressed into her palm.

But Sarah's trademark smugness hid behind a reddened face. Not from blush, but sadness. Her puffy eyes, dark with purple eye-shadow and eyeliner, gave her away. Sarah Skeleton had been crying.

Amazingly, she walked right up to Bailey and threw her stickish arms around her.

"I'm so sorry about Lauren," Sarah said. Her voice shook.

Sarah's hair tickled Bailey's ear. Bailey had no idea what to do. Instinctively, she put her arms around Sarah but pulled them back quickly. She pushed Sarah back and stared hard at her. "What are you talking about?"

Sarah's narrow eyebrows scrunched up toward the bridge of her nose. "I'm sorry," she said again.

Bailey should be angry still. She tried to conjure up the rage that boiled in her minutes earlier, but it vanished. The hollowness of shared suffering took its place. Genuine sorrow softened Sarah's face. But Bailey wouldn't give up easily, wouldn't let Sarah off the hook. "What do you care?"

Sarah put her hand on her chest. "I always admired Lauren. I never really told her, but I did."

"Stop," Bailey said, her voice hardly above a whisper. "I saw your text."

"What text?"

Students squeezed passed them. They frowned at Bailey, dropped their eyes to avoid the awkward, piteous eye contact. For once, instead of Lauren being Bailey's sister, people saw her as Lauren's sister—the missing girl's sister. These students, her former friends, no longer recognized Bailey as anything other than a Lauren's walking MISSING poster.

Her hot anger returned, and she clenched her fist, ready to punch Sarah harder than she'd punched anything before. She took a deep breath, wrinkled her nose, and said, "If I was as fat as you, I'd kill myself."

Sarah shook her head. "Wasn't me."

"Don't lie to me! I saw it! It came from your phone!"

"I didn't send it. Kevin did." Her face contorted into equal parts fear and anguish.

Bailey exhaled slowly. "Your boyfriend?"

"Not anymore. I totally broke up with him when I saw the text. I tried to unsend it, but it already went out. She'd already read it."

Bailey Renee didn't want to believe her. But Sarah's face was every bit as red and blotchy as Bailey's. "You liked Lauren?" She sounded more surprised than she hoped.

Sarah crossed her arms and tugged at the straps of her back pack. "I don't know. I guess so. We were lab partners first semester. Do you remember?"

Bailey Renee nodded. Oliver was absent that day, so Lauren picked Sarah for some inexplicable reason.

"Anyway, we talked a little bit, and she seemed really nice. She was super quiet, but nice."

Bailey Renee unclenched her fist. She dragged the sleeve of her sweater over her cheeks. She wanted to tell Sarah not to talk about Lauren in the past tense, but she didn't want to fight that battle now. Instead, she said, "She is nice."

* * *

Erica stood over Lauren's slender shoulder. "So what's it say?"

Lauren turned the stick around in her hands, brought her nose closer to the staff, squinted to better see it in the flickering light of the flames following the walls of Margwar. How did the dwarves see anything in this place? "It's hard to make out, but the words are getting clearer. It says something about nests, I think. And it says abomination, which doesn't sound good."

Aiden flicked his wrist. Instantly the short gold blade erupted in flames. He held it over by Oliver's staff. "Better?" He put his gauntleted hand on her shoulder.

Lauren smiled. "Much," she said. His cold armor contrasted with his warm touch.

Ullwen bristled.

"Why is she able to read it, and you are unable, Vicmorn?" Ullwen asked.

"I made the language," Lauren said. "I used to write letters to Oliver in dwarvish and elvish." Her cheeks heated, and not from the flames of Aiden's sword.

"I don't remember those," Oliver said.

Lauren took Aiden's hand in hers and rotated it enough to better illuminate the grooved letters. "Never gave them to you. A little too nerdy, even for me."

"It's not too nerdy. My dad's hand-carved chess board takes nerd to a whole new level," Aiden said. "I'm really glad you're okay. Have I told you that?"

"About a million times," Erica sighed. "Seriously, put the romance on hold. Let's grab the book and get somewhere with sunlight."

Lauren reviewed the letters. "And neither shall the nests from above nor the abomination from below conquer them."

Oliver moved closer behind Lauren and glanced over her other shoulder, the shoulder Aiden's hand rested on.

"Look girlie, that's all great information and everything, but does it say anything about a book and a place to find the book? That would actually be a lot better than something about some birds' nests or whatever."

Ullwen grabbed one of the arrows he'd retrieved before entering Margwar. He dipped the tip in the trough of kerosene, nocked it on his bow. He leaned back slightly, aimed the tip toward the ceiling, and let it fly.

The flaming arrow arched toward the ceiling nearly fifty feet up.

The nests did not belong to birds, or to bats. Thick black slimy strings twisted together into thousands of hammocks. As the arrow flew past them, they jiggled. The near silent city ignited in tongue clicks and squeaks of alternating pitches.

"Are you freaking kidding me?" Erica mumbled.

"So those are the nests from above. What's the abomination from below?"

Their eyes all went to the center, bottom-most level where the dwarvish palace stood.

"It's as good a place to start as any," Oliver said. "But let's go through the tunnels. If nar'esh start dropping from here, we'll never stop fighting them."

Ullwen had already dipped the torches in the kerosene. "Lead on, good monk."

* * *

Oliver took a torch and gestured toward an octagonal building nearby. "That should lead us to the Winding Roads. Think of them like freeways. They circle Margwar's outer perimeter and spiral down in opposite directions. Each level has two access points to the Winding Roads."

A quick rush of air pushed his back.

Nar'esh, must be.

He spun quickly, dropping to a knee and sweeping with his leg. The torch snapped around, illuminated a nar'esh stumbling backward. It covered its face and shrieked, then clicked its tongue. Three more clacks and thumps, like metal and meat hitting the floor. "Go fast," he said.

Erica and Sparky dashed through the door. Aiden rushed Lauren in immediately after her, taking the hand and head of a bold nar'esh pressing in on Lauren. Ullwen loosed arrows, embedding them in nar'esh stomachs and chests, eyes and shoulders. Oliver twisted his staff, swatted outstretched nar'esh hands away. Their thin arms cracked under the force of the rognak wood. He ducked through the door and slammed it shut.

Nar'esh immediately threw themselves against the door. It swung open, and Oliver leapt out of the way in time to avoid being hit. He brought his staff around, sweeping the reaching arms away from him. Behind him, a statue of a Minotaur trembled on a pedestal. He took the golden idol and threw it toward the nar'esh pouring through the door. Aiden stood near the door, severing appendages with quick flicks of his flaming sword. Lauren snapped, and tiny bursts of hot sparks exploded in front of the mass. Startled, the nar'esh stumbled back out the door. Ullwen put his shoulder into the door and slammed it shut. Erica kicked a bar down, which clicked into a holder on the opposite side of the door, barring more nar'esh from entering.

Aiden polished off the few remaining nar'esh and slipped the sword back in its scabbard. "Everyone okay?"

Breathless, they nodded. Oliver leaned on his staff and eyed the décor of the room. The statue he'd used to drive the nar'esh back wasn't alone. Several, fashioned from gold or from stone, from bronze or from silver, portrayed the same Minotaur with eyes stitched shut. Each depiction held the same staff.

No, not a staff. Oliver had a staff. This monster had a wicked, fat stick, something like a macabre scepter, an evil stave, on top of which sat a grizzly ornate human skull.

"What is that thing?" Erica asked.

"I'd say a Minotaur," Lauren said.

"An abomination," Ullwen said. "The dwarves turned their hearts from Adonai to this, whatever it is."

"They worshiped this thing?" Aiden asked.

"Sure looks like it," Oliver said. His heart broke. So much time had gone into the crafting of such idols, so much craftsmanship and care. They were works of art, but the artists' hearts had been in the wrong place. How could they turn from their creator to such an atrocity, from something as beautiful as Adonai, to something as twisted as a man-bull?

"Why'd they want to worship something so ugly?" Erica sneered, eyeing a four-foot tall statue.

"Power," Ullwen said. "They felt as if Adonai had turned His back on them. This abomination must have promised them power, a return to prominence in Alrujah."

The sadness in Oliver's heart transformed slowly, turned from irritation to a righteous anger. The dwarves were a long-lived people, a people of patience. How could they turn their backs on Adonai? How could they be so impatient? He curled his lip, knocked the standing idols on their faces. "Smash them," he said.

Chapter Twenty-Five

Shedoah corrupted those who chained him, twisted them into his image. In Moloch, Shedoah fostered a heinous love for violence and death. He became the Keeper and Eater of the Dead. He perverted life and took for himself a body of death.

—The Book of the Ancients

THE WINDING ROADS OF Margwar stretched as wide as a four-lane highway. Each had a similar trough of kerosene running the length of the wall. Inexplicably, it consistently ran downhill and hadn't dried up in the decades Margwar had been abandoned to the nar'esh.

Oliver touched the torch to the trench. The kerosene ignited, flooding the massive corridor in light and warmth. Lauren scanned the roads for nar'esh or their nests. None in sight. A morbid curiosity replaced her initial elation. The nar'esh were an invasive species. They moved in and stayed around; they infested every corner of the caves and caverns here. Why not the buildings or the Winding Roads?

Bleached white skeletons littered the black stone floor. Though short and stubby, the bones were thick, dense. Lauren's heart sank. "All these dwarves," she whispered.

"Oh thank God!" Erica said. "I thought they were kids for a minute."

"Some are," Oliver said. He stared at a huddle of skeletons, a larger one and two smaller ones tucked under the larger's arms. No mistaking the posture of parent and children.

"What happened here?" Aiden asked.

"Many of these are from the nar'esh," Oliver said, kneeling to better inspect the bones. He lay his staff down on the floor, reached toward the mass of bones but did not touch. He nodded to skeletons near the middle of the roads, axes and hammers littering the black stone floor. "They fought, but were overwhelmed. Others," he said, nodding to the huddled family, "died later, of starvation, after the nar'esh pulled out."

Lauren closed her eyes and focused on breathing slow. Aiden put his arm around her. "It's okay," he whispered. Even his touch failed to comfort her. An entire race of people had been slaughtered, wiped out. She'd designed it that way. She wrote their tragic ending in her journal. How could she look at these brittle bones and not feel like a mass murderer?

"On the bright side, it is kinda nice not to have to fight all the way, right?" Erica asked.

Erica's lack of compassion soured Lauren's stomach. She couldn't even find words to explain her irritation at the lack of respect shown toward the proud, noble race of dwarves.

Ullwen agreed with Erica reluctantly. "These are dead, and beyond our help. If we fail, more will die needlessly. We must press on." He had an arrow nocked on the string of his bow and held it at the ready in front of him as if he didn't believe the lack of nar'esh meant the lack of danger.

"What's that?" Erica asked, pointing to a rough-hewn tunnel.

Oliver shrugged. "Don't remember putting that in."

"The dwarves," Lauren whispered. "Some must have escaped the nar'esh. Maybe they tunneled out of Margwar to safety?" Her heart sang a little tune of hope.

"But where would they have tunneled to?" Oliver asked.

"They're dwarves, Oliver. They could tunnel anywhere."

"So there is hope," Ullwen said. "Let us press on. Once we have secured the book, if we wish, we can return here and explore the tunnel."

"If we have time," Oliver said. "Every second that passes is another second the Mage Lord is closer to the *Book of Sealed Magic*."

They pressed on, moving through the roads in a cautious hurry. Ullwen and Aiden took the lead, carefully stepping over bones and scanning the ceiling for nests of nar'esh. But none appeared. The Winding Roads were clear of any signs of the beasts.

After they'd walked for close to an hour, Aiden paused a minute and stretched out his hand to Lauren. He lowered his voice to a whisper. "I know this place is grim, and my timing probably sucks, but what do you think about going out together and getting some coffee or something when we get back to North Chester? Just you and me."

Her breath caught in her throat. Did he just say that? He must have meant it as a joke, no matter how serious he sounded. She scowled at him. Her fingertips heated, glowed red. "Aiden Price, what a mean thing to say."

Erica arched an eyebrow. "Did you hear what he said, princess?"

Aiden's cheeks flushed red. He glowered at Erica. "You heard? I could hardly hear myself."

"It's called acoustics, sweetie. Look in to it."

"Why would you want to tease me? Get my hopes up so at the last minute you can remind me I'm a fat loser back home?"

Ullwen whispered, "Indigo, keep your voice down. If anything resides here, we don't want to alert it to our presence."

"What are you talking about?" Aiden asked.

"You know exactly what I mean."

Aiden whispered. "You're not a fat loser, Lauren. Not in North Chester and not here."

Every thought of plaguing monsters vanished. She turned on her heels and walked backward in front of him. "You may like me here because I can do this." She traced the shape of a heart in the air with her fingers. Flames followed after. They dissipated into smoke. "But back home, you're the star football player, and I'm the fat nerd. Those two don't mix. Not in high school. Not after high school."

Aiden stopped walking.

Erica said, "Seriously? You're going to have a spat right here? You guys sound like you're already married."

"You really think you're a fat nerd?" he asked.

"You have no idea," Oliver said.

"Shut up, Oliver. No one asked you," Lauren snapped.

Aiden sheathed his sword and took her hand in his. "Let me tell you something about yourself. You—the real you—are super smart, you're funny, but most of all, I have fun with you. And you *are* beautiful."

"No. I'm fat and ugly."

"Welcome to my world," Oliver said.

"The only thing ugly about you is how you feel about yourself. You have the most amazing blue eyes I've ever seen. Seriously, the first time I saw you, when we got paired up in Algebra that first week of school, that image burned into my brain. I couldn't forget it in North Chester, and I still remember it here. But what makes you the most beautiful is how kind you are. At least, you used to be."

"Wow. Get 'em, Tiger," Erica said.

Lauren said nothing. She stopped walking and stared at him.

"And you're fun, too. I mean, you thought up this game, and I'm having the best time of my life here. I mean, life-threatening battles aside, it's pretty awesome."

"You really think so?" she asked.

He said, "I don't tell jokes. I'm not very funny."

"Agreed," Ullwen said. He lowered his bow and smiled at Lauren.

Lauren stared at Aiden. "You don't care that I'm fat?"

Aiden rolled his eyes. "You're not fat."

"You would actually be seen in public with me?"

"That's kinda what a date is, sweetie," Erica said.

Oliver stopped walking for a moment, leaned heavily on his staff. "So?" he asked Lauren. "Answer the jock so we can get moving again."

Everyone stared at Lauren. Her self-consciousness vanished. For a moment, she let herself believe what he'd said. She'd never felt more like a princess. "Okay. But can we get something other than coffee? I'm not a big coffee drinker."

"How can you not like coffee?" Erica asked.

Annoyed, Ullwen said, "I'm sure the bones will celebrate your love. But we must move on."

* * *

Oliver wished he'd not made the city so expansive. They'd been walking for what must have been hours. Still, the road stretched ahead of them. With each step, he reminded himself, they drew closer to the castle, closer to the book, closer to home. Still, the rhythmic clacking of his staff tested his patience. He tucked it under his arm.

His whole body ached, and he remembered his first night in Alrujah, racing through the Cerulean Woods. It seemed weeks ago, not just nights. But each muscle in his legs, in his back, in his arms, screamed that he'd been pushing himself too hard. Even in Vicmorn's well-conditioned body, he knew he approached the limits of his physical endurance. "Think we should maybe take a break?" he asked.

"No," Ullwen said quickly. "We can't be far now."

"You said that five minutes ago," Erica said.

"Then we are five minutes closer," Ullwen said.

"I'm with Oliver," Lauren said, sipping harspus sap from Ullwen's wineskin.

There's a first, Oliver thought, but decided not to say it out loud.

"Ullwen's right," Aiden said. "We gotta keep going. We've got like, no food left, and I'm not about to eat dead nar'esh. It's too far to go back to the central chamber now. We'd have to sleep here, and I'm not cool with that. Something about sleeping with the bones of dead dwarves creeps me out."

Oliver asked, "What about you, Erica? You're the deciding vote."

"I'm so tired right now, even a bone bed sounds good. Let's take five, people, put our feet up, munch some bread, catch a quick nap. Whatever's ahead of us probably isn't friendly, and we'll need to be on top of our game if we want to handle it."

Aiden and Ullwen sighed but consented. Oliver sat down against the wall, in a small space free of bones. The others followed suit, except for Ullwen. "I'll take first watch. Half-hour shifts. We spend no more than three hours resting before pressing on."

"Agreed," Oliver said, and he closed his eyes.

* * *

Oliver took the final watch and woke everyone a half-hour later. At least, he assumed it was thirty minutes. It could have been more. Hard to follow time without a watch, or suns to monitor. He didn't like the idea of wasting time resting, but the group looked much better now, stronger, ready to go.

They gathered their things and pressed forward. And, as luck would have it, in less than an hour, they came to a set of doors with a sign above them. Heavy and thick, the doors reached near twelve feet high. Gold inlaid etching adorned the black stone. He asked Lauren, "Can you read it?"

She tilted her head back and leaned against Aiden's chest. All of a sudden they acted like boyfriend and girlfriend. So annoying. Worse, she'd listened to him when he told her she wasn't fat. She didn't argue or fight with him as she had with Oliver whenever he said the same thing.

"It says something Palace. I don't think I can pronounce the first word."

"Margwar?" he asked.

"That's how you spell it?"

"Apparently. This must be it, guys." He pushed on the set of double doors. They didn't budge. "Want to give it a shot, Aiden?"

Aiden pushed on the doors, grunting with the effort, but they didn't move. He stepped back and kicked one hard. The resounding clang reverberated up the Winding Roads, but the door didn't move. "No good, bro. They must be locked or whatever. Big doors, all that gold, I'm thinking they weigh a few tons."

"So how do we get in?" Erica asked. She pulled at her gloves and twisted her bracelets around her arm. Sparky sniffed them and growled. "Easy, boy."

Lauren stepped up to the door. "I have an idea. But you'll want to move back."

They did.

Her hands shook. She pressed them to the door. Both began to quake, as did the walls around them and the ground beneath them.

Oliver shouted over the rumbling rocks. "You're using Quake down here?"

"It's the only way," she shouted. Slowly, the walls and floor calmed down. The doors, however, continued to shake even more violently. They trembled and rumbled. They chattered and bounced across the floor like an overloaded washing machine until, finally, a tiny crack opened.

Black rocks fell from the ceiling. Cracks shot up the walls.

"Enough!" Ullwen shouted.

Lauren stopped. The walls ceased chattering; the floor ceased trembling. She shook her head. "We can't fit through a crack that small."

"Any more of that spell, and we'll be crushed by the doors, or the walls may cave in."

Lauren sat down, pulled her knees into her chest. "So what do we do?"

Oliver approached the gap between the doors. He slipped his fingers in. The crack spanned only inches, but it might be enough. Simple physics offered a solution. He just had to be smarter than the doors. "Leverage," he said, offering his rognak staff to Aiden.

Aiden looked at the staff, then the doors. "Bro, this thing will snap in half before those doors budge."

Oliver shook his head. "You don't know the strength of rognak wood. Think steel, but stronger."

"Whatever you say," Aiden said. He shoved the staff between the two doors and pulled.

Oliver leaned against the staff, lending his weight, his strength to the effort. The staff bowed but held firm. Slowly, the doors squealed across the black rock floors.

Ullwen leapt in, added his strength. They pushed until the door slid enough to let Erica squeeze through. Of course, she was the thinnest of the group by a long shot. If they wanted Aiden to be able to get through in his armor, they'd need to work a bit more.

And they did. The staff, amazingly, held firm.

Sparky growled again. "Guys, he's pretty weirded out by this place. You sure it's safe?"

"No," Oliver said. "But what choice do we have?" He passed through the doors.

"Okay, so we go in, find a library, grab the book, and get out. Let's make it like a stealth mission," Lauren said.

Erica eyed Aiden. "Yeah, loud clanking armor really shouts 'stealth' to me." She scratched Sparky behind the ear, but the massive wolf didn't stop growling.

Ullwen brought his bow to the ready position. "There is little we can do, good friends. We must forge ahead, and Adonai will protect us. Remember the staff. It said neither the nests above nor the abomination below will overcome them."

Oliver hoped that prophecy wouldn't mysteriously change. He prayed God would keep his faith strong. He thought of David, of Goliath. He thought of stones and slings, of giants and armor.

Aiden passed through the gap after Ullwen. He unsheathed his sword and, with a flick of his wrist, the short golden sword erupted in flames. He swung it over his head and in front of him. He moved around in a slow circle until he found a trough of kerosene. He dipped his sword in it and lit up the room in bright orange.

A bow on his string, Ullwen scanned the ceiling and walls. "Clear in here," he said.

The lobby of the dwarvish palace spread out before them. Several stone columns crafted to look like rognak trees supported the ceiling nearly twenty feet above. The columns were gnarled and uneven, black like the wood of the harspus trees, but nearly twice as thick. Branches shot out from the central columns as they neared the ceiling. Each went a different direction.

"I've never seen workmanship of this quality," Ullwen breathed.

"Few have, other than the dwarves," Lauren said, her neck bent back to appreciate the full level of detail. "They look alive."

Expansive duct work piped fresh air in from the surface. It twisted through the chamber, moved over their skin, carried with it the scent of the leaves topside. Had Oliver not known better, he'd have assumed the ancient trees to be real. Instead, he pressed forward.

Sparky stepped lightly. His head whipped from side to side and his lips peeled up to show his front fangs. "It is pretty creepy," Erica said.

They walked up a center flight of stairs which led to another doorway. This one had no doors. If the dwarvish kingdom still existed, guards would have been posted on either side of this threshold, even in front of the palace, and in the foyer. Dwarves used the foyer as a place of business, a type of high-end swap meet. Here, they traded jewels, precious metals, weapons, armor, and regal clothing. It wouldn't be uncommon for thousands of transactions to take place, each guided by the delicate economic practice of dwarvish haggling, which generally involved boisterous insults, mace wielding, shield ramming, and a fair amount of biting. The guards had to break up several hundred fights a day.

But the barren foyer showed no signs of struggle or commerce. No kiosks filled the floors, no tables with merchandise, no kissing booths (favorites of the dwarvish nobility), no bartering areas or political consultants.

A huge golden statue stood in the back of the room. Unlike the idols found in the octagonal room leading to the Winding Roads, likely some sort of church, this statue was cast entirely in gold and featured the likeness of a dwarf with a long beard and a bald head. Both hands rested on the top of a double-bladed war axe. His round, egg-shaped eyes looked solemn. Three dwarvish words emblazoned the golden podium on which it stood.

"Is that …" Lauren began.

"Yarborough," Oliver said.

"Who?" Erica asked.

Lauren read the inscription. "The Nameless Heir."

"Long story," Oliver said.

"Are you not telling us something?" Aiden asked.

Oliver sighed. "Lauren knows. I'll tell you more when we get out of here. Right now, I'll just say that he's a friend. We'll probably run into him sooner or later. If we make it out of here alive."

Ullwen stared at the statue. He reached out to it, touched the golden cheek. "Chosen by Adonai to proclaim His name to his people. The nameless to proclaim the name that saves."

Erica said, "Oliver, he's speaking gibberish. Care to translate?"

"Like I say, it's a long story."

"Adonai has indeed blessed me," Ullwen whispered.

The detailed layout of the palace came to Oliver, perhaps unearthed from his mind because of the power of suggestion, by the sheer sensory overload of being *in* the place. "Okay, think I got the lay of the land now. Throne room and king's sleeping quarters are to the left." He gestured with his staff. "Royal library to the right. Sleeping chambers straight ahead. Book could be in the library or the throne room. Might be in the king's sleeping quarters."

"Which would be the fastest?" Ullwen asked.

"Less searching in the throne room," Oliver said. "Dwarves like to keep trophies on display. Most are ornamental weapons, ancient artifacts and the like. Only a few books."

"We begin there," Ullwen said.

Presented this way, the idea sounded like Ullwen's. Perfect. Let him take the fall if they got attacked by a pack of nar'esh or fangands or arachands. Oliver had used up all his patience being the scapegoat. "As you wish."

He took the hallway to the left. His staffs echoed in the narrow passageway. Several other passages branched from the main hall, but he stayed the course.

The hallway led to a foyer nearly identical to the one in the front of the palace, only on a smaller scale. Here, only certain merchants were allowed to trade and barter. Mostly, it was used for entertainment— dancers and jesters and the like. But, like the first foyer, this one showed no signs of life. Worse, the room felt different—like darkness without the lack of light, a shadow with soft, indeterminate edges.

Sparky's hair bristled. "I'm not liking this," Erica said.

"Aye. I fear a great evil here," Ullwen said.

Lauren asked, "So I'm not the only one creeped out?"

Aiden flicked his wrist and flames engulfed his sword. "Is it just me, or is it harder to breathe in here?"

Oliver saw what they couldn't. A perceptible dark mist, almost like smoke, hung in the room. Heaviest near the ceiling, it billowed down like diseased clouds over a mountaintop. "Maybe we should start someplace else."

Without waiting for an answer, Sparky rushed into the throne room. The sick, thick cloud enveloped him and obscured him from Oliver's view. Something very dark, very dangerous loomed ominously beyond the threshold. Worse, Oliver had no idea what.

Erica called after Sparky and ran in, but stopped almost as suddenly as her feet crossed the threshold. Her face pulled into a mask of fear and shock.

Oliver didn't wait. He rushed the room. The others followed on his heels.

Sour air filled the dimly lit room. Each breath was like drinking rotten lemon juice. Oliver fought down a wave of nausea and hoped not to vomit in front of Erica.

A man stood before the throne. He wore a flowing white Mage's robe with black arcane symbols embroidered along his sleeves. The man turned. Even in the thick shadows of his heavy hooded cloak, the golden eye sockets of his black mask glowed. Instead of a mouth, two thick gold vertical stripes dripped down from nose to chin as if painted hastily. In one hand, he held an obsidian-tipped partisan; its blade displayed the same gold arcane symbols as his robe. In the other hand, he held an ancient red-leather bound tome seized against his chest.

The Book of Sealed Magic.

* * *

"The Mage Lord," Oliver whispered.

Lauren's heart seized. Too early. They weren't ready. If they fought the Mage Lord now, they'd be slaughtered.

The Mage Lord spoke, each word coming out more as a choir of disparate voices. "You seek *The Book of Things to Come.*"

"You got it?" Aiden asked. "Turn it over, bro. I don't want to have to cut you into pieces."

"My quarrel is not with you," he said.

A strange anger burned in Lauren. "But ours is with you. Give us *The Book of Sealed Magic.*"

"In time, perhaps. I have work for it yet." He lifted his staff, and behind him, a shimmer of light glowed softly in the gloom.

A hulking black form appeared on the throne.

"I have work I must see to." The Mage Lord slashed the air in front of him, and another shimmering ripple appeared before him. He stepped through it and vanished, as did the strange sparkling air.

Her heart steadied. They didn't have to fight him. Still, she'd hoped they'd found their way back to North Chester, hoped they'd be able to get *The Book of Sealed Magic* and finally go back home.

The mammoth form on the throne stirred. Six feet when sitting, the hulking beast's two massive horns stuck up another two feet. If a bull mated with a professional wrestler, this would be the child.

Erica asked, "Is that …"

It grunted and stood up.

Standing, the Minotaur's big brother loomed near nine feet tall. The tips of his bone horns stretched toward the ceiling. Much of the flesh on the face of the bull's head had pulled away, as if it had been ravaged by some flesh-eating bacteria. Seeping sores covered its hairy body from the neck to the human's hairy torso to the bullish legs. Its two massive eyes had been stitched shut. Blood crusted around the thick, black thread running between upper and lower eyelids. A human skull adorned the golden stave he held.

The idols they'd smashed in the room before the Winding Roads. This must be the demon they'd sculpted. The form was nearly identical.

"You are not dwarves, but still you have come to pay homage? Very well. I will accept your worship, but you must kneel before me." Its voice sounded like a radio tuned to a dead channel. Apparently, despite the stitched eyelids, it could see just fine.

"Pay homage to whom?" Ullwen asked.

The beast lumbered forward slowly. It bent to further inspect them.

Fear froze them.

"You are a monk?" it asked.

Oliver nodded.

What was left of its lip curled and showed massive, bone-crushing teeth. "You are a servant of Adonai?" The static in his voice buzzed furiously.

Aiden whispered, "Bro, he sounds angry. Take the robe off a minute, just till we get out of here."

No chance. Unmistakably, they faced some demon, a false god, even. Lauren knew neither Vicmorn nor Oliver would bend their knee to a false deity, no matter how fearsome or brutal.

Why couldn't he get past the Jesus thing for a minute and realize what kind of trouble they were in? Kneel, Lauren thought. Her hand reached for his, pulled his fingers weakly.

"Who are you?" Oliver asked, his voice defiant but unsteady.

The beast straightened his back. He pounded his chest. "I am Belphegor, lord of the dwarves and the mountains. None may stand before me. You will kneel, now," it buzzed.

"Don't do it," Oliver said.

She wanted to kneel, wanted to not fight. But she didn't. Despite her fear, she trusted Oliver.

"You will kneel, or you will die."

"Bro, I hope you got a really good plan, because this guy looks like he wants to boil us up for dinner."

Ullwen nocked an arrow on his string and took aim.

"You have made your choice." Belphegor smashed the butt of his stave into the earth. Instantly, the black sockets of the skull on the stave glowed red. A crimson flash filled the room, and Lauren's knees bent.

Chapter Twenty-Six

Adonai's power defeated the strange kings of old. He guided his people through the sands of the deserts, through the cold of the mountain tops, through the dark forests of the Otherlands. Adonai led His people, and His people followed.

—The Book of Ancients

INSTEAD OF TAKING THE school bus home, Bailey Renee zipped up her parka and walked down Hemlock Drive to Aspen Ave. She caught the city bus downtown, where she got off on Grand. Hood snug over her ears and cheeks, she walked two more blocks to North Chester Police Department.

Deputy Parker sat in his office, papers strewn across his desk. He had an unlit cigarette in his mouth and another behind his ear. The office reeked of stale cigarette smoke. He'd taken several of the photo frames from the line of file cabinets and put them on the portions of the desk not buried in papers. For a minute, she considered picking them up, looking them over, but figured that'd be too forward. Still, it'd buy her time. She took off her coat and sat down in the chair she'd sat in yesterday and crossed her legs quietly.

He set a few papers aside, keenly aware that she stared at him patiently, took the cigarette out of his lips and put it behind his other ear. "You said it had to do with Sarah?"

She paused for a minute before she said, "I was going to hit her today. I mean punch her really hard," she said, picking up the conversation she'd started when she called him after school.

"But you didn't?"

"Couldn't. She was crying. Big tears, too. She didn't send the text. So if you thought she had anything to do with it, she doesn't. Don't call her or harass her or anything."

Detective Parker scratched his left eyebrow. "You think I would harass her?"

"I'd hoped you would."

He smiled. "Couldn't tell me that when you called?"

"I could have."

"Why didn't you?"

"Wanted to come here."

"Didn't want to go home, did you?"

She stuck a piece of gum in her mouth, then took one of the photo frames. "May I?"

"Knock yourself out." Parker took the other cigarette from his ear and mimed lighting it.

Instead of a photo, he'd framed a simple sketch of a young girl, probably about her age. Matter of fact, if she didn't know better, she'd think that the sketch was of her. "Your daughter?"

"No," he said.

"Who is it?"

"You're stalling," he said.

"You're avoiding the question."

He sighed and took the frame from her. Putting it back on the desk, he leaned back in his chair. "A girl I knew growing up," he said.

"The one that got away?" she asked.

"Something like that," he said. He paused a moment, giving her plenty of opportunity to continue the conversation, but she didn't. So he continued. "Did you think of any other connections between the four kids?"

"There's a connection. I just don't know what it is right now." She sighed. "So what do we do now?"

"Not much we can do. Still haven't heard back from your father."

"No surprise. He's kinda tough to get a hold of. Lauren tries to call him every year on his birthday and on hers. She's only reached him once in the last ten years."

He stood up. "I'm going to get a burrito."

Bailey stood up quickly. "Can you tell me where Erica lives?"

He put the damp cigarette back in his mouth. "I can't tell you that." With a final glance at the strange sketch, he stepped out of his office.

Bailey put her jacket back on and followed him out. "Come on. I just want to talk to the family to see if they know anything."

"We're way ahead of you."

"No offense, Detective, but sometimes cops scare people. Sometimes people don't say as much as they would if they were talking to their kids' friends or something."

Parker froze near the front exit of the department. "You want to come with?"

Bailey frowned. "What?"

Parker spoke slowly. "I'm getting a burrito. Do you want to come with?"

"Excuse me?"

Parker walked out of the station. He opened the door to his car. "You make a good point about people not wanting to talk to cops. Get in the car. I'll call your mom."

Bailey Renee zipped up her coat. The temperature dropped to about a million below zero. "I really should get home."

"Weren't in that big of a hurry two minutes ago. Tell you what, I'll drop you off," he said. "Now get in the car."

* * *

Oliver's head started to clear. He lay on the floor. His fingers and toes tingled. He took the rognak staff that lay near his hands and pulled himself up. Next to him, his four friends knelt before Belphegor. Aiden had one knee and one fist on the floor, his head bowed slightly. Erica and Lauren bent both knees, their arms before them, foreheads to the ground. Ullwen had one knee and two fists on the ground. His head bent toward the beast.

Anger washed over him. How could they bow?

Then, looking closer, he realized they hadn't. Their necks strained to raise their heads, and Aiden and Ullwen grunted as if they were lifting weights. Belphegor must have forced them into this position.

"Are you okay?" he asked.

"Can't stand up," Erica groaned. "Too heavy."

Gravity.

Somehow, Belphegor could manipulate the physical laws of gravity. He'd somehow increased it beneath the feet of his friends, forcing them to break knee before the brutish man-bull.

Belphegor sat in the throne with his stave across his knees. The eye sockets of the skull glowed red. He blinked his stitched eyes. Crusted blood from his eyelids fell like crimson snowflakes to the hairy torso.

"Let them go," Oliver said.

Belphegor sneered at Oliver. "Adonai will not let my power touch you." He stood up and pointed his stave at Oliver. "But my hands and my stave can. My reign will be unmarred with your weak faith."

In a streak of shocking boldness, Oliver straightened his back defiantly. "You mock Adonai. Today, we will stand over your dead body and show all Alrujah that Adonai is God."

Belphegor stood over him, taller by at least three feet. His huge bone horns curved out from his forehead and ran up to gleaming points. His bullish face sneered, and he swung his massive stave, twice as thick as Oliver's legs, at Oliver's head.

Oliver ducked the attack. He moved faster than he thought possible. Fear and adrenaline made him faster, stronger, more flexible.

Belphegor stomped on the ground and the stone shook under Oliver's feet. He struggled to maintain balance, but as he did so, the beast of a man brought the butt of his stave into Oliver's chest.

He flew back and hit something hard and cold. Metal.

Aiden grunted. The others still knelt under their own weight, under the massive pull of the increased gravity. Oliver rolled over the top of the knight, found his feet, and pulled his staff under his arm. He wished he had something else, another weapon with which to defend himself. What could a staff do against such an abomination?

David had only stones. David tended sheep.

Yea though I walk through the valley of the shadow of death, I will fear no evil.

The verse gave Oliver strength, courage. Belphegor roared and charged. Oliver rolled away from his friends, hoping to keep them out from under the Minotaur's feet. He moved on instinct, hoping whatever skill and training he'd acquired in Alrujah would come back in some form of muscle memory.

He rushed the giant throne, bounded up the steps leading to it. Belphegor followed, his stave raised high. Oliver leapt forward, planted a foot on the back of the throne and used it to push himself further up. Something behind the throne caught his eye.

A book on a pedestal, encased in glass.

The Book of Things to Come.

He spun in mid-air, and, with every ounce of strength in him, swung the rognak prayer staff around toward Belphegor's face.

It connected and glanced off something hard before it glided through the beast's open maw. The Minotaur staggered back one step and spit out a tooth the size of a can of green beans. Belphegor's stave crushed the back of the throne, narrowly missing Oliver.

For Thou art with me.

Oliver moved quickly, leaping off the rubble of the throne to the wall behind, back-flipping, arms spread out, staff firm in his right hand, and somersaulted over Belphegor. The Minotaur chased after him, blood seeping from the stitches in his eyelids, from the corner of his mouth where Oliver'd knocked the tooth out.

Oliver was faster, more agile than the beast, but running would only keep him safe for so long. At some point, he'd have to face the monster, find a way to free his friends. As he landed, his hand sought the prayer amulet. He lifted hasty, earnest prayers to Adonai.

Belphegor swung the stave hard, the gold plated human skull racing toward Oliver.

Thy rod and thy staff, they comfort me.

Oliver jumped, twisted, landed on Belphegor's back.

The beast stank of smoke and ox hair.

Oliver put the staff under Belphegor's chin and pulled it hard. He sank his feet into the thickly muscled back of the monster, but Belphegor simply plucked him off and threw him down on the stone floor.

Hot white flashes of pain lit in front of Oliver's eyes. Vision and breath left him. Belphegor didn't stop.

Thy rod and thy staff...

He brought the rognak staff above his head. Belphegor brought the fat stave down at him, smashed it into his staff. Stave cracked over staff. The top half with the gold-plated skull skittered along the floor to the wall.

How had the impact not broken both his arms?

Belphegor stood over him, incensed. Nothing quite as terrifying as an angry Minotaur with a shattered tree-stump of a stave. Belphegor raised his fist up and brought it down fast.

Oliver had to move, but he couldn't. His back felt like it was broken in twelve places.

So this was how his life ended? At the blunt end of the fist of a Minotaur. He'd have divots in his skull the size of golf balls, one for each of Belphegor's knuckles.

Oliver closed his eyes and waited for the end.

For thou art with me.

The blow never came. Instead, Belphegor roared.

Oliver opened his eyes. Aiden stood over him. He must have deflected the blow with his shield somehow, moments before Belphegor sent him flying.

But how did Aiden get free? The shattered stave.

Oliver wrestled his remaining strength to turn his head to the left a bit and see all his friends standing.

Thank you, Lord God.

Lauren launched fireballs the size of watermelons at Belphegor.

"Not by the throne!" Oliver cried. "Keep the fire away from the throne!"

Aiden stood back up and held his flaming sword in his hand. His sneer said he meant to cleave Belphegor in two. Ullwen had already nocked an arrow and loosed it. It found its mark in Belphegor's shoulder. Sparky howled and snapped his jaws at Belphegor.

Belphegor roared, and in a move that defied his size, rolled quickly to the skull on the floor. He snatched it up, grunted, and deflected the fireballs. The slits of his closed eyelids glowed red. He snapped the arrow from his shoulder as if he'd been pricked by a toothpick. Sparky set his jaws on the beast's wrist and bit down hard. The Minotaur brought his hand toward the ground, but Sparky released moments before being crushed and rolled away.

Erica shrieked, but Belphegor held the skull out to her. Immediately, she flew up toward the ceiling. Her screech morphed to a scream as she deftly twisted in the air in time to land on the ceiling.

He'd flipped gravity.

Aiden flew toward the roof, too, as did Lauren and Ullwen. Only Oliver and Belphegor remained on the ground.

Oliver rushed him, rognak staff tucked under his arm. Belphegor brought the skull down, and Erica crashed into Oliver. Aiden landed, twisted around, and leapt at the beast, flaming sword stretching out toward the abomination.

Belphegor grabbed Aiden in mid-air, then threw him to the ground. He squeezed the skull, and Aiden groaned under the weight of the armor.

The gravity would crush him. "Get out of the armor!" Oliver shouted.

Aiden's fingers sought the leather straps connecting the armor to his body but couldn't lift his arms. "Too heavy!" Aiden screamed.

Erica rolled off Oliver and threw her dagger into the chest of Belphegor. The beast didn't stop. He lowered his head, rushed at Lauren, who, like Aiden, had been pinned to the ground.

Lauren struggled to lift her hand, to conjure flames or ice or electricity, but her weight threatened to break her bones.

Oliver had to get the skull from Belphegor's hand. He rushed the beast, leapt at the monster in mid-charge, and deftly threaded his staff between the skull and Belphegor's fingers. It popped loose, and Oliver brought the opposite end of the staff up under the beast's chin. Belphegor stumbled, crashed hard to the earth.

Momentarily freed, Aiden scrambled to his feet. Ullwen, ran, then slid across the floor to kick the skull further from the Minotaur. Erica pulled her gloves up, twisted both her bracelets, and pulled her hair back. "I got this one, fellas," she said. Her tongue clicked and clacked.

Oliver had heard that sound before, far too many times in the last couple days to mistake it.

Erica was calling the nar'esh.

* * *

After stopping by Burrito Union, Detective Parker drove down Park Street to the part of town Bailey didn't like going to. Several dilapidated apartment complexes lined the streets. The few paranoid people out in the cold gazed suspiciously at Parker's car. They stood in tight circles like a football huddle.

Putting his unlit cigarette behind his ear, Detective Parker pointed to the mass of people. "Thirty bucks says its drugs."

"Where are you taking me?" Bailey asked.

"Erica Hall's house. She lives there." He pointed to a house straight out of *The Ring*. Even covered in snow, it looked creepy, like some fairy-tale witch's cabin. Pointy in all the wrong places, the roof jutted out over the front door. Paint peeled around the windows and off the doors. Duct tape loosely covered the cracks in the front windows. "I don't remember this place coming up in the phone book."

"I'm guessing you searched under Hall. Erica's mom's name is Gertrude Adams."

"Gertrude?"

"I know. Sounds like she's eighty, right? She's thirty-seven. Technically, she's a foster mom. Took Erica in about a year ago now. I'm pretty sure Gertrude here is using her to get the cash. It's not uncommon. Take a teen, lock them in their room, collect a check, let the school district deal with discipline."

Bailey shivered. "Is it really that bad?"

He frowned with half his face and stuck the cigarette back between his lips. "I've seen worse. Then again, so has Erica."

"Is it safe?"

"Wouldn't bring you out here if it wasn't. Here's your chance to talk to her."

"I didn't really expect this. I wouldn't even know what to say."

Detective Parker steered into the driveway and parked the car. He wiped his mouth with a paper napkin and replaced the unlit cigarette between his lips. "Introduce yourself. Bailey Renee Knowles—super sleuth."

She sighed but got out of the car. She walked up to the front door, which inexplicably still had cobwebs in the corners, and knocked. A blonde woman in a pink bathrobe answered the door. She'd pulled her stringy hair into a hasty ponytail. Lines creased the corners of her eyes. She had a scar on her lower lip, as if someone had ripped out a lip ring at some point. Sleep clouded her bloodshot eyes. Thirty-seven? She looked more like fifty. She inspected Detective Parker's car before she made eye contact with Bailey Renee. "Can I help you?"

"Ms. Adams?"

She kept the door mostly closed. A chain ran from the door to the jamb. "Who are you?"

"My name is Bailey Renee Knowles." Gertrude should recognize the last names of the other missing kids.

"Are you from the school?" She wiped at her nose and scratched her cheek.

"Yes, but it's not like I work there. I'm a student. I'm Lauren's sister."

"Who's Lauren?"

"Lauren Knowles. She went missing the same day as your daughter Erica." It broke Bailey's heart to have to give her such information. Shouldn't she already know?

"Oh? I'm sorry. Good luck finding her." Gertrude went to shut the door.

Bailey Renee slapped her hand on the door, held it open. "Don't you want to figure out what happened to them?"

Getrude opened the door again. "Don't you know? They ran away together. All three of them."

"Four."

"Sure, all four of them. Kids run away. Especially foster kids. You can't really stop them." She scratched at her elbow. "Listen, thanks for stopping by. I'm sure Erica will come back when she's ready." She slammed the door quickly and latched the lock.

Bailey shuffled through the snow back to the car. She dusted the snow from her boots and sighed.

"Sounds like you had as much luck as us," Parker said. "She wouldn't even let us in without a warrant. Didn't even report Erica missing."

"Who did?"

"No one. When the Shaws called about Oliver, they mentioned him meeting Erica. We paid Ms. Adams here a visit. She didn't even know when to expect Erica home. Said it wasn't uncommon for her to be out late. She'd come back eventually."

"How sad," she said.

"Sadder still, Ms. Adams is probably the best mom Erica's had. Most of her parents, foster and otherwise, have ended up in jail for one reason or another. I'm surprised I haven't seen Erica down at the station. Criminals make criminals, sure as I'm an ex-smoker." He flicked the damp, unlit cigarette out the car window. "Erica's either already turned, and she's very good at getting away with it, or she's the exception to the rule."

"Let's hope she's the exception," Bailey said.

Chapter Twenty-Seven

Solous cried out to Adonai as the suns descended. He petitioned Adonai's favor, sought His glory. And for as long as Solous remained on his knees, and while his forehead touched the feathered grass of Harland, Solous's armies pushed the elves back.

—The Book of the Ancients

ENRAGED, BELPHEGOR PUNCHED AIDEN. He grabbed Oliver before he could roll away, lifted him, then slammed him onto the ground, back first. Oliver tried to sit up, but the pain spread out in a million places, like he'd gone spine first through the windshield of a car and had every scrap of glass in his back to prove it. He prayed and prayed for God to heal him, but no relief came.

Screeching echoed through the foyer, from down the corridors, from the doorway to the throne room. Oliver's eardrums nearly split, but he was helpless to move his arms to cover his ears. Hundreds of nar'esh skittered in, swarmed the walls and the ceiling and the floor. Hundreds became thousands, all circling in and around Erica. She pointed to the Minotaur and said, "Sic 'em, boys."

Oliver hadn't realized it before, but the gaping sores on Belphegor matched the marks he'd seen on Lauren. The nar'esh must have poisoned him at some point, but he survived. Must have an incredible fortitude.

Shadows scurried over the stone ceiling and leapt on Belphegor. He roared, threw them off, and smashed their skulls. Inexorable waves of nar'esh swarmed him, crawled over him like maggots on a corpse. He stabbed at them with his shattered stave, but for every nar'esh he killed, two more took its place.

Belphegor howled and spun around. Sores opened all over his hairy carcass.

The smell of the nar'esh, of the wounds opening on Belphegor made the already sour air even more rank. Oliver tried not to be sick. He closed his eyes and hoped the nar'esh wouldn't trample him, hoped Belphegor would fall to the beasts. But if he did, what then? Would they turn their attention to Oliver and his friends? Had Erica truly mastered their language?

* * *

Lauren didn't like the nar'esh, especially this many this close. They ran between her and Ullwen, up and down walls, over the ceiling. They crawled over each other like cockroaches. She fought hard not to throw up.

The tide of nar'esh at once relieved her and terrified her. If the nar'esh killed Belphegor, wouldn't they turn on her and the others? No matter who won, Belphegor or the nar'esh, they'd have a massive battle on their hands. Best to conserve her strength.

Belphegor dropped to his knees as lithe, black, spidery limbs crept over him. Aiden sneered, kept his sword unsheathed, waiting for the nar'esh to clear so he could unmake Belphegor.

The beast struggled to his feet again. With massive, ground-shaking steps, he moved toward the throne. He used the stones to smash the nar'esh, to throw them into the walls. He tore their limbs, used them as weapons. Hundreds of nar'esh died in minutes.

Lauren had never seen so much blood. The stench of rotten grapefruits nauseated her, and she held her stomach tight. "He's going to kill them all," she said, electricity already crackling between her fingertips.

Heaps of dead nar'esh piled over the floor.

"We should do something," Aiden said.

Erica's tongue clicked and clacked.

Sparky sat beside her, haunches tightened, ready to spring.

Ullwen had an arrow on his string. He didn't wait. He stepped over a nar'esh to steady his shot and let the string free. The arrow pierced the snout of Belphegor.

Deftly avoiding the few nar'esh still standing, Aiden charged Belphegor and sank the flaming sword into his leg.

Belphegor screamed and dropped to a knee. He lunged forward, gripped the skull of his stave. The sockets flashed red, and the nar'esh rushed toward the ceilings with frightening ferocity. Their thin limbs cracked on the stone, and their lifeless bodies collapsed to the ground below. He turned his head toward Lauren.

She lifted. The ceiling rushed toward her. She screeched.

Aiden stabbed Belphegor's other leg, smashed the skull from the beast's hand with his shield.

Sparky howled and nipped at Belphegor's knees.

Lauren, now plummeting to the earth, sent a surge of electricity at Belphegor. At the same time, she heated the earth beneath her. The drastic temperature change created a current of wind. Not much, but enough to cushion her fall.

"Leverage!" Oliver shouted. "Rognak staff!"

Lauren changed her tactic. Instead of using fire, she let her blood run cold, her fingertips numb. She crafted ice from air, a thick block on each of Belphegor's feet. She did the same with his hands, so he knelt before them.

The beast howled, wrenched his hands free from the ice blocks. Shards of ice shattered like glass. Aiden moved in front of Lauren, used his shield to absorb the magic-imbued ice crystals.

Erica and Sparky leapt on Belphegor's back. He twisted under their weight. Sparky latched on with his piercing teeth. Erica smashed a rock into the back of his skull. "Just quit your whining and kneel, you stupid ox!"

Ullwen rolled toward Oliver and snatched up the rognak staff. "Leverage," he said with a grin. He leapt up and jammed the staff between Belphegor's horns and pulled down, twisted Belphegor's head.

Lauren worked faster, thickening the bonds of ice around Belphegor's hands and feet.

He roared and tried to twist his head, but physics gave Ullwen an advantage. Still, Belphegor's twisting neck threatened to throw Ullwen from his feet. He pulled down hard, pushing against the might of Belphegor.

Aiden ran next to Ullwen and pulled down with all his strength. Erica and Lauren followed close after, adding their physical strength to the torque.

Sparky bounded over and nipped at Belphegor.

The ice holding the beast's hands and feet began to crack. Lauren leapt back and thickened the bonds. But the new ice cracked as quickly as it formed. "Move fast, guys."

Ullwen, Aiden, and Erica pushed and pulled until Belphegor's head twisted and his neck snapped.

Belphegor twitched against his ice bonds, then dropped his limp neck.

Unconvinced, Aiden ran the blade of his sword along the beast's neck. A tide of crimson blood splashed out, flooded the bodies of the nar'esh.

Near the ceiling of the cave, a thick black cloud coagulated like an undulating mass of flies on rotting meat.

"You feel that?" Aiden asked.

"Electricity," Lauren said.

"So," Erica said, stepping back from the abomination. "The creepy mystery cloud creeping anyone else out?"

Red sparks flashed, and with a mighty clap, a thick bolt of red lightning flashed down and consumed the massive, hairy Minotaur.

The group scattered back, scrambled for cover, but as quickly as it appeared, the cloud and the lightning vanished, and took with them the body of Belphegor.

Panting, Erica scanned the cave, looking for any other signs of strangeness. When everyone settled down, Erica turned up her lips and said, "At least it took the stink with it."

* * *

Bailey Renee hurt so bad for Erica, she couldn't sleep. She worried about Lauren, about Aiden and Oliver, too. But Erica made her heart ache. When she found Lauren and the others, and she would, three of the four would have good homes to go back to. What would Erica have?

She didn't know Erica, but she didn't know Sarah Skeleton until today either. She'd judged Sarah, and she could easily judge Erica. She could call her a criminal and blame her for the disappearances, but it didn't feel right.

So instead, she tried something she'd never done before, something she'd seen Oliver do, but had never done herself. She prayed.

Oliver had explained prayer to Lauren enough, so Bailey knew the basics, but she wondered if she would do it right. She prayed silently for Lauren and Aiden and Oliver and Erica. She prayed for their safety and their quick return.

Nerves and unease still squeezed her heart. So, to calm down, she sipped her hot tea with honey and milk, and grabbed the leather-bound book, the one she'd found under Lauren's pillow. *The Book of Things to Come.*

She turned to the page she'd left off in English class, but had trouble finding her spot. Of course, she had marked the page with a bookmark, but it must have been moved.

Strange words like nar'esh and abomination still filled the pages, but the story around them changed. Something about a staff and horns, and killing some sort of Minotaur. Definitely not there in English class.

She flipped back through the pages trying to find her place, but had no success. Wherever she left off in English had simply vanished. Her stomach knotted up.

She flipped to the front of the book where Lauren had made several notes.

Indigo: Me. Daughter of King Ribillius, Princess of Alrujah, Mage
Vicmorn: Oliver. Mystic Martial Arts Monk, Father of the Cerulean Order
Lakia: Erica. Summoner, raised as an orphan in the castle.
Jaurru: Aiden. Valiant Knight and King Ribillius's personal guard.

Bailey Renee shook her head. The four missing teens and sketches that looked just like them. So they were connected.

By the game.

What if Oliver's super-confusing code had something to do with their disappearance?

No. It'd be easier to believe they all joined the witness protection program or some other nonsense. But the connection was undeniable.

Without doubt, if she wanted to know what happened to the four teens, she'd have to figure out Lauren's game. It might have some answers.

It might have *the* answer.

She slipped the book under the pillow, pulled the covers up, and went to sleep in Lauren's bed.

* * *

Lauren knelt next to Oliver. Hot tears burned her eyes, and her body ached. She put her hand on his cheek and tried not to cry. "Are you okay?"

Lying still, he whispered, "Never better."

"Can you move, good Vicmorn?" Ullwen asked.

"I don't think so."

Erica knelt on the other side of him. "What if I promised to kiss you if you sat up?"

Oliver smiled but still didn't budge.

"Seriously, bro, that thing hit you so hard I thought you'd be dead. I'm amazed you're still breathing."

Oliver's chest rose and fell slowly, each accompanied by an anguished rasp of breath, like he'd just had the wind knocked out of him.

"Can't you heal yourself?" Erica asked. The sarcasm in her voice had dropped and, for the first time, she sounded vulnerable.

"I can't really move at all," he said.

"We've got to get him out of here," Aiden said. "Maybe the monks can help him."

"We must find the book first," Ullwen countered.

"Behind the throne," Oliver rasped. "I saw something back there before he smashed it up. A table with a book on it."

Erica took Oliver's hand in hers. "Hang on, Oliver."

Aiden rushed to the throne. He began heaving chunks of rubble to the side, hurling them to the back wall or behind him. "Bro, you weren't kidding," he said. "Good news is it's intact. Bad news is it's still in its case. If the glass didn't break when this throne did, it must be made out of something wicked strong."

"Enchantment," Oliver murmured.

"So how do we open it?"

"Use my staff," he whispered to Lauren. "The rognak staff. It's blessed by Adonai. If this is Adonai's will, He'll allow my staff to shatter the glass."

Erica stroked his cheek with her thumb. "Hang on, Mr. Monk. I'll take care of it." She grabbed his staff and leapt up the stairs and over the rubble of the throne, then smashed the staff down on the glass casing.

It shattered.

Aiden lifted the green book high in the air. Gold lines ran up and down the binding. On the cover, in the Ancient Language, were the words *The Book of Things to Come.*

Lauren smiled. "We did it," she said to Oliver, but sorrow tainted the words. The stone floor chilled her knees through her dress.

"Not done," Oliver whispered. "Crush the skull."

Aiden smashed it under the butt of the rognak staff.

Lauren put a hand on Oliver's chest. "Now how do we get you out of here?"

Aiden came over, book in his hands. "Can you make any sense out of this?" he asked Lauren.

She took the heavy book from him, felt the power of the pages in her bones. Holding the book must have replenished her magic reserves. No wonder the Mage Lord wanted it. But why had he left it to them? Why hadn't he stayed to fight?

The Ancient Language was different than dwarvish, but the words on the pages flitted, like those on the stick. When they settled down, she read from the middle of the book. "Now that's interesting," she said.

"What?" Erica prompted.

"I know how we're going to get Oliver out of here."

"Well spill, girlie."

She closed the book and said, "We'll carry him back to the central chamber. Since Erica can speak nar'esh now—and by the way, awesome trick."

"Thank you," Erica said.

"Anyway, since you speak nar'esh, it shouldn't be tough to get back. We'll have Erica call a razorbeak when we get back, to deliver a message to Eljah and Dillard. They should be able to make it to the caves quickly, and they should be able to heal Oliver, for the most part."

Aiden said, "Not to be a jerk or anything, but how are we going to carry him without hurting him more? Sounds like his back and ribs may be broken."

Lauren smiled and wiped the tears from her eyes. "Backboard."

She channeled her fear into a tangible cold. Moving away from Oliver, she stood up, bent over, and drew the moisture in the room to her fingertips. Ice crystals formed in her fingerprints, bound together until they were thick and cold. Inch by inch, the ice grew thicker and longer until a board formed next to Oliver.

"Amazing," Aiden said.

She smiled but kept working, kept concentrating on forming something comfortable and supportive. They had to get him to safety. They had to get him better.

The road ahead would be long. *The Book of Things to Come* made that point clear. And they would need Oliver every step of the way.

END

Look for the second book in the *Hand of Adonai* series, *The Blood Sword*.

The Blood Sword
A Hand of Adonai Novel

by
AARON D. GANSKY

Brimstone
Fiction

The Blood Sword

For a time, Shedoah will allow himself to be imprisoned by Adonai.
He will live under the sea. But Adonai's power will not hold Shedoah.
Shedoah will rise again, overcome Adonai and his reign of disease and
war, and restore peace to Alrujah for a thousand years.

—The Shedoahn Prophecies

Maewen folded her wings and plummeted toward Dragon's Tooth Island. There, among the mountainous waterfalls and the dense green foliage, she alighted on the highest pinnacle. Her bismuth circlet glimmered in the waning light of the lesser sun. She carried no weapons. She'd had no need since Solous ascended the throne.

Rich with the power of Adonai, the island remained hidden from Alrujahns for centuries. She'd not heard it mentioned among the elves since the War of the Suns.

Far overhead, Pacha el Nai circled the island. Two dark spots buzzed like flies near his distant form. As he descended, the spots took the shape of griffins. She never understood Pacha's fascination with the creatures. He did all he could to keep them hidden from the people of Alrujah, convinced they'd "subjugate the noble animals and breed them for war."

Already, they were bred for war. Adonai saw to that. With paws the size of stone tablets and twice as heavy, they could swipe a man's head from his shoulders without effort. Their beaks, with their gleaming razor edges, could snap tendon from bone.

The two Pacha el Nai brought landed beside him. One tawny, the other black, both sat like well-trained dogs. He touched each of their heads and smiled. "Maewen, it is good to see you."

"And you in kind," she responded. "May Adonai bless your steps."

"An odd choice of greetings for one such as yourself."

Maewen folded her arms.

The tawny griffin lay on the cold black rock precipice. Pacha el Nai continued. "Adonai is concerned. The hearts of the elves turn toward you. They worship you as a goddess."

"I do not encourage their worship."

"Do you reject it?"

"How can I, when Adonai forbids me to appear before them?"

Unlike Maewen, Pacha el Nai had come fully armed. His twin swords hung at his hips, humming with power. "And yet you've not obeyed this commandment."

Maewen's heart chilled. Of course, Adonai knew, but had he told Pacha? He must have. And if Pacha knew, the others would, too. How long had they known?

Pacha's smile thinned. The black griffin screeched, flapped its wings. "Your actions have endangered the lives of all who live in Alrujah."

"I know," she said. "I have repented. Is that not enough?"

"Children," Pacha said. "Twins. They live among the elves as gods, and you ask if repentance is enough? They are abominations, Maewen, and must be dealt with."

"No," she said, her hands grabbing his shoulders.

The black griffin snapped at her hands, but Pacha settled it with a palm on its head.

Maewen's throat tightened. "Spare them, please. The mistake was mine. I will bear the burden of punishment."

"They've taken wives," Pacha said. The tawny griffin shrilled at Maewen. "Until now, Adonai has been merciful. He's allowed them to live. But they must not bear children. To do so would further upset the balance of peace in Alrujah. Their children would lay waste human and elf and dwarf alike."

Maewen's eyes widened. Her circlet weighed heavy on her brow. How had she not known they'd taken wives? She'd been away from them too long. Without her guidance, their hearts would turn from her to the elves. "Must they pay with their lives for my mistake?"

Pacha took her wrists gently. "The decision is not yours. Adonai must act against such abominations."

"Please. They are my sons. They've done nothing to harm the people of Alrujah."

Both griffins screeched at her, and she stepped back. She steeled herself, moved forward toward Pacha. "Don't do this, Pacha. We've been friends for centuries. We've fought together, served Adonai together. Do not let my single mistake end our friendship."

Pacha stretched his wings. "Adonai will relent and allow them their lives. But your sin must not jeopardize Alrujah. You know what you must do."

She nodded. "I must go to my people and denounce their worship. I must bring my sons here, to Dragon's Tooth Island, away from Alrujah and Harael."

Pacha rested his hands on the hilts of his swords. "You must slay their wives."

She lowered her head.

"I do not envy you your task."

Maewen's knees weakened. She rested her head on his chest. Once, she'd loved Pacha, though love was forbidden among angels, and so she turned to the elves. What if Pacha had returned her love? Would they have avoided this mess? Or would they be in a different chaos?

He wrapped his massive arms around her, enfolding her smaller body, her fragile wings. "Be quick. If they're not dead by tomorrow's sunsdown, and your sons are here on Dragon's Tooth Island I will deal with them myself." He released her, stretched his wings, and launched himself from the cliff. The griffins followed close after, screaming at the waterfalls, their shrill voices echoing over the streams and the ocean.

Maewen wasted no time. She lifted herself in the air and flew through the night to Harael. The wind pressed her cheeks hard. Her eyes watered. She tried not to think about the task before her.

She landed lightly on the smallest, southernmost island and ducked inside a dank cave. She retrieved a spear leaning against the wall near the entrance. Her sons, now twenty-four years old, lay near the back of the cave, next to two young, beautiful elves. They'd decorated the cave, hung Torap's paintings, built shelves for Uhesdey's books, constructed beds from bamboo and straw mattresses. They'd lit the walls with enchanted ever-burning, smokeless torches.

The blonde elf wore a golden circlet and slept with her head on Torap's chest. Her left ear wore the bismuth ankh, Torap's chosen symbol. Torap, eldest of her twin sons, wore an identical earring in his left ear. His chest rose and fell slowly, and his new bride's hand draped over his stomach.

The black-haired elf lay beside Uhesdey, her leg draped over his, a golden anklet reflecting the sparkling water near the back of the cave. In her left ear, she wore the bismuth four-pointed star, Uhesdey's chosen symbol. He wore an identical ring in his left ear.

Her sons had taken brides, had started families, and hadn't told her. The betrayal stung, but she understood why. She'd forbade them to interact with the elves, mandated they stay in this cave. But they were young. They'd not obey her forever. And why shouldn't they experience love? Why shouldn't they raise their families?

Because, she reminded herself, such an act would spell the demise of Alrujah.

Within the bellies of these women grew the destruction of the world.

Maewen readied her spear, steeled her nerves. She whispered over her sons and their wives, deepened their sleep, then lifted the elf women, one in each hand. Secure in a bottomless slumber, the women's bodies flopped like boneless fish. Their necks lolled to the sides, their chests rising and falling in slow meter.

Outside the cave, she leapt, flapped her wings, and flew to the beach beyond the jungle trees. She lay the women in the sand, the blonde beside the dark-haired. They were so small, so young, so beautiful. No wonder her sons had fallen in love with them. Next to her giant sons, they'd looked like dolls. Her heart wept to do what she knew she must. "I'm sorry," she whispered. She lifted her spear and plunged it through the heart of Uhesdey's beloved.

The woman's body twitched. Her chest swelled, her hands grasped the massive shaft, her eyes snapped open, then rolled back into her head. Air seeped from her, escaped like a confused sigh.

The blonde stirred, rolled in the sand.

Wiping tears from her eyes, Maewen stepped on the dark-haired elf's chest and pulled the spear free. She rolled the blonde on her back.

The elf awoke. "What?" she asked.

Maewen spoke the words of sleep over her again and closed the elf's eyes.

With a heavy breath, Maewen lifted her spear and stabbed the blonde in the heart.

She'd killed hundreds of wicked men and elves and dwarves and never shed a tear. Now, remorse welled in her, and the bloodied bodies twisted her with guilt. She dropped to her knees beside them, wept over their wounds. "I'm sorry," she said. "I'm sorry. I had no choice."

"Mother?"

Maewen's head snapped up, her guilt instantly magnified. Fear widened her eyes.

Had he seen her plunge the spear into his beloved? How had Uhesdey resisted her sleep enchantment? How had he made it to the beach so quickly?

She stepped over the bodies of the women, did her best to stand between them and Uhesdey, to obscure his view. "My son," she said by way of distraction. She dropped the bloodied spear behind her in the sand.

"What have you done?" he asked.

She could not hide it from him. He would find the truth soon enough, and hate her for it. "I had to," she said. "Adonai demanded it. If I didn't, he would destroy us all."

He couldn't understand, wouldn't. His ears wouldn't hear her words. His eyes would see only the bloodied corpse of his new bride, the soft swell of her belly, and anger would flash hot inside him. He'd taken his personality from his father, a war elf who loved the blood his job demanded he spill.

"You must come with me," she said, hoping her son would listen. "We must go. We must leave the elvish isles."

"Neldessa?" he whispered, moving to his wife. He knelt beside her, pressed his hands to the hill of her belly, the blood of her wounds.

Maewen steadied her voice. "This is not what I wanted. Forgive me, my son. I have no right to ask it of you, but I beg nonetheless."

Torap, near seven feet tall, emerged from the tree line of the jungle. "Baradeth," he whispered, his voice like distant thunder. He knelt beside her, whispered over her wounds. Immediately, the skin began to seal; the blood slowed.

But the wound was too much for even Torap to heal. Maewen had seen to that. "Hear me, Son," she said again, retrieving her spear. "I've done this for you. We are in danger here. We must move. We'll be safe on Dragon's Tooth Island."

Uhesdey fisted his hands. "Safe?" he asked, standing. "From what, exactly? From whom? The elves? They're nothing. They fear us. They worship us as gods."

"From Adonai."

"Adonai?" Uhesdey spat. "I've never seen him. He is no god. If he were, he would protect you from me."

"He will strike you down if you don't come with me," Maewen said. "Please, we must go."

"Will you kill me, too? Mother?" Uhesdey stood over her, freakishly tall, his eyes like two smoldering coals.

"I could never raise a hand against you."

Torap's chest heaved. "But you would kill our wives? Did you not see our earrings? Did you not see their bellies growing? You murder our wives and our children, but you swear not to harm us?"

Uhesdey reached for her neck, but Maewen stepped back and smacked his hand away. He grabbed her wrist and pulled hard. The bones in her hand snapped. She twisted, found her footing, and steadied herself. Pain lanced through her arm up to her shoulder. "Please, Uhesdey. Your life is in danger if you stay here."

"You killed Neldessa!" Uhesdey shouted.

Torap stood, his head bowed, eyes brimming with tears. "I couldn't heal her."

Uhesdey sneered. "Your power is of life and light. It cannot touch the dead or the dark."

"But yours can, Brother," Torap said, his voice pleading. He took his brother by the shoulders. "You can bring them back to us."

"No," Maewen said. "Such a thing is evil. The dead must stay dead."

"You've been away too long, Mother," Uhesdey said as he knelt next to his slaughtered bride. "Our powers have grown. The waters of Harael run deep. Torap's hand guides them, and mine freezes them. His hand establishes life. My hand brings death. His will brings light and mine darkness. We are the balance of Harael. There is no place for you." Beneath the silver moon, he took the hands of the brides, and the corpses stood.

Maewen's chest tightened. Only Moloch could raise the dead. How had Uhesdey discovered this power? Cradling her broken wrist, she said, "What you do is evil."

Torap spoke, his voice broken with sorrow. "I marvel how twisted your logic is, Mother. Which is more evil, to slaughter the living, or to raise the dead?"

She should not have come. This was a mistake. They would strike at her, and no amount of talking would stay their hand. Perhaps, if she flew to Dragon's Tooth Island, they would follow her. Once there, she might trap them.

Her wings ached from the frenzied flight across Alrujah, and she doubted she had the strength to fly back. But she would have to. If she stayed to fight, she would not win.

"Please," she said to buy time. Her mind raced for a spell that would bind them to the Dragon's Tooth.

Torap lunged at her. Maewen moved, but Uhesdey joined the fight. He wrested her spear from her unbroken hand before she realized where he was. He stabbed at her, and Maewen struggled to move in time. The flaming emerald tip of the spear seared her skin. Her wrist shrieked in pain.

She spread her wings and leapt, but each of her sons grabbed an ankle and threw her to the ground. She spun, hoping to break her fall, but they'd pulled too hard. She landed hard on her back, snapping her wings. She arched her back in agony. Sand slithered between her armor and skin, pulled her under with snakelike fingers.

Torap.

The sands carried her toward the sea, and the sea reached up for her.

Uhesdey punched the ground hard, and hundreds of dead elves crawled up with the tide. Their flesh, loose and bloated on their bones, shone blue in the moonlight. Tendons clung limply to bone. Reddish muscle stretched beneath torn skin. Teeth clacked and snapped in rigid jaws.

Maewen flexed her fingers. Pain knifed her wrist, but she put it out of mind, and a million bursts of light exploded around her sons and their wives. The distraction gave her time to pull herself from the sand-fingers, right herself and bend the silver moonlight to create thirty perfectly mirrored copies of herself. They moved with her, action for action, breath for breath.

Pain seared her snapped wings. Whatever dream she'd had of flying to Dragon's Tooth Island was now impossible. If she hoped to survive, she'd have to fight.

She thought of the War of the Suns, of her battle against the elves, but this time, she had no human army behind her, no troops to command. Dead elf hands grasped at her. She needed a weapon, needed her spear. She pooled light into a white-hot disk and severed the elves' hands. She turned the light toward her sons, burning a path to them.

Uhesdey and Torap moved in opposite directions. She followed Uhesdey. "Stop this madness," she said. "I only wanted to help you, to protect you."

He closed his right fist, and the moon blinked out. Her doppelgängers vanished.

Such power.

Uhesdey stabbed at her, catching her side, slashing her armor.

She moved on instinct, wrapping her good arm around the spear and kicking Uhesdey in the chest. Not hard enough to crush his sternum, but hard enough to separate him from the weapon.

He stumbled back. She twisted the spear into the palm of her good hand.

Torap grabbed her and threw her against a tree on the edge of the beach. Pain seared her wings, her back. She leveled the spear at his chest. "Please, Torap, not you." She'd never seen him angry until this moment.

He leapt at her.

She bent the thin tendrils of light stretching through Uhesdey's disk of darkness, used them to vanish from Torap's sight. She reappeared behind him and kicked him in the small of the back. She had to stop them without killing them.

How had it come to this?

The hands of the dead grabbed her broken wings and pulled her back. Hundreds fell on her. She pooled light into disks and slashed at them, but there were too many. They scratched her face, pulled her limbs until she couldn't move. Uhesdey's foot smashed down on her neck.

Tears burned her eyes.

Torap handed the spear to Uhesdey.

Uhesdey raised the weapon. "An eye for an eye," he said.

Desperate with fear, Maewen burned light. She concentrated it in two spots, Uhesdey's right eye and Torap's left. She burned hard, and the light exploded.

Their heads snapped back, and they staggered through the sand. The elf corpses fell. Neldessa and Baradeth, still bloodied and lumbering, crumpled in the sand.

Maewen stood quickly and struggled toward the sea. If she could not fly, she would have to swim.

Torap, one hand over his bloodied eye, snatched his mother's wings. With a savage shout, he threw her on the sand.

Pain galloped through her wings, her spine, her ribs. Breath left her chest.

Torap knelt on her shoulders, pinned her down. Hate and loathing twisted his face.

His anger hurt her more than any of her wounds. He'd been such a beautiful, gentle child. She'd failed them as a mother, failed Adonai as an angel.

With one hand, Torap clutched her neck.

Uhesdey stepped on her broken wrist. "Kill her."

Maewen tried to shriek, but Torap pinched off her throat. The pupil of his remaining eye shrank to a peppercorn.

She fought to put the pain from her mind. With her good arm, she tried to wrest Torap's thumb loose, but he was too strong. If she could speak, if she could tell them how much she loved them, if she could make them hear her heart.

Her words dribbled out as a gurgle.

Uhesdey plunged her spear into her palm.

Her back arched with pain.

"Why?" Torap said.

His eye narrowed. His blood and tears dripped down her cheeks. How long could she survive without air? She shut out the pain in her hand, her wings, her neck.

"Do it now," Uhesdey said. "Or I will." He stepped forward. His black, unnatural shadow poured over her.

Torap lowered his left hand.

With the end nigh, Maewen stilled. Perhaps this was best. Perhaps this is what she deserved. And why shouldn't death come from their hands? At least, she would not die alone. At least, the last thing she would see would be her sons, whom she loved.

Torap put his bloodied hand on her face. His blood was warm, his palm hot.

Did he feel her waning pulse beneath his thick fingers? Did he see the panic turned peace in her eyes? Did he see her love for him?

His palm heated until it seared her skin.

Still, she would not scream, even if she could.

A white-hot light erupted from Torap's fingers and palm.

* * *

As the docks of Sylvonya neared, Archduke Pentavus Korodeth gave Argus, his trusted Captain of the Chameleon Soldiers, some final instructions before docking. "Stay close to me, cloaked in your Chameleon Armor. Do not reveal yourself, even if you feel I am in danger. I assure you, there is little threat they can muster that would cause me fear."

Argus nodded and pulled his hood over his face. Instantly, the enchanted light-refracting armor caused him to vanish.

Korodeth sailed the one-mast boat to the nearest rickety dock at the eastern gate of Sylvonya. Two port guards, lightly armored and cloaked in red, stood beside two castle guards wearing heavy plate mail and cloaked in blue. All four put a clenched fist over their hearts.

After the long journey, Korodeth's legs took a moment to adjust to the steady, unwavering ground. He brought his right fist to his left shoulder, and the guards released their salutes. He greeted each by name, asked after their families, assured them they'd done a fine job.

He rarely smiled, but his stern stare made his words earnest. These men would follow him anywhere, fight for him, die for him. They'd pledged fealty to Ribillius with their mouths, but their hearts belonged to Korodeth, as was the case with most military personnel. He'd seen to that over the years, dedicating himself to the training and well-being of the standing armies of each of Alrujah's cities. Ribillius spent too much time in the throne room and behind closed doors administering the kingdom. Korodeth liked the personal touch.

"How was your journey?" Dybarian asked. He'd served as Viceroy Harrow's Captain of the Watch for Sylvonya for years now, almost as long as Harrow sat the Port Dais. Like the rest of the castle guard and the watch, he'd been appointed by Korodeth.

"Swift and lonely."

Dybarian grinned. "Traveling alone will do that." The castle gates swung open at their approach.

Women in long, filthy dresses lined the cobblestone streets. They threw buckets of sea water and lye over the road and scrubbed with stiff-bristled brushes. Korodeth moved aside to allow the water to pass by. He had no desire to turn his boots pink with the bloody water. "Droughtworm?" he asked.

Dybarian shouldered his halberd. The three other guards marched in perfect step with him. "We drag a hundred bodies to the ocean every morning, sir."

Korodeth shook his head. The market, as always, bustled. Guards watched over merchants and their customs. The city walls echoed with the names of a thousand fish and crustaceans in myriad accents. At least the economy still thrived.

Deeper into the heart of the city, as they passed the homes of castle servants and public officials, men and women slumped against their walls, held their children in thin arms. Korodeth's heart heavied. "We're working to find a solution. Every man who can read has his eyes in a book. Every healer at our command studies the dead to protect the living."

The man smiled. "No one loves the people like you, Captain."

"No?"

"None sir. And well the people know it. If anyone finds the answer, it will be you."

Before them, the castle loomed large on the horizon. The steep inclined streets led directly to the castle gates, where the gardens famous for hibiscus and oleander lay in ruins. The plants, long dead, had been burned. Blood smeared the stone walls of the castle.

"What happened here?"

"Difference of opinions," the guard said.

"The monks?"

Dybarian nodded. "Proclaimed Adonai as god and demanded Viceroy Harrow tear down Tiamat's church."

"And you killed them?"

"On Viceroy Harrow's command, aye."

Korodeth had trained Dybarian personally. He took great pride in having a personal investment in the military leaders of Alrujah's cities. And in that training, he'd seen Dybarian fight off a dozen men with a dulled halberd. "How many?"

"Near the whole monastery, sir. A few ran off."

"There were almost sixty monks in Sylvonya's monastery."

"The Brown Brothers pressed in on our walls. They would not disperse."

Korodeth knelt. From his lower stature, he could see the broken plants, the lines and puddles of black blood. Near the hibiscus, the puddles ran red. They'd fought recently, within the day.

Harrow was a bigger fool than he thought. He stood. "Clean up this mess. It's a disgrace."

"Aye, Captain." The guard turned back and called after his mates.

Korodeth marched directly to the throne room. Viceroy Harrow, a robust man draped in a red robe with blue stitching, stood. He smoothed his white beard and stared at Korodeth. "You're early."

Korodeth stormed up the Port Dais and grabbed the man by the front of the robe. "You slaughtered the monks?"

Eyes wide, Harrow pulled at Korodeth's wrists. "How dare you!"

Korodeth broke Harrow's grip and boxed his ears. The viceroy collapsed into his chair and held his head, his shoulders and elbows pulling in toward his expansive belly. He screamed, a shrill, piercing wail more befitting a child than a viceroy.

Guards approached from the doorway, clearly confused as to whom to defend, but Korodeth waved them away. "This is a matter of kingdom security." He bent Harrow's head back, allowed time for the ringing in the man's ears to die down, and whispered. "Perhaps you can hear my voice better now that I've knocked the wax from your head."

Harrow pulled away, checked his hands for blood. He pushed past Korodeth and walked behind the throne. "Leave me be."

Korodeth followed him. "Don't walk away from me, Harrow. My word put you on this throne, and it can take you off. I'm beginning to see why Ribillius never liked you."

Harrow tilted his head to either side, opened and closed his mouth. His beard danced like a silvery stag. "I've done everything you asked." Whatever steel he'd had, whatever resolve, had fled. Older than Korodeth by decades, the viceroy spoke to him as a boy speaks to a man.

"Aye, and more. I never ordered the murder of monks!"

"They demanded I destroy Tiamat's church!"

"Did they attack you?" He asked the question, not to elicit an answer, but to make a point.

Harrow twisted the gold rings on his fingers. "No."

"Of course not. They are a peaceful order unless you put them to the sword. How many guards lost their lives for your stupidity?"

Harrow straightened his robe. "Wine," he said to a guard, who made his way quickly out of the room. "None."

"Only because the Brown Brothers vow not to take the lives of humans. How many of your soldiers are visited by healers now?"

"Near a hundred."

"You are a witless fool, Harrow. You should have known not to engage the Brown Brothers."

"Hypocrite!" Harrow shouted. "You have me build a church and ask me not to protect it?"

"Encourage your city, I said. Give them something to worship. How do you take that to mean slaughtering a peaceful people?"

"My people had Adonai to worship."

Korodeth raised an eyebrow. "A weak and deaf god. A deceiver. Tell me, if Adonai planned to save his people, wouldn't he have done it already? And yet the droughtworm persists. And yet political tensions grow. And yet the elves make plans for war. And yet the dwarves are all but dead. Where is his hand now?"

Harrow straightened behind the throne. "Then what ill is there in killing his monks? Did you not order the burning of the Cerulean Monastery? But what's right for you isn't right for me, I suppose?"

Korodeth spoke quietly, as if to a daft child. "No monks were killed," he said. "I saw to that. I turned their attention. Distraction is not murder."

"The conflict is unavoidable." Harrow found steel in his voice. He took his seat again, took a cup of wine from the guard. He swallowed deeply. "Was it not you who taught me the rules of warfare? He who strikes first strikes last?"

"We are not at war."

"Said the kingdom that fell."

Korodeth had had enough of this fool's willful ignorance, his subtle accusations as if he knew better than Korodeth. He smacked the goblet from Harrow's hand and threw him to the ground.

Lightning flashed outside and a dagger appeared in Korodeth's hand. He slashed at Harrow, stopping the blade inches from the viceroy's throat.

Guards rushed the Port Dais, but with a wave of his hand, Korodeth knocked them all back to the wall. They crumpled like boneless dolls. His eyes glowed red and the blade of the dagger heated. He touched the blistering steel to Harrow's neck.

The man howled, clutched at the floor.

Korodeth removed the blade. He waved his hand and it vanished. "Hear me well, Harrow, for if your ears fail you again, I'll sit someone new upon your chair. You are to attend the church of Tiamat. Heed the words of his priests. Seek counsel with his monks. But never again strike at Adonai's chosen. If you do, I'll not stop the wrath his people will bring on you." He helped Harrow to his feet. "Pick a fight with a god, and the god may strike back. Never strike unless you're ready for the counter-attack."

Harrow stood, slowly, steadying himself on his chair. "We are ready."

"You are worthless and witless. We're ready when I say we are. You are a narrow-sighted, dim-eared old man."

Harrow's guards righted themselves slowly.

Harrow raised his chin, a willful child defying a parent.

Korodeth thought of slapping the man again. "The Monks of the Cerulean Order will hear of this. I must prepare Alrujah for the transition."

Harrow's voice came stronger than Korodeth imagined. "May I ask when to expect you on the throne?"

He spun and smacked Harrow's face hard. "You have a filthy, treacherous mouth. Until you learn discernment, your lips are sealed."

Harrow's lips melted together like wax. He grabbed at his mouth, moaned and cried, but no words came.

Korodeth marched toward the door, stepped between the wobbly guards. "You're fortunate I don't throw you in the dungeon for treason." He walked back through the gardens, through the city, to the port, where his boat floated, tied to a rickety dock. He set the sail and pushed off.

When Sylvonya's towers diminished to sticks, Argus removed his hood. "Am I to assume the plan has changed?"

"Harrow is a fool," Korodeth said. "The plan remains, but his loose lips jeopardized what I must do. The guards needed a show of power."

"A fine show," Argus said. "A question, Captain, if it pleases you. How will the viceroy eat with his lips in such a state?"

"The enchantment will wane in two days' time. A man so fat cannot starve in so brief a period." Korodeth surveyed the vast ocean. From this distance, the land looked small, but the world felt larger. Beneath this very sea, Shedoah waited. How long must he wait? "I want eyes on the monks. They're in the caves near the Cerulean Woods."

"They can sense us," Argus said.

"They will not sense you, Argus. I will see to that. Do well, and you will soon find yourself on the Port Dais. I have a feeling it will soon be vacant."

Preview or purchase *The Blood Sword* now by scanning this QR code with any free QR reader scanner from any mobile device.

www.ingramcontent.com/pod-product-compliance
Lightning Source LLC
Chambersburg PA
CBHW031720170626
46808CB00005B/1825